BEFORE NOW WAS NOW

ANGELA MARIE WALTERS

Next Level Rebel Press

BEFORE NOW
WAS NOW
ANGELA MARIE WALTERS

For Robin,

who exists in all my parallel universes.

CHAPTER ONE

Rae woke up in fight-or-flight mode, the phone that lay twisted in the coils of her bedsheets banging and clanging like a sinner at the gates of hell. It was her mother who'd convinced her that the ringing of an old-fashioned alarm clock would make it easier to get out of bed in the morning. Maybe if you enjoyed waking up in a stress-induced sweat.

She wrenched herself away from her strange dream of knitting rainbow-colored hats for a raft full of baby river otters and hit the dismiss button before rolling over and opening her eyes. It was still dark out. What kind of people got up before the sun? Farmers. High achievers. Influencers. Lawyers, hustlers, entrepreneurs. Her mom was none of those.

Controlling people, then. Worriers. Old people.

Right on cue, her mother knocked out a "Shave and a Haircut" on her bedroom door, pausing to allow Rae time to respond with the "two bits" reply on her headboard. It was a stupid routine they'd had since Rae was a kid. But today, she squeezed her eyes shut and prayed her mom would disappear.

"Rae? Are you awake?"

Rae could hear her breathing with one ear pressed against the other side of the door. "Go away!"

"But what about smoothie bowls?" she asked in the most played-out version of her favorite victim voice.

Rae flopped on her stomach and groaned loudly.

"Come on, Rae. You can't pour from an empty cup!"

"Oh my god, stop talking in memes. I'm coming."

Rae reluctantly abandoned her bed and trawled through the heaps of clothes on her bedroom floor until she successfully fished out her favorite hoodie, a black, faded pullover with ragged, stretched-out cuffs. She was cold because her mom refused to turn the thermostat above sixty-eight degrees. The woman was obsessed with saving money.

She pulled the hoodie over her head and yanked open her bedroom door, trying not to laugh when her mom practically fell inside the room.

"Good morning," her mom said, as if she was trying to sound happier than she really was. Her eyes widened at the mounds of dirty clothes, shoes, and candy wrappers behind Rae.

"Do you mind?" Rae asked, wedging herself between her mom and her stuff.

Her mom's mouth twisted into a sanctimonious little *O*—she was definitely on the verge of dropping some wisdom about how much better Rae's life would be if only she kept her shit organized—but she switched tactics at the last minute and awkwardly held out a mug of what smelled like lemon-ginger tea.

Rae felt anger crawl up her spine like a fat spider before it leaped and landed in her brain with a messy *splat*. How long had her pathetic mother been standing in the hallway with that phony fucking smile plastered on her face?

"Jesus, Mom, step off and give me some space, will you?" Rae spat.

Her mom flinched, spilling some of the hot tea on her forearm as she pulled back.

"Ow," she whispered, wiping her arm across her chest.

Rae felt a little guilty as she glared at her mom in her hideous, faux-African-print caftan, no doubt purchased on Amazon from a third-party seller who bought cheap, nasty clothes from some child-exploiting, environment-destroying clothing manufacturer in China. She'd paired it with red-and-white-striped fluffy socks and ratty blue slippers. Her brown hair was pulled back into a stumpy ponytail, at least a half inch of gray growth showing at the scalp. Her face looked old in the yellow light of the hallway.

Everything about her screamed defeat. She didn't need her own daughter making her feel worse.

"Way to consume consciously, Mom," Rae scoffed as she stepped around her, gesturing with her chin toward the despicable caftan. She wanted to be nice, but sometimes the mere sight of her mother enraged her.

Her mom looked down at her outfit and then back at Rae with a confused expression on her face.

Rae ignored her and shuffled down the hallway toward the kitchen while she watched Cosima's newest Story, a perfectly edited review of Fenty's hybrid lip gloss plumper in Hot Cherry.

She stood on a square of cold linoleum, wishing she'd remembered slippers, then checked her Snaps and switched over to TikTok.

She avoided looking at the selfie she'd posted on Instagram last night, which had been a major fail: she and Cosima had just decided selfies were the exclusive domain of pathetic, attention-seeking losers with self-esteem issues. They'd made a pact that if they absolutely *had* to post a picture of themselves, someone else would need to take the photo. Posies were okay. Posies proved you were an adequately socialized person with friends, not some freak sitting alone in your room, trying to pass off a phony, filtered version of yourself to the world.

The problem was that yesterday, Rae had finally gotten up the nerve to persuade her dad to Venmo her a hundred bucks so she could walk into the salon in the strip mall and ask the stylist with the neck tattoos to cut her straight, brown hair—the hair she had worn almost to her waist for her entire life—into a dramatic A-line bob with bangs. She was sick of Cosima asking her if she meant to look like a preteen, and thank god for that because now she looked like Anri Sonohara from *Durarara!!*, only more glam. Honestly, it was such an upgrade, it would be weird if she didn't post *something*, but the idea of asking her mom to take her picture was gross. She couldn't do it. So after taking a bunch of selfies at her desk while pretending to do homework, she picked a shot of herself chewing on a pencil eraser with her head tilted and her eyes squinched, added a filter with a grimy vibe, and posted it with a #newhairwhodis tag before she had time to process what she was doing.

Of course, she'd regretted posting as soon as she hit Share. Cosima was going to be disgusted with her. But was it worse to post and delete? She wasn't sure. She'd closed the app and hadn't allowed herself to think about it until now.

Since Rae only had four hundred and sixty-eight followers on Instagram and a decent engagement rate was anything over 3 percent, she needed at least fourteen likes to validate her repulsive need for approval. She opened the app and peeked through half-closed eyelids.

Eight likes. A familiar pain gripped her stomach.

"Well, what do you think?" her mom asked.

Rae looked up from her phone and found herself in front of their ugly, aqua kitchen countertop, where her mom had set up glass bowls filled with goji berries, shredded coconut, chia seeds, granola, blackberries, and raisins.

"Mom, seriously? Raisins? We're having smoothie bowls, not *oatmeal*." She rolled her eyes hard. Why did old people put raisins in everything? Her mom was clueless as usual, and Rae was sorry she'd ever agreed to this stupid breakfast ritual. It was supposed to make them bond somehow, only now her stomach was cramping like crazy. Eating would make her want to cry and crap her pants. Maybe she had posted too late in the evening?

"Honey?" Her mom was staring at her, biting her bottom lip. She looked like *she* might start crying.

"Oh, for god's sake, let's get this over with," Rae grumbled. Maybe an aesthetic food post would help her move past the selfie shame.

They blended frozen bananas and blueberries in her mom's professional-grade Vitamix and scooped the amethyst slush into fancy dessert bowls. Rae arranged fruit, seeds, and granola in alternating rows across her smoothie bowl, using everything except the raisins.

"Your new hair is adorable," her mom said as they sat at the counter to eat. "I love it."

"I hate it," Rae replied. She'd loved it yesterday. It had been sleek and smooth and made her look way older than sixteen. But if her hair looked as good as she thought it did, why did she only have eight likes?

"Change can be hard. You'll love it in no time."

"My mom, the walking inspirational poster."

Rae ignored her mom's sad face and turned back to her phone. She'd recently read that you shouldn't eat while watching TV or scrolling through your phone since it doubled the dopamine released in your brain and caused overeating, but she had to know how many of her friends had liked her post so far.

Her grandma had liked her post, of course, along with every one of her school friends—except Cosima.

"—so I won't be able to drop you off. Are you listening to anything I'm saying, Rae?"

"Huh? What?" she asked, looking up from her phone.

"Let me explain again. I can't take you to school because I have to deliver a last-minute continental breakfast for a group of forty to an office building in Uptown by 9:00 a.m., and I still need to go to the Center to cut fruit and bake off the pastries. This guy originally wanted breakfast tacos." She sighed, shaking her head. "Can you imagine? On such late notice? Typical entitled douchebag lawyer."

She was being dramatic about work to distract Rae from the shittiness of what she was saying, but it wasn't working.

"Are you for real, Mom? You're telling me this *now*?" Rae threw down her spoon and shoved her bowl across the counter. "I'm not taking the bus."

"It's just this once, Rae."

"*It's just this once, Rae,*" she mimicked, jumping out of her seat. The barstool fell over, clattering across the kitchen floor.

Her emotions had blended into a toxic smoothie of their own. Anger at her mom combined with her insecurity about the selfie and her stupid hair, and all that combined with her paranoia about what Cosima was going to do now that Rae had defied her. Sprinkle in some anxiety about getting on the bus while a bunch of people she didn't know sat in silence and stared at her as she walked down the aisle avoiding eye contact, and the combination was just too much. She couldn't hold it in. Purple rage, bits of shame, and pieces of social anxiety gushed out of her.

"How many times have I seen you grab a bottle and say those *exact* same words, Mom?" She picked up an imaginary bottle off the counter and mimed pouring the contents down her throat while her mom's eyes widened. "*Oh, it's-s-s jus-s-s-t this once, Rae,*" she garbled in her best version of her mom's slurred speech, staggering around the kitchen.

Her mom put her spoon down on the counter as she watched Rae bang into a wall and ricochet off in the opposite direction, tripping over her own feet.

"What's wrong with you?" she shouted, shaking her head. "Why are you so hateful? What do I have to do for you to forgive me? How many times do I have to say I'm sorry?"

"How can I forgive you?" Rae yelled. "I can't even trust you anymore! I'm always wondering if today is the day you'll start drinking again!"

It was true. Whenever Rae started to relax and feel good about the way things were going, dark thoughts crowded into her head like a herd of twisted, eyeless monsters. Maybe her mom was just pretending to be okay. Maybe she was drinking while Rae was at school or hiding in her closet with a bottle after Rae went to sleep. Rae had no choice but to constantly monitor her mom for signs that she might be hiding something. The minute Rae stopped worrying would be the day her mom picked up the bottle again.

"Oh, honey," her mom said, her face crumpling as she reached toward Rae.

Rae shook her head and stepped backward. "No."

"You're only hurting yourself by hanging on to this anger. You need to forgive me so you can move forward."

"Screw that shit!" Rae yelled, running to her bedroom and slamming the door.

Her heart pounded from the confrontation. She had never talked to her mom like that before. She was scared but exhilarated. It felt good to tell her mom the truth.

Perched on the edge of her bed, she reopened TikTok and scrolled through makeup tutorials. Though she didn't wear a lot of makeup, there was something strangely soothing about watching her favorite creators selecting the right brushes and sponges to apply their layers of foundation, concealer, highlighter, and blush, blending and smoothing until their faces appeared flawless. The series of transformations calmed her down until it was almost possible to accept what a train wreck her life was.

Until nearly two years ago, Rae's mom had been the owner and executive chef of a bougie farm-to-table restaurant in Nob Hill called Ensalada. She was kind of a major food celebrity in Albuquerque and had even been nominated for a James Beard Award for Best Chef in the Southwest two years in a row. She hadn't won, but still.

The year her mom ran her life off a cliff, she'd been married to Rae's dad, a senior architect at Elevated Design, for almost twenty years, and the three of them had lived in a big rammed-earth house with enormous picture windows and a Japanese soaking tub overlooking the Sandia Mountains. They'd been flush with cash, and even though both Rae's parents practically lived at work, life had been chill. She'd been fine staying with her grandma when her parents worked late because her grandma was the GOAT, and when she was at her grandma's house she didn't have to listen to her parents constantly bitching about space and quality time and authenticity. Rae had been living her best life back then and she hadn't even known it.

Her entire life disintegrated into meaningless little pieces when she was almost fourteen years old and her self-sabotaging mother had smashed into the back of some couple's car while driving home drunk after a late night at work. The news anchor had said it was a miracle she hadn't killed them.

Because it had been her third offense—Rae hadn't even known about the first two times—*and* it was aggravated, the judge had sentenced her mom to either a year in jail or a year in residential rehab. The choice was hers. Rae's grandma had told her the judge didn't have to give her mom the option of rehab, but a lot of her mom's customers and employees had written letters saying what a great person her mom was and the judge had decided to show her some mercy, which Rae thought was bullshit. What kind of mom worked all day and night and then got wasted before driving home to be with her family?

The only rehab center that had accepted her mom's insurance was run by a bunch of shady bastards who were in it for the insurance check and couldn't care less about her actual recovery. At least, that was what her mom had said. So Rae's dad had liquidated the restaurant and sold their house and that was how her mom had ended up in a fancy private rehab in Scottsdale, Arizona, for a year, while Rae had been practically homeless. She'd never understood why her mom hadn't volunteered to go to jail instead so they could at least keep their house.

But the shit show hadn't ended there. One day, while Rae and her dad were driving around supposedly looking for a smaller place to live, her dad confessed that he'd accidentally fallen in love with one of the paralegals at his architectural firm. Her name was Elia and she was thirty-one years old. Rae's dad was seriously geriatric—like, almost sixty—and he swore he'd never had any intention of getting involved with Elia. He'd turned to her for emotional support after Rae's mom was arrested and it had just happened, that was all. He wasn't a bad guy; he hadn't planned to betray the mother of his only child. Only now he couldn't imagine his life without Elia, so he was going to move with her to Northern California to help her run the small vineyard she'd recently inherited from her childless great-aunt. Rae would have to live with her grandma the entire time her mom was gone, but she could come out and visit her dad as soon as he got settled. He was really, really, *really* sorry.

It had ended up being okay, living with her grandma. Rae didn't have to listen to her parents fight anymore, and her grandma gave her a lot of space and didn't nag her about her phone or her homework or her messy room. They usually cooked dinner together and ate in front of the TV while watching old mystery shows like *Murder, She Wrote* and *Matlock*. Her grandma had helped her with her homework on the weekends, and Rae had gotten straight As in school for the first time ever.

By the time her mom got out of rehab, her dad had petitioned for divorce and proposed to his cheugy girlfriend with the ginormous plastic boobs, and it looked like her mom would have to figure things out on her own. She deserved it, as far as Rae was concerned.

Actually, both of her parents were dirtbags and she'd been totally fine with all three of them going their separate ways as long as she could stay with her grandma. But her mom wouldn't even think of it, no matter how much Rae had begged and cried. Instead, her mom had literally forced her to blow up her life one more time and move with her to this crappy apartment downtown. Rae had had to switch schools at the end of freshman year and lost all her friends and hardly ever saw her dad, who was almost as much of an asshole as her mom anyway.

Rae hated her new school and their jacked-up apartment, and most days, she hated her mom too. Her mom wanted to pretend all of the issues in their relationship were Rae's fault because she was having a hard time forgiving her, but how fair was that? She harassed Rae about it constantly, always trying to get her to read whatever stupid self-improvement book she was into now, books with gross names like *Heal Your Inner Child* and *Rising Above Shame*, and always pushing her to open up, write down her feelings, go to therapy with her. But Rae wasn't the one with all the problems, and she was tired of feeling like it was her responsibility to help her mom feel better about the mess she'd made of their lives.

With the tragic story of her life playing in the background of her brain for the millionth time, Rae switched from watching makeup tutorials to watching food-snatching videos until her mood improved, which took exactly twenty-three minutes and left her with just enough time to get ready for school. She sprinted through her shower and dried her hair with a blow-dryer and a round bristle brush, using the pull-and-roll technique she'd learned on YouTube last night, and finished with a smoothing cream to get her bob as glossy and angular as possible.

She looked good. Not as good as she had when she'd left the salon but hopefully good enough to help her cope with the embarrassment of having everyone notice her now that she looked so different. Until yesterday—pretty much her first real haircut, unless you counted trims—she'd always worn her hair straight down her back and parted in the middle or in a ponytail with a scrunchie.

Cosima was right: It was time to switch up her stale persona. And she really did want to stand out from the crowd a little bit, just not so much that she didn't fit in with everyone else. Most of her friends at the new school were into the soft girl aesthetic and she didn't want to stray too far from that.

Cosima had already made her feel weird about shopping at thrift stores. Everyone at her old school had been into thrifting, but not Cosima. The first time she'd hung out at her house, Rae had been shocked by the size of Cosima's closet, a walk-in literally as big as Rae's room, stuffed with clothes and shoes from Urban Outfitters and ASOS and Forever 21, clothes Rae had only ever seen her wear once, if at all. Feeling a little jealous as she watched Cosima pick out a pair of shoes from her floor-to-ceiling wall of choices, Rae had reminded herself that fast fashion was wrecking the world.

Rae had been almost strictly thrift since her grandma had suggested she watch a documentary about fast fashion on YouTube a couple years ago and Rae had learned about the man-made mountain of discarded clothes growing bigger every day in the Atacama Desert, made of exactly the kind of cheap, trendy, made-in-China clothes from SHEIN and Zara that had filled her closet at the time. Most of the garments in the Atacama Desert had been donated to charities by Westerners after wearing them only a handful of times, charities who sold what they couldn't use to salvage buyers and merchants hoping to resell the clothes in the tax-free port of Iquique. Thirty-five thousand tons of those clothes were ultimately dumped in illegal landfills in the Chilean desert every year.

What Rae kept thinking about after the documentary was over, no matter how hard she'd tried not to, was the footage of the local people, babies on their hips or at their feet, picking through the horrible mountain of dirty, discarded clothes, searching for something good enough to wear or sell. But there was too much of this crap in the world and most of it couldn't be resold or repurposed, anyway, so the mountain sat there every year, growing bigger and bigger until someone decided to burn it. Who knew how many poor kids ended up inhaling the toxic smoke from cheap clothes that had looked so fire when they'd hung on a rack at H&M.

As if the mountain wasn't bad enough, Rae had also learned that millions of seals and turtles and sharks and seabirds died every year from eating the plastic fibers of cheap clothes that ended up in the ocean, and that garment workers worked up to sixteen hours a day, seven days a week, in unsafe, inhumane conditions. Many of them were children and less than 2 percent of them made a living wage. The documentary had made her cry even more than *A Dog's Purpose,* which she hadn't thought possible, so she'd made up her mind to buy all her clothes from thrift stores or fashion resale shops like Buffalo Exchange from then on.

Even though she didn't stick to it 100 percent of the time—it was hard to turn her dad down when he visited Albuquerque and offered to take her to the mall—she knew that every garment she bought used instead of new had a positive impact on the environment. She didn't shop at thrift stores because she was poor, no matter what Cosima said. Cosima had also given her shit about the way thrift stores smelled and told her she smelled bad, too, but Rae knew that wasn't true. She washed everything she bought as soon as she got it home.

Her thrifted fit of the day was a vintage *Rainbow Brite* T-shirt French tucked into baggy Levi's 505s and a pair of black Chuck Taylors. She considered elevating the look with a blazer or her Army-green utility jacket but decided to stick with the hoodie she'd fished from the depths of her textile sea earlier. It was old and shabby, but she felt protected when she wore it.

Rae gathered her homework and the pile of textbooks from her desk and organized them in her backpack so the overall shape of her bag was as smooth and streamlined as possible. She slid her laptop into its designated pocket before arranging all of her binders, notebooks, and textbooks from largest to smallest within the main compartment. Pens, pencils, lip balm, earbuds, and one emergency tampon went into the small front pocket.

Just as she was about to leave the house and walk to her bus stop, Rae had the wicked idea to call for an Uber instead. Her mom had helped her set up the app with her debit card number when Rae had first started at her new school, in case her mom ever ran late to pick her up or her grandma forgot it was her day. Her mom had warned her that she was only allowed to call an Uber if it was a true emergency, since money was tight. Even though they were both almost always late, Rae had never used it.

It would serve her mom right to have to pay for an Uber today. Why should Rae have to suffer through a humiliating, claustrophobic bus ride to school because her mom had made poor life choices?

She closed her bedroom door behind her quietly and tiptoed down the hallway, hoping to sneak out of the house before her mom noticed. But she was in the living room, putting on her ugly Profi-Birkis.

She'd changed out of her embarrassing lounge outfit and into black pants and a white chef's coat with the Ensalada logo embroidered in yellow and green over the left breast pocket. Her hair was stuffed under a Nusenda Credit Union dad cap.

"I'm going to the Center," she said. *The Center* was short for the South Valley Economic Development Center, which rented out commissary space and commercial kitchen equipment to people like Rae's mom, who now ran a small catering business but couldn't afford a professional kitchen of her own.

Rae tried to silence her mom with a dead-eyed stare, but she kept talking. Didn't she care that Rae had cussed her out? Or had she not noticed?

"I talked to your grandma. She'll pick you up from school, but you'll have to take the bus there. You can't expect her to do both."

"No worries. I called an Uber," Rae said. "It should be here any minute."

Her mom, who had been straightening the seam on the toe of her right sock, stood abruptly. "Are you freaking kidding me right now? You know I can't afford that."

"You can't afford ten bucks?"

"No, Rae, I can't afford ten bucks just because you're too much of a princess to ride the bus! Have you considered walking, Your Highness? When I was your age, I walked everywhere."

"No one is interested in the way things went down back in the Stone Age, Mom."

Her mom took off one of her clogs and threw it across the room right at Rae, who ducked just in time. The shoe hit the wall with a *thunk* as Rae's phone chimed with a notification from Uber. Her driver was here.

"Peace out," Rae said, throwing her mom a peace sign and racing for the front door. She slammed it shut before she could see her mom's expression.

A white Toyota Prius idled at the curb in front of their apartment. Rae walked in front of the car and checked the face of the driver against his profile picture on the app to avoid climbing into a car with a sex trafficker. The gray-haired, bespectacled man in the front seat matched the photo and passed the vibe check, so she opened the back door and climbed inside, half expecting her mom to come running out to stop her.

The driver's name was Antonio. He offered her a bottle of water and a stick of Wrigley's Spearmint gum, which she refused. As he pulled away from the curb, he told her he was a retired elementary school teacher who drove for Uber to help pay for his wife's acupuncture treatments for her chronic back pain.

Rae didn't know how to respond to his oversharing and blushed with discomfort. The task of making small talk with some rando boomer while she recovered from a fight with her mom was too much. She smiled politely and responded with monosyllables until Antonio finally took the hint and shut it down.

Using the deep-breathing method her grandma had taught her to deal with her anxiety, Rae closed her eyes and focused all her energy on not showing up to school a stressed-out mess.

CHAPTER TWO

R ae had been a happy public-school kid from kindergarten through fifth
grade. She'd gone to Bandelier Elementary, where most of her teachers had
been idealistic women in their early thirties who'd assigned interesting projects
like designing poster-sized maps of imaginary worlds and making homemade
slime out of Elmer's glue and borax. Her best friend, Julia, had been a crafty bo-
hemian who'd taught her to make friendship bracelets out of embroidery thread
and glass beads and introduced Rae to elaborate role-playing games inspired by
watching her older brother, Chase, play *Dungeons & Dragons* with his friends.
They'd LARPed their own versions of games like *Laser Monks in Outer Space* and
riffed on *The Princess and the Dragon*, acted out in a hidden corner of the play-
ground while wearing headpieces woven from Mexican feather grass. Sometimes
Rae still found herself thinking about the delish grade-school lunches her mom
would pack for her in her stackable, stainless-steel bento box—special things like
pita pizza with pesto and Greek olives, or cream cheese, tomato, and cucumber
pinwheels—before she'd decided Rae was old enough to fend for herself.

When Rae was in fifth grade, her mom had started researching the middle
schools in their district, comparing things like student-to-teacher ratios and na-
tional test-score rankings to decide which school would be best for Rae. But her

research had turned into an obsession, and pretty soon all she could talk about was how American public schools were contributing to the collapse of society. Before she'd even discussed it with Rae, she began announcing to anyone who would listen that her daughter would be going to a private school for sixth grade.

In between all her flexing, her mom had made sure everyone understood she did not identify as a privileged member of the liberal elite—far from it. She'd actually grown up poor as dirt, but now her husband's firm was thriving and her little restaurant was beginning to turn a profit. They weren't *affluent* or anything; they were average parents who worked like dogs to be able to afford to send their daughter to one of the best private schools in Albuquerque, where she would be challenged to an academic standard more appropriate for her intellect than she would be at some piece-of-shit public middle school. And if Rae also happened to be enriched by a strong sense of community in a positive group setting and exposed to an array of cocurricular activities that would broaden her interests and enlarge her world, well, fantastic. It wasn't wrong or elitist to want the best for your children, was it?

Rae could never understand why her mom had always apologized for having money. Her dad sure didn't feel bad about it, and he'd gone along with the whole private school thing like it had been no big deal at all.

At first, Rae had hated Ponderosa Prep. Everyone else seemed smarter than her, and it sucked to be in the youngest grade with no friends. But when a field trip to the Middle Rio Grande River watershed opened her eyes to the unique natural environment running through her own city, she'd realized that whoever had come up with the school's core values had totally nailed the whole inquiry-based learning thing. Over five hundred species of animals lived in the cottonwood forest bordering the Middle Rio Grande Valley floodplain and Rae learned how to identify dozens of them, like the iconic North American porcupine, the Cooper's hawk with its short, rounded wings, and the New Mexico whiptail, a female-only species of lizard with a pale blue throat and a long, slinky tail that reproduced babies all on their own. No boy lizards required.

During her four years at Ponderosa Prep, Rae became an expert at gathering water samples from the Rio Grande and testing them for pH levels and cleanliness before submitting her data to the Bosque Ecosystem Monitoring Program. She even learned how to make homemade pH paper out of poinsettia leaves leftover from Christmas. Who knew? Maybe when she grew up, she would become a field scientist and work for the EPA.

Then again, maybe not. Turned out, she was good at a lot of things: she joined the swim team, made a life-sized bust of herself out of papier-mâché that her grandma kept on her bureau and still used as a hat rack, and competed nationally with the seventh-grade speech and debate team.

More importantly, she made the best friends of her entire life while she was at Ponderosa Prep.

She, Jordan, Madison, and Alma had first bonded during a school camping trip to the Jemez Mountains, when they were assigned together as a team to look for rocks, branches, and pieces of bark they could use to make land art sculptures. By that summer, Rae felt as close to her new crew as she did to her own mom and dad, who were usually working or, if they were home, arguing over stupid things like who asked who more follow-up questions when they talked about their days. The four of them ate lunch together and signed up for classes together and had group sleepovers at someone's house at least once every other weekend, where they stayed up past midnight doing nail art, kissing pillows, eating Doritos with hummus, and ranking the kids in their school from highest to lowest according to appearance, intelligence, friendliness, and style, until a parental unit threatened to take their phones away.

That all changed after her mom drained their life savings on her fancy attorney and bougie rehab and her dad apparently decided he wasn't all that concerned with the quality of Rae's education after all. Rae had begged and cried for three days straight when he told her she would have to go back to public school—she'd even offered to get a job and help pay for her own tuition. But nothing she said mattered, and she was forced to transfer to Zia High for her sophomore year of high school, right when she, Jordan, Madison, and Alma were almost old enough to join Ponderosa's Medical Reserve Corps and start their training as first responders.

Rae had thought the training might inspire her to become a doctor. Even though she'd never held a baby before, she was pretty sure she would be a great pediatrician. She would wear colorful scrubs printed with sea horses or donuts, and she'd let her patients use her stethoscope to listen to their own heartbeats.

Zia High didn't have a Medical Reserve Corps, and even if it did, Rae wouldn't have had anybody to join with. It wasn't fair. Jordan, Madison, and Alma still had each other and she had no one. She'd cried herself to sleep every night for a week until her grandma had convinced her that if her friendships were strong enough, they would survive the challenge of going to different schools.

At first, it had seemed like her grandma might be right. She, Jordan, Madison, and Alma would meet up on the weekends at ABQ Uptown to hit their favorite shops. Rae would brief them on Zia High and how wack it was while they searched the clearance rack at Lululemon for anything smaller than a size eight, and then Jordan, Madison, and Alma would spill the tea on their latest crushes over affogatos at Frost Gelato.

As the weeks became months, Rae had a harder and harder time following along with their conversations. Jordan was totally in love with a transfer student from Florida who Rae had never even met. Alma had filed an official complaint with the principal about a new teacher who'd made it a policy to never give out As, but Rae was the only one who didn't know what a jerk the teacher was. The more time that passed, the less interested her friends seemed in hearing about her new school and the more they ignored her constant requests for backstory. They kept talking, talking, talking, and Rae had to piece it all together on her own.

Pretty soon, they started ghosting her Snaps. Madison didn't even seem to notice when she broke their six-hundred-and-eighty-six-day Snap streak. Six hundred and eighty-six days! It had been the longest streak of Rae's entire life.

One Saturday, her Snap Map had revealed that Jordan, Madison, and Alma were all together at Rude Boy Cookies. Rude Boy Cookies had been Rae's thing before it was anyone else's—she'd first visited the ska-themed cookie shop with her grandma when she was five years old and had been legit addicted to snicker-doodles and cereal milk ever since—but no one had thought to invite her. They hadn't even bothered to turn off their locations.

Maybe it had been for the best. Being around her old friends didn't feel good anymore; it actually made Rae feel sorry for herself. How was it fair that their lives hadn't changed at all, whereas her life was a total shit show? Jordan, Madison, and Alma were taking college prep courses and three-week immersives in art and social justice and generally becoming their best selves during their sophomore year, while Rae was forced to downgrade her whole existence. Her mom had laughed so hard when Rae had shared her college shortlist that tears had actually rolled down her face. "Swarthmore?" she'd choked out, her face red. "*Pomona?*"

It appeared that Rae would be forced to stay in Albuquerque and attend the University of New Mexico, where tuition was free for all resident undergrads and basically anybody with a pulse was accepted. What had been the point of private school anyway? What good had all that homework done her if she was going to end up at a public university? Even more humiliating was the fact that her mom had told her she'd have to live with her while she was in college. They couldn't even afford a crappy dorm room.

This was who Rae had been when she'd first met Cosima: a miserable, pathetic, friendless reject three weeks into her sophomore year at Zia High. She'd noticed Cosima on the very first day of school. Who wouldn't? She was tall and blonde with expensive clothes and a glittery mean-girl vibe that shot sparks from across the room.

What had surprised Rae was that Cosima had also noticed *her*. One day, while Rae stood behind her in the lunch line, admiring the back dimples she had on full display between the edge of her low-rise jeans and the hem of her shrunken T-shirt, Cosima had turned around and said that Rae's vintage Levi's patchwork denim jacket was dank as fuck. Rae had blurted out that Cosima's Fjällräven Kanken backpack was dope as shit, which it was, and Cosima had asked Rae to eat lunch with her right there on the spot.

Rae couldn't stop looking at her beautiful, cherry-red mouth that first day they ate lunch together, as Cosima nibbled on a mustard-smeared burger patty freed from its bun and told Rae all about her family. Her dad was a film location manager who'd been a pretty big deal in Hollywood before his mind was blown during an ayahuasca ceremony in Costa Rica and he decided to relocate his whole family to Albuquerque. He'd wanted to pursue a more "authentic existence," which apparently meant selling their mansion in California and forcing his children to attend basic public school so they wouldn't grow up alienated from the "more ordinary aspects of the human experience," whatever that meant—which sucked for Cosima but couldn't have worked out better for Rae.

Cosima was an early adopter of all the latest trends in West Coast music and fashion, and she shone like a beacon among Rae's Albuquerque classmates. She played on the varsity tennis team even though she was only a sophomore, and she had been personally invited by Demi Taylor, cheer captain and by far the most popular person in the whole school, to try out for the team. She wore real cashmere and had a Vespa and a swimming pool, and she sometimes hung out with her dad on set, and she knew Millie Bobby Brown and Lexi Underwood and B. J. Novak. She could probably even get someone a walk-on part in a movie if she really wanted to.

Even with all that going for her, Cosima had chosen Rae to be her best friend, and Rae still couldn't figure out why. She wasn't popular, she lived in a run-down neighborhood, and she didn't have an interesting life. When you looked at their friendship in those terms, was it really that big a deal if Cosima could be a little extra at times?

Now, as Rae walked to the cafeteria to meet Cosima for lunch, the butterflies that had been hibernating in her stomach sprang to life. Cosima was going to make her suffer for breaking their selfie pact.

There she was, leaning on the wall outside the cafeteria, scrolling through her phone and broadcasting her disinterest to everyone who walked by, snatched as ever in slouchy, wide-leg jeans with ultrawhite booties and a pale lavender V-neck cardigan falling off her shoulders with only the two middle buttons fastened.

She wasn't wearing a shirt underneath so her black bra straps and flat tummy were exposed to the world. Rae was way too self-conscious to wear anything that revealing, but not Cosima.

Cosima had swagger. She looked amazing and she knew it.

As soon as she was within reach, Cosima grabbed Rae by the elbow and dragged her into the cafeteria.

"What were you *thinking*? What is up with that selfie? I thought you were better than that."

"I know, I know. It was a compulsive decision," Rae groaned. "Thanks so much for liking the post, by the way."

"I'm sorry, but I honestly cannot condone such thirsty behavior. You screwed up your grid too."

Rae's shoulders slumped as she followed Cosima to the salad bar. It was true. For months now, she'd been alternating her Instagram posts between inspiring quotes on a pink background and outdoor shots with a black-and-white filter, which together created a pink-and-gray checkerboard layout that made the hair on her arms stand up in pleasure every time she looked at it. Last night's selfie post had butchered her Feed and made her need for approval that much easier to spot.

"Should I delete the photo?" Rae asked as they picked among the vegetables from the salad buffet. Honestly, she would have preferred packing her own lunch from home, but she hadn't wanted to deal with Cosima's criticism of whatever she was eating. She'd learned her lesson the hard way when Cosima had almost unfriended her for bringing a peanut-butter-and-honey sandwich wrapped in foil to school one day.

Oh hell no! she'd screamed as Rae unwrapped her sandwich. *What are you, a mentally disabled third grader?*

Plus, Cosima was literally obsessed with micros and macros and grams of sugar and counting calories. Rae had figured out pretty quickly that the only way to avoid her contempt was to eat exactly the same thing she was eating.

"Look, I get it," Cosima said, scrutinizing a stalk of broccoli. "You made an embarrassing plea for public validation. You know how desperate and vain it made you look, so now of course you want to delete the post. Destroy all evidence or whatever. But that will only make you look more pathetic. Deleting a post is a sign of weakness. You have to resist."

As usual, Cosima's insight into the unwritten laws of power on social media was spot-on. Rae sighed loudly and placed five cherry tomatoes on her tray.

"Your grid is looking cheugy anyway," Cosima said. "Maybe the universe is trying to tell you something."

That was news to Rae; Cosima was the one who had suggested the pink-and-gray design scheme in the first place. It was nearly impossible to keep up with her rules about what was cool and what was embarrassing.

The construction of their twin salads complete, Rae trailed behind Cosima as she sauntered to their usual table outside in the courtyard.

Evani and Olivia were already there, unpacking their lunches. Cosima exhaled loudly to make her irritation with this fact crystal clear. She preferred to be the alpha who decided which side of the table belonged to whom.

"Oh god," Olivia groaned as they dropped their backpacks on the ground. "Your salads are triggering me. Stop it with the diet culture already."

Cosima batted her eyes and shrugged. "Guilty as charged," she responded proudly.

Olivia rolled her eyes.

"Your new hair is fire, Rae," Evani said, unzipping their Adidas lunch bag.

"Thanks," she said, glancing at Cosima for some kind of reaction.

Nothing.

Rae had been eating lunch with Olivia and Evani since the third day of the semester, when they'd taken pity on her and waved her over as she walked around the cafeteria, looking for an empty table. They wouldn't have been her absolute first choice of lunch companions, but they were nice enough and they were both new to Zia High—Olivia had had to transfer from a performing arts charter school when her parents found edibles hidden in one of her socks, and Evani had just relocated to Albuquerque from Madison, Wisconsin.

Rae had planned on permanently switching from their table to Cosima's when it became clear that it was what Cosima wanted, but it was more awkward to break up with Olivia and Evani than she imagined. The four of them ended up sharing a table, and at first it felt like they'd had enough in common to at least eat lunch together. Lately, Rae had noticed some weird tension creeping into the group dynamic.

Despite the funky vibes, she made herself as comfortable as she could while she picked at her plate of cold vegetables. #Crudité, this was not. She had no appetite anyway. Not only was she depressed about the selfie but she was also starting to feel guilty about the way she'd yelled at her mom this morning. Her grandma would be so disappointed in her.

"Hey, where's your head at?" Cosima asked her in between bites of cantaloupe. "You didn't even say anything about my fit." She raised one irritated eyebrow and gestured toward her jeans and gleaming white boots.

"Love," Rae replied, making the shape of a heart with her hands.

It was pretty funny that Cosima was demanding props for her outfit, even though she still hadn't said a word about Rae's haircut. Sure, Rae had messed up with the selfie, but shouldn't her best friend at least acknowledge a major hair transformation?

As much as she was dying to call her out on her withholding behavior, Rae kept her mouth shut and focused on Olivia, who was unpacking her cheddar-and-sprouts sandwich and arranging it on the table in front of her next to a banana and a ziplock baggie full of Oreos. If only she could trade lunches with her! But Olivia would never be satisfied with a low-fat salad for lunch. She was always going off about how everyone should honor their hunger and how well-being was more important than appearance. Ha! It was easy for her to say it didn't matter what people looked like. She was a walking golden ratio.

"Hamia is going to eat lunch with us today, if that's okay," Evani blurted as they ate around the bright pink maraschino cherries in their fruit cup. They were addressing the whole group, but they were looking at Cosima.

"Hamia?" Cosima said, screwing up her face as if the name tasted bad.

"Yeah, you know—we have her in bio? She just moved here from New York?"

"The Lebanese girl? She's gay too? Wow, a Lebanese lesbian. That's so progressive of her," Cosima snickered.

"She's not gay," Evani said, their face flushing red.

"Then why is she hanging out with you?"

"Maybe because Evani is undisputedly awesome!" Olivia interrupted, her voice angry. "Did you think about that? It's not always about sex."

"You might want to tell *them* that," Cosima replied, nodding her head at Evani.

It was weird that Cosima would throw shade at Evani, who was not only smart and friendly but was also a member of the Gender and Sexuality Alliance, had a huge collection of activist T-shirts, and was always encouraging everyone to stand up for their rights. They weren't exactly easy prey.

"Um, hello," said a girl standing by the table, clutching a purple neoprene lunch tote.

"Hamia! I'm so sorry!" Evani said, jumping up. "Please, sit down."

Evani introduced everyone at the table while the shy girl sat and began removing glass containers filled with pita bread, pickled vegetables, and some kind of creamy sauce from her bag.

As tasty as her food looked, Hamia herself was so pretty that Rae found it hard not to stare. She had dark, curly hair and eyebrows so perfect, it actually hurt. Rae's eyebrows were thin and sparse, and if she didn't fill them in with an eyebrow pencil, you'd hardly notice they were there at all. On top of that, Hamia had flawless skin, pouty lips, and long, thin fingers with exquisitely shaped nails that she used to pry open the largest of her glass containers, unveiling little brown balls of something fried. Rae recognized them right away as falafel. Her mouth watered as the savory aroma of cumin and cilantro wafted into the air.

Cosima shoved her tray aside and cleared her throat. "What is *that*?" she asked.

Everyone looked over at Hamia's lunch at the same time.

"It's falafel," Hamia answered with a self-conscious smile.

"Oh, I love falafel," Evani said. "I get the falafel sandwich whenever I'm at Olympia Cafe." They were vegetarian, so maybe it was true.

"But Olympia Cafe is Greek, isn't it?" Cosima sneered. "Aren't you Lesbonese or something?"

"Hey! What's with the microaggression?" Evani snapped, dropping their fork.

"It's okay, Evani," Hamia said, straightening her back and turning to face Cosima. "I was actually born and raised in upstate New York, but yes, my family is originally from Lebanon. As far as where falafel came from, that's actually disputed within the Arab community. Most likely Egypt, since they were a major trade partner with Greece for centuries—which would explain how it was adopted into Greek cuisine, along with hummus. It's now eaten literally everywhere, but falafel definitely originated in the Arab world." She took a deep breath and smiled at Cosima. "So your confusion is forgiven."

All heads swiveled to Cosima.

"But Egypt—Egypt is in Africa," she blurted.

"Which was conquered by Arabs in the seventh century and is one of the original members of the Arab League, whose citizens speak Arabic and identify as Arabs," Hamia spoke in a slow, steady voice, like she was speaking to a child.

Wow. Cosima had been thoroughly schooled. Everyone turned back to her for a reaction.

Cosima narrowed her eyes into razor-sharp slits of meanness. "I've personally never tasted falafel," she said. "I'm always put off by the awful *stench*." She waved her hands in front of her face and made an expression like she wanted to puke.

Rae almost choked on a spinach leaf. Cosima's culture shaming was coming as a total surprise, and she wanted to say something that would make it clear to everyone she didn't share her opinion, like how she'd made falafel from scratch with her mom before, or that one of her grandma's favorite books was written by Kahlil Gibran, who she was pretty sure was Lebanese. She wanted to say something, but she heard herself laugh out loud instead.

It was nerves. Nerves made her do that.

"Seriously?" Evani's cheeks were red, and they were now clenching their fists at their sides. Rae had never seen them this upset before. "You're a fucking bigot now too?"

Cosima ignored Evani as she stared at Hamia, who had her head down. Tension engulfed the table as everyone waited to see what would happen next. Out of nowhere, Cosima threw her head back and started laughing.

"I'm just kidding, Hamia! I'm just hazing you." She slapped her knees like she'd made the funniest joke ever.

Hamia looked up and smiled hesitantly. Olivia and Evani glanced at each other, at Rae, and then back at Cosima, frowning.

"C'mon, fam," Cosima said. "You know I'm not a racist." To prove her point, she reached across the table and plucked one of Hamia's falafel balls from its glass container and popped it in her mouth.

Hamia's eyes widened.

Cosima stood and stretched her arms above her head like a lazy house cat without a care in the world. "Not bad," she said, licking her lips. "C'mon, Rae, let's scope out some hotties before the bell rings."

Avoiding eye contact with the others, Rae stood and started to gather her belongings. Evani, Olivia, and Hamia sat in stunned silence.

Had Cosima really been teasing, or had she only pretended to be teasing once she felt everyone's bad vibes?

Rae reached for her tray and Cosima grabbed her by the wrist. "Leave it."

Rae dropped the tray. It clattered on the table.

"Later, haters," Cosima called over her shoulder as she linked arms with Rae and skipped away from the table.

They walked around the courtyard arm in arm like everything was normal. Rae waited for her heart to stop pounding in her chest.

"Why did you do that?" she finally asked.

"Huh? Do what?" Cosima was watching a group of senior boys kick around a soccer ball in the middle of the grassy courtyard, waiting for them to notice her.

"Why were you so mean to Hamia?"

"Oh. That," Cosima said, smiling as the boys looked up to watch her pass by. "People have to learn to be less sensitive, don't you think?"

She turned to look at Rae with the fake smile meant for the boys still plastered on her face. Rae shuddered as Cosima's bleached-white teeth gleamed in the afternoon sun.

Chapter Three

As if her day wasn't shitty enough, Andy wasn't in fifth period.

Rae had had a thing for Andy since pretty much her first day as a sophomore, when he was assigned to be her lab partner for fifth-period chemistry and she discovered that, on top of being a popular football player with obvious rizz, he was also funny and smart—maybe even smarter than her. It didn't hurt that he was super cute and smelled like grass and fresh laundry and made her stomach flip over every time she saw him. He was probably the only person in the entire world who could have made her feel human again, and she was shattered by the emptiness on his side of the desk. He was a wide receiver for the Zia Raptors, and she'd totally forgotten that the team had left by bus that morning for an away game in Las Cruces.

She sent him a Snap of his empty chair with a black heart emoji before she got down to extracting bismuth from crushed-up Pepto-Bismol tablets all by herself, wondering if she would've told Andy about the incident between Cosima and Hamia if he'd been in class today. What would she have said? That her best friend was a racist?

At the sound of the dismissal bell, Rae bolted to the less-used bathroom upstairs and locked herself in a stall with her feet up on the toilet seat in case Cosima came looking for her.

Lately, they'd been meeting in the downstairs foyer and walking outside to wait for their rides together, spilling the tea on anything interesting that had occurred between lunch and last period before they went their separate ways and carried on a stream of almost uninterrupted communication through Snapchat. Not today. The episode with Hamia was really confusing. Had Cosima casually revealed a never-before-seen prejudiced side to her personality? Evani and Olivia sure seemed to think so. The aching dread Rae felt in the pit of her stomach suggested they were probably right.

But Cosima was her friend. Wouldn't a loyal friend decide to believe that she'd been joking?

The only plan that made sense was to avoid Cosima until she could figure out if she was a racist bigot or not.

After the pandemonium unleashed by the bell subsided to a low hum, Rae crept downstairs and situated herself at the bottom of the concrete stairs leading to the school entrance. Her stomach lurched when she finally took out her phone and opened Cosima's Snap of the empty lobby, followed by one of the pointy toes of her booted feet waiting on the sidewalk outside, and lastly, a disturbing Snap of her glossy, frowning mouth. Rae's disappearing act had definitely landed her on Cosima's shit list.

Oh well. She had all weekend to beg for forgiveness.

The November afternoon had warmed up at least ten degrees since lunch, with an occasional thin cloud stretching across the pale blue sky overhead. She took off her hoodie and allowed the feeling of the sun on her face and arms to take some of the tension out of her shoulders as she scrolled through Snapchat, Instagram, and TikTok—and then, when her grandma still hadn't shown up, YouTube, Facebook, and X. She even scrounged around on BeReal for a while.

As the last few students drifted out of her peripheral vision, Rae realized she might actually be the last student left on campus.

If it were anyone else, she would have been furious. But she couldn't get mad at her grandma, whose running-late problem was getting worse every day. She knew she would eventually show up—smiling to hide how flustered she was, going off about how she had gotten lost in some book or misplaced her purse or car keys or forgotten that she'd needed to stop for gas.

Rae's mom complained nonstop about how spacey her grandma was getting. Sometimes she even said right to her face that it might be time to put her in a nursing home, which, in Rae's opinion, was just mean.

A full forty-five minutes after the bell rang, her grandma's little blue Honda pulled up to the curb. Sure enough, her grandma waved and smiled as if everything was normal.

"Grandma, you're *really* late," Rae said as she opened the passenger door and got inside.

"I know, honey, I'm so sorry! I was looking for something I misplaced and I lost track of time. First things first, give me a kiss." Her grandma leaned over and offered Rae her cheek.

Rae's grandma was her favorite person in the whole world. Not only was she always positive and nice to everyone she met but she was also an interesting person who knew a lot about all kinds of different things, like chakras, homeopathic remedies, the history of Hawaii, and the best way to poach an egg. She had a ton of hobbies—gardening, painting, and sewing—and she wasn't trying to be like everyone else. She had her own unique style and she totally owned it.

Today, for example, she was wearing a white Mexican Puebla dress embroidered with bright orange-and-pink flowers on the chest and around the hem, paired with green cargo pants and big, black Army boots. Her gray hair was cropped very close to her head, almost shaved. On her fingers she wore multiple silver rings, each with a different semiprecious stone—turquoise, lapis lazuli, and tourmaline, which had special healing properties she knew about from her dad, Rae's great-grandpa Ignacio, who had been a curandero in northern New Mexico when her grandma was a little girl.

Rae didn't know anyone else who had a grandma like hers.

She settled in her seat and plugged her dying phone into the car's USB charger. Her grandma wasn't a control freak about the time Rae spent on her phone, unlike her mom, who would randomly force her to put her phone down and make eye contact when she was talking to her. These hypocritical episodes of moral superiority were almost too much to bear.

Rae was trying to think of something cute and funny to say in response to Andy's last Snap when she noticed that her grandma had driven right by Tenth Street, where she would normally take a right to get to Rae's apartment.

"Grandma, you passed my street!"

"I'm taking you to my place first," her grandma explained. "For tea."

"But I've got so much homework—"

"It's the weekend, Rae. It can wait," her grandma said, patting her knee.

Rae dropped her phone in her lap and crossed her arms over her chest. Her grandma had no freaking idea how much homework kids had to deal with in the modern world—or how essential it was for Rae to stick to her schedule. She was supposed to visit her grandma on Sunday after she'd completed all of her assignments, not on Friday before she'd even started.

Her stomach hurt just thinking about everything she had to do. Besides the outline for her chem lab paper, she had to complete an entire set of algebra problems and finish reading *The Catcher in the Rye*, which she couldn't get into. Holden Caulfield was supposed to be this amazing savior of innocence, but in Rae's opinion, he was sort of a douche. His judgmental point of view stressed her out. Plus, he was always saying how phony everybody was, and it secretly made Rae wonder if she was a phony too.

She would probably be forced to use SparkNotes, which wouldn't be the first time. Was it her fault her teachers assigned way more homework than one person could possibly accomplish in one weekend? Was it her fault her English Lit teacher only assigned old-ass books that had nothing relevant to say about contemporary society? Enough with this constant obsessing over the past.

She peeked at her grandma, who was driving in silence and chewing on her bottom lip, oblivious to Rae's distress. Normally, she would have been asking Rae a million questions about how her day was and what she had learned in school.

"Highs and Lows?" Rae suggested. Highs and Lows was a game she and her grandma had been playing for as long as Rae could remember, where they took turns describing the best and worst parts of their days.

"Sure," her grandma said. "You go first."

"Well," Rae began, "it's hard for me to pick one low because there were so many of them. I found out at lunch that Cosima might be racist and possibly homophobic, too, and the boy I'm sort of crushing on wasn't in school today. But the lowest of the lows is that I got into a fight with my mom this morning and I said things to her that I feel bad about now. It was her fault, though."

"What happened?"

"She changed our morning plans at the last minute . . . again! She knows it triggers me when she messes with my routine."

"Well, that's understandable," her grandma said. "You're still learning to trust her again. Maybe you never will. Who knows? She has to learn to accept the consequences of the choices she's made in life."

Rae was surprised. She'd expected her grandma to remind her to be compassionate and forgiving. "I shouldn't be mean to her, though, right?"

"Of course not, sweetie. Don't be mean. But I know you're trying." Another pat on the knee. "What about your highs? Any of those today?"

"Right now. Seeing you."

Her grandma smiled but didn't reply.

"What about you, Grandma?" Rae asked as they pulled into her apartment complex.

"I had a big low today, honey, a big low. I lost something precious. Well, I lost it, misplaced it, or someone took it from me, but I only realized today that it was missing. Come inside and I'll tell you all about it."

Rae followed her grandma up the stairs to her second-story apartment and wondered what had gone missing this time. Her grandma misplaced something at least once every time Rae visited—her car keys, phone, credit card, a pair of her favorite earrings—and of course, Rae usually had to stop everything she was doing and help her find it. It stressed her out. And today she noticed her grandma was going extra slow up the stairs, pausing every third step to catch her breath.

Rae pushed the worry out of her head and leaned over to scratch behind the ears of her grandma's skinny orange cat, Kazak, who was waiting by the front door. She and Kazak followed her grandma inside.

Her mouth dropped open when she saw the condition of her grandma's apartment.

Receipts, letters, and pens were strewn across the surface of her grandma's vintage writing desk, which normally stood so dignified in the entryway, and scraps of paper lay all over the floor and across the sectional in the living room, which someone had pulled apart. Her grandma's collection of cozy cushions and lap blankets were scattered around the room and the coffee table was standing on its side.

What the actual fuck?

When she walked further into the small apartment, Rae discovered that the hall closet was open, with boots and raincoats spilling into the hallway. Every shelf and drawer in the kitchen had been emptied, their contents scattered everywhere: measuring spoons, dried oregano, toothpicks, AAA batteries. The apartment looked like a TV crime scene, only without the blood.

"Grandma, what *happened*?"

Her grandma opened the fridge and for a second Rae thought she might start ransacking that, too, but she just grabbed a pitcher of iced tea.

"Sit and we'll have a little snack and a chat," she said, gesturing to the yellow Formica breakfast table piled with random junk.

As her grandma poured them both a glass of tea and arranged some mint Milano cookies on a plate, Rae dropped her backpack on the floor and sat at the table. Her eyes were drawn to a rusted metal box that looked out of place on the table. She'd never seen it before: it was about the size of a large shoebox, weathered green with spots of rust and two large metal clasps, a plain handle, and a plaque on the outside that read BARCO SWIVEL JOINTS with some manufacturing information printed underneath.

Rae unlatched the squeaky lid and opened the box to inspect the two compartments inside. The first compartment held a small bundle wrapped in an old paisley-print scarf and the second compartment contained stacks of strange cards, smooth and shiny as glass but not as fragile. Each card was hand-painted in tiny strokes of brilliant colors, depicting different landscapes and people Rae had never seen before. Some of the cards were painted with numbers, symbols, and letters that didn't make any sense.

Rae unwrapped the paisley-print scarf to reveal a worn leather belt with a silver case that functioned as a buckle, about the size of a pack of cigarettes, with a blank LED display and three slots just big enough to hold the cards. Two of the slots already had cards inserted, and Rae tried to pry one out with her fingernails.

"Here, here," her grandma said, putting the cookies on the table. "That's not how you do it. Hand it over."

"What is it?" Rae asked. "An old game?"

Her grandma grabbed the case and sat down in the chair beside her. "This, my dear granddaughter," she said, spreading her arms toward the old toolbox and everything in it, "is the key to the triple world."

"The triple world?"

"The triple world, the space-time continuum, the fourth dimension—there are a lot of names for it. When I was your age, we just called it the Block." She chuckled and bit into a cookie. "Normally, I wouldn't initiate you on the fly like this, but I've lost my personal travel card and you're the only one who can help me find it. At least you're sixteen, that's what really matters."

"I'm all ears," Rae said, taking a big drink of her iced tea. She wasn't sure what her grandma was talking about, but she had a feeling deep in her bones that it was something serious, kind of like how it felt when her mom and dad had sat her down to tell her they were getting divorced. Her palms were sweating, just as they had then.

"*Space-time*," her grandma continued, "is a word used to talk about the three dimensions of space and the one dimension of time merged together to create the four-dimensional, unchanging block universe. It's every place and every time that ever was and ever will be, for everyone who lives. We call it the triple world because it contains the past, present, and future—all equally real, all happening simultaneously."

The idea that the past and future were as real as the present didn't make any sense to Rae. In her experience, the present moment was the only thing that felt real. The past was a fading memory and the future was just a dream, but everything that actually happened was happening in the present moment. How could the past, present, and future occur at the same time?

As she thought about her grandma's definition of space-time, Rae watched her take cards out of the metal toolbox and sort them into separate stacks on the table. She made one pile of cards with locations and dates and one pile with time quantities on them: *one month, two days, four hours,* and so on. The cards that didn't fit into either of these categories, her grandma set aside.

She found the card she was looking for and held it up, face out, so Rae could see it.

The woman on the card had long, straight hair the same shade of brown as Rae's. If she squinted her eyes, the woman sort of looked like her, too, only she was older and wearing an indigo space suit and holding a white cat in her arms.

"This is your personal travel card," her grandma said.

When she looked closer, she saw her name written at the bottom of the card in old-fashioned cursive: *Andrea Aragon.* Whoever made the card had decided not to include her dad's half of her hyphenated last name, and they'd painted a border of tiny sunflowers around the image.

"I love sunflowers," Rae whispered.

"I know you do, honey, and so does your great-grandpa. He painted this portrait of you."

"How could he know I love sunflowers? He died before I was even born!"

"Your grandpa is a space-time traveler, Rae, just like you. He can move through space-time to visit different people and places across human history. He may not be present in the particular slice of space-time we currently inhabit, but he's certainly not dead. You'll meet him one day."

Rae realized with a terrible pain in her heart that her grandma had straight up lost her mind. Here she was, worried about her grandma misplacing her car keys and forgetting what time it was when the situation was actually much, much worse. She was completely delusional! Something would have to be done right away.

Rae pulled her phone from her back pocket to text her mom. Maybe her doctor could prescribe some kind of emergency Alzheimer's medication to help her.

"Hey, hey, gimme that," her grandma said, swiping the phone out of her hand. "You think I've lost my marbles? Well, of course you do." She closed her eyes and rubbed her temples the way she did when she was thinking really hard. At last, she said, "The only way you'll ever believe that what I'm saying is true is if you experience it for yourself. It's time to take a little trip, Rae."

Her grandma picked up the stack of cards with the dates and numbers on them.

"Here," she said, passing them to Rae. "These are space-time locations, or destination cards. They indicate a specific point of space and time somewhere in the Block that we can visit if we want to. I inherited all these cards from my dad."

Rae flipped through the destination cards, most of which were pictures of ordinary places: a mountain slope, a park bench, somebody's living room. There weren't any people in most of the pictures, so it was hard to tell what year they depicted just by looking at them.

"Most of the destination cards in this box go backward in time from this point," her grandma explained. "Not many go forward."

"Why not forward?" Rae asked. She knew it was all made up, but even so, she was intrigued by her grandma's story.

"It's harder to blend into the future than it is to blend into the past," her grandma replied. "There's nowhere here to buy the clothes you would need to look like you belong in the future. And once our civilizations stop using cash, it's tricky to get your hands on essentials like food." She gestured to the pile in Rae's hands. "Pick one of those."

Rae flipped through the stack of cards, breathing in through her nose and out through her mouth to avoid an anxiety spiral.

The first card that caught her attention was a picture of a group of huge outdoor fountains shooting different-colored streams of illuminated water into the night sky. *Lima, Peru* was written above the painted fountains in ornate script, with the date and time *October 5, 2017, 7:38 a.m.* written below in slightly smaller letters. Below all of that were the numbers *–12.04318, –77.02824-0999 .76.0000876.*

"What do those numbers mean?" Rae asked.

"Those are the space-time coordinates for the specific time and geographical position this card would take you if you could go. You can't, though." She snatched the card out of Rae's hand. "Sorry. I thought I removed all those."

"Why can't I go?" Rae asked, suddenly overwhelmed with an indescribable longing to stand in front of those beautiful fountains and feel the cool water spray on her face.

"You see that symbol there?" Rae's grandma pointed to an orange crescent moon about the size of a sunflower seed painted in the lower left-hand corner of the card. "That's your symbol. It means your personal world line extends through 2017, so you absolutely cannot go there. Any chance of meeting up with yourself at another point in space-time must be avoided at all costs, no matter how remote."

"What would happen if I met myself?" Rae asked. It was hard to imagine what that would feel like—to walk up to yourself and say hello.

"Never mind that now," Rae's grandma replied, taking all the cards from Rae and spreading them facedown on the table in front of her. "How about we let fate decide instead? Try this. Hold your hands a few inches above the cards and slowly move them across until you feel one trying to get your attention."

Rae hesitated, unsure if it was the right thing to do. She was interested in the cards, but she didn't want to encourage her grandma to go deeper down the rabbit hole.

On the other hand, if she continued to play along, she could gather information to pass on to her mom later.

With her hands above the table, she began to move them across the cards.

"Slower," her grandma instructed.

Rae slowed her hands down until they were barely moving. She moved them across the whole row of cards and was passing back in the other direction when, all of a sudden, she felt a warm tingling in both her palms.

Her hands froze in midair. What was happening?

"There!" her grandma exclaimed. She plucked the card directly below Rae's hovering hands and turned it over to reveal its face. It was a picture of a large sagebrush in the middle of a desert plateau, set against a clear blue sky with fluffy clouds and a mountain range in the background.

Taos, New Mexico, May 15, 1984, 2:45 p.m., the card read. Definitely no orange moon in the lower left-hand corner.

"That's absolutely perfect!" Her grandma clapped her hands together. "My father lived in Taos in 1984, and he's the man you need to see! How interesting that you picked 1984. That's a transformational year, you know, and it attracts a lot of energy. Everyone is always returning to 1984 in some way or another. Can you believe it?"

"No, I . . . I can't believe it," Rae said, shaking her head. She turned her hands over and stared at her palms. Was it the power of suggestion that had caused them to tingle like that?

"This first trip will be a short one, just to make a believer out of you." Her grandma flipped through another pile of cards. "Here—this should do the trick." She passed Rae a card with the words *three hours* written in fancy purple letters across the top.

"The time here," she explained, tapping the numbers on the card, "refers to the passage of time in whatever space-time zone you start from. You have to remember that you'll experience time differently depending on how far your visiting point is from your current space-time position. The further you travel, the more time will pass for you in comparison to your home base. You can add five minutes to every hour for every year away you travel to, in order to calculate approximately how much time will elapse in whatever space-time zone you visit. In this instance, you'll be gone for three hours from our current location in space-time, but over there you will be gone for . . . "

Her grandma's voice trailed off as she did the math.

Watching as she used her fingers to figure out the equation, Rae was amazed at the complexity of her delusional world-building. How had she managed to keep her dementia hidden from them for so long?

"Ten hours!" her grandma exclaimed. "You will spend approximately ten hours in 1984, but only three hours will pass here. You'll be back in time for a late dinner."

Rae glanced at the clock on the wall. It was 5:15. "Does my mom know I'll be time traveling?"

"Oh no, honey, she doesn't have a clue about any of this stuff."

Her grandma picked up the silver case from her metal toolbox and pressed the two indents on its otherwise smooth sides. The two cards inside popped out. She put them on top of her pile of cards facedown so Rae couldn't see them and replaced them with the sagebrush card and the three-hour card. The case made a mechanical whirring sound when it sucked the new cards inside, reminding Rae of the bill slot on a self-checkout register.

"Those are your destination and duration cards." She held up the third and final card, the Andrea Aragon card. "This is your personal traveler card. You can't activate a space-time portal without some variation of these three categories of cards inserted into the itinerary case."

She looked like she was about to say something else but changed her mind and shook her head instead.

"Okay, are you ready?"

"Actually, I don't feel ready at all," Rae confessed, forgetting for a moment that she was playing make-believe.

Her grandma looked surprised. "Not ready? Hmm. Right. I suppose you'll need some travel tips before you take off. Okay, let me think. Whatever you do, don't mention time travel to anyone. You might end up in a mental hospital or even in jail, depending on what year you visit. Don't reveal any information about the future. Don't even mention the future. And don't call any attention to yourself."

"Jeez, Grandma! I'm not exactly feeling reassured over here. Time travel sounds scary."

"No, no, no. You'll be fine. You're a viajera del tiempo by blood! Go with the flow. Don't resist anything too much. You'll want to blend into your environment as much as possible. Think of yourself as a scientist—you're there to observe, not participate. Even if you feel that you should try to change a situation, resist the urge, okay? As much as possible."

"But what about the observer effect?" Rae asked.

Her grandma cocked her head to the side.

"It's the theory that observation alone will change something," Rae explained. "We just learned about it in science class. Mr. Quintana said observing a situation or phenomenon always has an effect on whatever is being observed, no matter what."

"Really? That's fascinating." Her grandma rubbed her temples again. "I'm giving you the same advice my dad gave me when I started my travels, but in my experience, it's actually much harder to change the past than the movies will have you believe. But the old man was right about one thing—it's a mistake to try. I don't want you to learn the hard way."

Rae wasn't too sure about that. Mr. Q was really smart. He said researchers always influenced the results of their experiments, even if they did everything in their power to control for it. What if Rae visited 1984 and said something stupid that would change the course of human history? What if she accidentally negated her own existence or caused World War III or something? The thought was beyond stressful . . . until she remembered that none of it was real.

Her grandma stood and handed her the leather belt with the case attached.

"Okay, honey, it's time. Put the belt around your waist and insert your traveler card into the itinerary case. This will open a space-time portal from here to Taos, New Mexico, in 1984. Right here in my kitchen! Isn't that exciting? And since you're wearing the belt, you'll be swept up in it."

Rae's face must have revealed her anxiety because her grandma put her arm around her and pulled her close.

"It doesn't hurt, don't worry." She gave her a pat on the shoulder. "Now, when the timer on the case counts down to zero"—she pointed to the LED display on the back of the silver case—"you need to get yourself to an isolated spot before the space-time portal opens again to bring you back home. People are pretty good at explaining away anything bizarre or supernatural they might witness, but it's less complicated if no one actually watches you disappear into thin air. All right, then. Do you have any questions before you go?"

Any questions? If she had actually been preparing to visit 1984, Rae would have had a million questions for her grandma. How did the portal work? Would she feel anything? What should she do once she got there? Wouldn't people be able to tell she was from the future? Should she pack snacks?

But since she wouldn't be going any further than her grandma's kitchen, all she had to do was play through the rest of this uncomfortable charade before she called her mom and broke the news that her grandma had lost her shit.

"I'm ready," she said, standing from her chair. She pulled the belt through the loops of her jeans, and her grandma reached over and connected one of the punch holes on the belt to the prong on the case, tugging on the leather to make sure it was secure. She nodded at Rae to indicate it was time to insert her travel card.

"Good luck, honey," she said.

Rae grew increasingly nervous as she inserted the Andrea Aragon card into the case and waited for what would happen next. Everything she had ever seen about time portals on TV made her imagine a swirling vortex of bright colors and laser-beam lights that would open right in front of her, a doorway through space and time made of pure energy that would whip her hair and clothes around as though she were standing in the center of a windstorm. In the movies, the hero who stood in front of the time portal had to choose whether they were going to step into the portal or run away.

The actual time portal was barely visible at first. She might not have noticed it at all if the air around her hadn't become thick and wobbly, like asphalt shimmering on a hot summer day. She felt like she was swimming in oatmeal, and she struggled to breathe in enough oxygen. Everything around the edges of her vision turned gray as the refraction of light around her intensified and the center of the vortex tugged at her like a huge magnet.

Her heart was pounding so fast, she was afraid it might burst. She tried to scream, but no sound came out. Her grandma leaned in close with a look of concern on her face. Her mouth was moving, but Rae couldn't hear what she was saying.

The ground beneath her feet suddenly dropped and Rae had the horrible sensation of endless falling that she had only ever experienced in nightmares. She thrashed her arms and legs about, hoping for something to grab onto as she fell and fell and fell through a tunnel of silent, brilliant light.

And then there was nothing.

Chapter Four

When Rae regained consciousness, she was lying flat on her back between two huge sagebrush in the middle of the high desert. She opened her eyes and watched the fat, white clouds pass across the expanse of brilliant, blue sky above her, searching her mind for any memory of how she got here. But it was as though her mind was a clean, blank slate. She remembered nothing.

When she turned her head to the right, she discovered that her nose was mere inches away from a massive prickly-pear cactus. She was close enough to count the sharp, slender needles that protruded in clusters from each individual areole on the dimpled flesh of every cactus pad. She felt like she was seeing a cactus for the very first time, and for a while, she could do nothing but admire the way the sprays of white needles reflected the sunlight.

Once her inventory of the cactus was complete, Rae sat up, stretched her arms, and wiggled her fingers and toes. Nothing hurt and everything was where it should be, so she probably hadn't fallen. Had she curled up in the sagebrush for an afternoon nap?

It was bright outside, but the air had a briskness to it. She was wearing her Converse and her favorite black hoodie, which she suddenly remembered picking up off her floor this morning. This sliver of memory led to a memory of fighting with her mom, which led to her shitty day at school and waiting on the curb for her grandma. But her memory of the day ended there.

Everywhere she looked was a vast blanket of sagebrush and scrubby piñon mingled with black rocks, spindly cholla, and low patches of prickly-pear cactus. Anthills teeming with tiny workers coming and going as they foraged for food were located everywhere among the cacti. To the east was a low range of juniper-covered mountains. The crisp air was filled with the fragrant, clean smell of dirt and cedar. A baby whiptail scurried across her shoe.

Google Maps would know this place.

She reached for her phone in her back pocket and screamed out loud when she realized it wasn't there. She jumped to her feet and began to circle the area, poking frantically through the dirt and brush with her Converse, praying for a glimpse of her phone. But every damn bush looked the same as every other bush and they all stretched on forever, which made it hard to keep track of where she'd started and which bushes she'd already checked. What if she wandered off too far and got herself even more lost? The thought made her hands sweat.

Every survivalist she'd ever watched on YouTube said the same thing: *In any emergency, the first thing you need to do is calm down and assess the situation, or you risk doing something stupid and probably dying.* The last thing she wanted to do was have a panic attack and pass out and die out here in the wilderness, so she closed her eyes and breathed in through her nose and out through her mouth until her pulse slowed. Turning in a circle to get a full view of her surroundings, she spotted a ring of tall trees on the horizon with buildings on the other side. All she had to do was walk until she reached them, and hopefully she'd be able to borrow someone's phone to call her mom. No biggie.

As she walked through the sagebrush toward the trees, Rae remembered her grandma sitting at her kitchen table in front of a metal toolbox filled with cards. They had a tradition of playing card games together—Uno and Go Fish and rummy—but the cards in this particular memory were unlike any she had ever seen before. Each one had a colorful picture of a strange person or place on its face.

The cards in this fuzzy memory reminded her of the cards in Magic: The Gathering, a game she'd discovered by accident in fifth grade when she purchased a hinged cookie tin filled with the cards from a thrift store. Mesmerized by the vivid illustrations of dragons, Swamps, and Dwarven Warriors, she'd been determined to master the game before she realized every other kid who played MTG belonged to a social group she would then need to become a part of if she wanted to play: nerd archetypes—boys, mainly—with greasy hair and mismatched socks who sat in the back of the classroom avoiding eye contact but lit up during conversations about the probability of finding a Black Lotus card in a vintage booster pack. As much as she'd enjoyed building decks and discovering new creature cards and spells, it was obvious such a move would ruin her socially. She'd wanted to be one of the popular, sparkly-eyed kids, not one of the untouchables, so she'd shoved the tin of cards in the back of her closet next to her oboe.

These other cards, though—their memory washed up in her mind with a residue of anxiety but also of wonder. Whatever she and her grandma had been playing, it hadn't been Go Fish.

As Rae stepped around brush and over clumps of cacti, extra careful not to poke herself through her Cons, she became aware of an unfamiliar weight around her waist. She lifted her hoodie and inspected the silver belt buckle that was really a case . . .

"An itinerary case!" she said aloud, though she wasn't sure what that meant.

She stopped, examining the shiny object. The LED timer ticked off one number as she stood and tried to remember what the case was and where it had come from.

Her efforts were interrupted by the voice of a girl yelling from somewhere nearby.

Rae sprinted toward the voice. Whether to offer help or find it, she wasn't sure.

She came to a quick halt when she reached the source of the yelling. Rae gasped at the unexpected sight.

Sitting cross-legged on a plaid blanket spread on the dirt was a lanky girl with black, spiky hair. She wore smudged sunglasses and wired headphones and was singing off-key to music Rae couldn't hear. She pounded out the beat with her hands on her knees.

The girl stopped singing when she saw Rae and yanked her headphones off her ears.

"Hi," she said with a huge grin that suggested there was nothing at all weird about sitting alone in the middle of the desert in the middle of the day, singing to yourself. "Who are you?"

"I'm Rae."

The girl lifted her sunglasses to get a better look at her. "What are you doing here?"

Rae opened her mouth to answer, but she didn't even know herself. Her mind was as empty as the terrain she'd found herself in. It was quiet, too, in and around her, except for the unhinged voice of a man still singing out of the girl's headphones.

"I'm not sure," Rae finally answered. "Walking around. How about you?"

The girl pressed the Stop button on her device. "I'm ditching school," she explained, gesturing to her backpack and the paper lunch sack beside her. She kicked the half-eaten peanut-butter-and-jelly sandwich laying at her feet and Rae watched it fly and land in the dirt.

"You can sit if you want," the girl offered.

Avoiding smears of strawberry jam, Rae sat on the blanket and pretended to take in the view of the mountains while she peered at the bizarre girl out of the corner of her eye.

The girl's hair was an unnatural shade of black that gleamed almost blue in the sunlight, cut short and sticking up everywhere in stiff, sharp spikes. She was wearing Ray-Ban Wayfarers and long earrings made of chains and safety pins. Some of her bright red lipstick remained on her mouth, but most of it had transferred to her now-punted lunch in half-moon shapes. Rae was almost positive her indigo jeans were vintage Levi's, folded in pinroll cuffs over an enormous pair of dirty combat boots. The whole fit was finished with a comically oversized men's herringbone suit jacket with the sleeves rolled up.

Rae tried to figure out where she was at from a fashion perspective: her vampy lips and blue-black hair said gothcore but with indie-grunge overtones and a dose of eighties-influenced big-suit vibes thrown in for good measure. Because why not?

"Why are you ditching school?" Rae asked. In her mind, ditching was the sign of a low achiever.

"I had to listen to my new tape," the girl explained, ejecting a cassette from the device on her lap. It was branded with the word WALKMAN in a retrofuturistic font. She passed the cassette to Rae tenderly, as if she were handling a baby animal.

Rae had seen an audio cassette before—in dusty stacks at Goodwill or, more often, as a cheugy graphic on T-shirts and tote bags carried by her mom and everyone else's mom she knew—but she'd never actually held one before. The plastic shell that protected the magnetic tape inside was lightweight and held together by the tiniest little screws. The name Simple Minds was printed in black letters below the window that separated two tape reels, and the title *Sparkle in the Rain* was printed below that. Each side of the cassette listed a set of different songs under Program 1 and Program 2, which were 21:50 and 22:55 minutes long, respectively.

She shook the cassette tape to hear its internal mechanisms jiggle before handing it back to the girl, who placed it gently back into her Walkman and closed the cover. She was pushing her retro vibe to the limit.

"Should we go back to my house and listen to it?" she suggested.

Rae reached for her phone in her back pocket to check the time before she remembered that she had lost it somewhere. "What time is it?" she asked.

The girl looked at the watch on her wrist, a bulky, red plastic thing with actual moving hands. She was certainly committed to her analog technology.

"It's 3:15," she said.

"Will your parents know you were ditching school?"

"Ha!" the girl scoffed as she wrapped the cord neatly around her headphones and Walkman before tucking it all into the inner pocket of her massive suit jacket. She stood and jammed her schoolbooks and a half-eaten apple into her backpack, and after Rae stood, the girl balled up the thin blanket and shoved that in there too.

"I'm Iggy, by the way," she said. "I turned sixteen in February. How old are you?"

"I turned sixteen in September," Rae responded. There was something significant about being sixteen, but she couldn't remember what it was. Something her grandma had said.

"What kind of music do you listen to?" Iggy threw her backpack over her shoulders and started walking toward the blurry cluster of buildings on the horizon, taking brisk, confident steps that made it obvious this was not her first time playing hooky in the sagebrush. Her legs were long and Rae had to run to stay two steps behind her.

"Oh, you know, a little K-pop, some hip-hop, but mainly shoegaze and dream pop."

"Hip-hop? Like Newcleus and the Sugarhill Gang?"

"Uh . . ."

"No, no, wait—how about 'Double Dutch Bus?'" Iggy turned around and started walking and skipping backward, shouting out nonsensical lyrics and waiting for a verbal response from Rae, who had no idea what the girl was doing or how she should respond.

She was beginning to feel embarrassed by her shameless singing, so she said nothing.

"*Ho! Ho! Ho!*" Iggy responded to her own call, jabbing the air with her fist and shouting each syllable with the full force of her lungs before turning around and calmly continuing their conversation as she led the way through the brush. "Okay, tell me this," she said. "Who are your top five favorite bands of all time?"

"I'd have to think about that."

"Not me! I've already thought about it plenty. They are"—she held up her hand and began ticking off fingers—"the Clash, Talking Heads, and Siouxsie and the Banshees as my top three, no question. Then probably the Pretenders and Violent Femmes after that. Or maybe New Order instead of the Femmes. Except on some days, I'd put Simple Minds up there, too, and definitely U2 has to be up there, you know what I'm saying? Their music has a similar feeling, don't you think? And what about Tears for Fears? Wait, maybe Bowie instead of Siouxsie, except—no, I'd feel really bad if I didn't have the Cure somewhere on my list. I love Adam and the Ants, too. Maybe we should do top ten? Hey, do you like ska? Two-tone? Have you heard of the Specials? The English Beat?"

Iggy didn't wait for an answer to any of her questions. It was like she was talking to herself, which was fine with Rae. The steady rhythm and up-and-down cadence of Iggy's animated voice had a soothing effect on her as she followed her footsteps through the desert.

Iggy was taller than Rae, with shoulders that seemed broader than they probably were thanks to the enormous shoulder pads in her ridiculous jacket. Her boots looked heavy, and she landed each step with unnecessary force. She was as loud and obnoxious as a British football fan, yet Rae couldn't remember the last time she had met someone this friendly and open.

"Where are we exactly?" Rae asked, straining to make her voice as carefree as possible.

"We're in Taos, about ten miles south of town," Iggy replied, unfazed.

How had Rae ended up in Taos? She hadn't had any plans to come to Taos. Her mom had been born here but Rae had only visited once before, when she was little. Why Taos? How long had she been here?

Oh man, her mom had probably put out an APB by now. If Rae had her phone, she could check for an Amber Alert.

"Hey, can I use your phone?" she asked. "I think I lost mine somewhere out here."

Iggy turned with a quizzical look on her face. "We're almost at my house," she said. "We have a phone there."

Now Rae was confused. Did Iggy not have a cell phone? Maybe she had strict parents who wouldn't allow her to take her phone to school or something. Rae had always wondered about those kinds of parents. How did they expect their kids to get help in an emergency situation?

At last, they crossed through the circle of cottonwood trees she'd seen from a distance, which had obscured the exact nature of things on the inside. Her eyes widened as she followed Iggy toward a sprawling adobe house that sat in the middle of the property next to an A-frame barn and a stand-alone garage with a sagging roof. Weird, long-haired people were walking around everywhere. Rae almost tripped over an abandoned tricycle as they passed a half dozen tents of different shapes and sizes pitched right there in the driveway. More people were standing around a fire pit dug in the ground. One woman had her shirt off and her boobs were just hanging out for everyone to see.

They passed a garden with handwritten signs identifying onions, carrots, and sugar snap peas that had recently been planted, then an amazingly ugly Chrysler Town & Country station wagon in a pukey shade of green with real wood paneling along the sides. It had to be at least fifty years old and three times the size of a normal car. It was literally as big as a sailboat! Rae wrote her initials in the dust on the passenger window as they walked by: *AA*.

AA? Those weren't her initials.

"That's our piece-of-crap car," Iggy said.

"It's . . . interesting," Rae replied.

"Yeah, that's the word." Iggy laughed.

Rae tried not to stare at the grungy people chilling out under the trees and around the camping area as they neared the barn. No one seemed to notice them. Everywhere she looked, something was happening. She heard dogs barking, chickens clucking, and someone playing a tambourine. Two long-haired children ran in front of them, laughing and screaming as they chased each other on bare feet that must have been as tough as leather to move so quickly over the sticks and pricklies that covered the dirt driveway. Iggy lunged toward them as they ran by and they both shrieked in pretend terror.

"Do you live here?" Rae asked, fascinated by the activity.

"Duh."

"With all these people?"

A woman in a tie-dyed skirt was leaning against the barn, sharing a joint with a fat man in a top hat. She winked at them and exhaled a long stream of strong, skunky smoke in their direction.

"My family lives here and my mom has a lot of friends who sort of sometimes live here too. You know, a bunch of hippies and artists who came to Taos to find themselves, which I think is code for *drop a lot of acid*. They stay with us in exchange for food stamps or whatever else they have—food, art, vitamins. Sometimes they'll give my mom money or trade shelter for things like babysitting or haircuts."

As they walked by the barn, Rae saw a vintage Ford truck with four flat tires taking up much of the space inside, which made her wonder what was in the garage. The rest of the barn was crowded with bales of hay and piles of junk—empty bottles, stacks of deteriorating cardboard boxes, rusty tools, an old bed frame. Everything looked like it had been gathering dust for decades. The only trace of the building's original purpose was four yellow chickens hopping from hay bale to broken box, clucking softly in the dim interior.

The whole place had such an out of pocket atmosphere, Rae would have been convinced she was dreaming if not for the very real blisters forming on her ankles and on the outside of her little toes. As much as she loved them, Converse were clearly not designed for long-distance walking in the desert.

While she considered her shoes, a stone fell from above and bounced off one of her white rubber toe caps. She looked up and saw two boys, maybe a couple years younger than her, perched in a tree branch that extended above the corroded metal roof of the old barn, tossing pebbles at her and Iggy and stifling their laughter.

Iggy ignored the boys and watched Rae instead. She seemed to be gauging her reaction to her unusual home environment, but Rae had decided to wear what her grandma called her poker face. She didn't want Iggy to know she thought her communal living situation was a little disturbing. Who was in charge here?

"We're hippies," Iggy blurted, as if that explained everything.

Most of what Rae knew about hippies was thanks to her ninth-grade civics teacher, Mr. Long, whose lectures about the sixties counterculture and the demonstrations against the Vietnam War were well-known for stirring up controversy. He'd devoted entire classes to who Timothy Leary was and how psychedelic drugs had influenced the hippie subculture, and he'd had a big section on Woodstock and how music could be a vehicle for social change. He'd even played protest music by Bob Dylan and Joan Baez and asked the students to write short responses to what they heard. Her grandma had been pumped when Rae had told her she was learning about the hippie counterculture, and she'd shared some of her own experiences marching at the White House and living in communes in the sixties and seventies, which Rae hadn't known about until then.

So Rae probably knew a little bit more about hippies than most kids her age, and she was pretty sure the movement was over. Sure, flared pants and oversized sunglasses had made a comeback, but Mr. Long had assured them that capitalism killed the counterculture a long time ago.

"I've never met an *actual* hippie," she finally replied. "Are they still a thing?"

Iggy stopped on the flagstone path leading to the back porch of her house and stared at Rae as if she couldn't believe what she was hearing.

"Is this your first time in Taos?"

"I've been before."

"Then you should know this is where old hippies come to die!" She slapped her knee and laughed at her own joke.

One of the many weird things about Rae's mom was that she didn't like to talk about her childhood, and she sure never wanted to go back and visit. Instead, it was her grandma who had taken Rae to visit Taos when she little.

The only thing she remembered about the trip now was visiting the Taos Pueblo for San Geronimo Feast Day. She'd been excited because her grandma had promised her food, dancing, and clowns, and since she was a kid and didn't know anything, she'd been expecting cotton candy and funny clowns with big feet and red noses. Although she'd been captivated by the Puebloan dancers in their colorful robes and moccasins with bells that made music when they stomped their feet, she'd been terrified to discover that the clowns were actually tall men painted in black-and-white stripes who ran around the crowd, pretending they were going to catch all the kids and throw them in the river that flowed through the middle of the pueblo. Rae wouldn't stop crying, and she and her grandma had had to leave the festivities early. She didn't remember seeing any hippies there, but what did she know? She'd only been six.

Iggy's backyard was a mess. Among the weeds and clutter, Rae identified overgrown hollyhocks and the woody skeletons of past years' pepperweed alongside this year's new growth. Hidden among drooping clusters of cheatgrass she saw twisted sculptures of turtles and frogs constructed from scrap metal and copper wire, along with a scattering of broken toys. Cloth diapers and faded jeans hung from a clothesline stretched between two juniper trees on both sides of the walkway. They had to duck beneath it to get to the porch, which was crowded with potted plants, a pile of old shoes, milk crates filled with gardening tools, rolls of chicken wire and an old washing machine. Next to the washing machine was a box of old-fashioned powdered laundry soap and two naked children jamming broken Barbie body parts into a big, dirty blob of Play-Doh. Iggy knelt and patted their heads, grinning as they wrapped their arms around her legs.

"This is my brother and sister," she said. "They're twins."

The twins looked up and smiled in unison, revealing matching gaps where their two front teeth had been. They had dark hair and big, brown eyes with long lashes. Traces of breakfast were left on their unwashed faces. Rae smiled at them and followed Iggy into the living room, where she paused for a minute to let her eyes adjust to the low light. After a few seconds, she realized there was a group of people sitting on big cushions right on the floor, talking quietly as they passed a bong back and forth between them.

Rae watched in amazement as a grown man with beads in his braided beard put his mouth inside the glass pipe and sucked thick smoke deep into his lungs, making the water pipe bubble and hiss. The other people in the circle noticed her staring at them and broke into laughter. The man with the braided beard made short snorting sounds as he tried to keep the smoke down.

Iggy took a deep breath, put her head down, and barreled through the people sitting on the floor. With Rae right behind her, Iggy raced all the way down a long hallway to a door that was locked from the outside with an actual padlock. Here she stopped and pulled a key from the seemingly bottomless inner pocket of her jacket.

"That's extreme," Rae said. She'd never seen a bedroom locked from the outside before.

"Trust me, if I didn't keep it locked, I wouldn't have anything to call my own."

They stepped into a bedroom that would have felt small even without the amount of crap Iggy had crammed in there. There were clothes and shoes everywhere. What wasn't blanketed with clothes—which was pretty much everything besides a tall bookshelf made from plywood and cinder blocks—was crowded with empty yogurt cups and candy wrappers, stale-looking coffee mugs, used plates with remnants of dried food, scraps of paper, bottles of dried-up nail polish, and an unexpected collection of *Smurf* and *Star Wars* action figures arranged in clusters among her books.

Not only was Iggy's room buried in junk but the bedroom walls were also plastered floor to ceiling with band posters, flyers, drawings, letters, photographs, postcards, ticket stubs, and every other kind of paper keepsake imaginable.

Rae didn't have a lot of room to judge, but the chaos in this room was next level.

"I guess I need to clean my room." Iggy laughed, setting her Walkman on her dresser carefully before taking off her jacket and tossing it on the floor.

Rae walked over to a massive boom box on the dresser beside a spinning plastic tower of cassette tapes.

"So you actually collect cassette tapes?" she asked. There had to be at least a hundred of them. "That's different."

Iggy looked at her as if she were speaking a foreign language. It was the same look she'd given her when they were walking through the sagebrush and she'd asked to borrow her phone. Which reminded her . . .

"Hey, can I use your cell?" Rae asked. "I need to call my mom."

"My cell?"

"Your *phone*?"

Iggy dug through the clothes on her bed until she located a light blue rotary-dial telephone attached by a cable to a small white box on the wall. She handed it to Rae without any explanation.

"Are you for real?" Rae asked. "Is this a *landline*? You don't have a cell?"

"What's a cell?" Iggy asked, furrowing her eyebrows.

As they stared at one another in confused silence, Rae became aware of the Billy Idol calendar hanging on the wall behind Iggy's head. She took two steps forward and rubbed her eyes to make sure she was seeing things clearly.

May 1984, it said.

There was a light knock on Iggy's door. Rae turned as the door opened and a woman with long, dark hair poked her face into the room.

She looked exactly like Rae's grandma, only forty years younger.

Iggy rolled her eyes at the intruder, and Rae realized for the first time that her eyes were the exact same brown with golden flecks as her mom's.

"How was school today, Ignacia?" the younger version of her grandma asked the younger version of her mom.

Rae knew she was going to pass out right before it happened. All she could think about as her knees buckled and the movie screen in her head went dark was how fucking heavy telephones used to be.

Chapter Five

When Rae opened her eyes again, she was staring at the handset part of the sky-blue telephone, which had fallen off the hook and was lying next to her on a pile of clothes on the bedroom floor.

She lay motionless as she struggled to process where she was and how she had gotten there. Like before, she remembered sitting at the kitchen table with her grandma and the strange box of cards, only now she also remembered what her grandma had been telling her.

She was a time traveler—they were both time travelers—and to prove it, her grandma was going to send her on a short trip to Taos. Across four decades. That was what the belt was for.

Rae remembered thinking that her grandma must have been suffering from late-stage dementia and deciding to play along so she could gather information to share with her mom.

It was starting to look like the joke was on her. Ha ha.

"If you'd like to make a call, please hang up and try again," a recording of a woman's voice repeated from the handset.

The younger versions of her mom and grandma were kneeling beside her with concerned expressions on their oh-so-familiar faces.

"Are you okay?" Iggy asked, putting the receiver back on the cradle.

"Your dirty clothes probably saved me from a concussion."

"They're not *all* dirty," Iggy clarified.

Younger Grandma grabbed Rae's hand, her brown eyes brimming with kindness. "What happened?" she asked.

Rae sat up and smoothed her hair down, trying to recall what her regular grandma had told her about time-traveling etiquette. Unfortunately, she hadn't believed a word she was saying at the time, so she hadn't paid much attention to the details. All she remembered was her warning not to tell anyone about time travel. Neither her younger mom nor her younger grandma seemed to have a clue who she was, and she would need to do her best to keep it that way. The less she said about herself, the better.

"I have low blood sugar," Rae explained, "I haven't eaten in a while."

"Oh, you poor dear!" Younger Grandma hopped up. "Let's get you something to eat right away!"

It was strange to recognize the deliberate movements of her grandma hidden in the more carefree movements of this much younger woman. She cocked her head to the side and swung her arms in the same manner as the grandma she knew, but she did everything faster, like she wasn't thinking about it. And while Rae thought her grandma was beautiful, she was shocked by how pretty she'd been forty years ago. She'd seen old photos, of course, but pictures couldn't really show you what a person looked like. Faces and bodies looked different when they were moving.

Her grandma's skin was tawny and smooth. She had big, brown eyes with long lashes and thick, bushy eyebrows. Her hair was almost to her waist, and it was the same dark brown as Rae's. As long as Rae had known her, her grandma had worn her gray hair cropped short.

Her smile was as big as always, though, and a little crooked, and as she watched her cross the room and close the door behind her, Rae was happy to see that she'd been repping the military-boho style as far back as 1984, with Army-green cargo pants tucked into long moccasins that almost went up to her knees and a burgundy macrame poncho over a white T-shirt.

Seeing her in 1984 explained a lot about her grandma's current fashion choices.

What Rae absolutely could not understand was how this strange girl with the black, spiky hair and the safety pins in her ears could possibly be her mother. Nothing—absolutely nothing—about her reminded her of her mom.

"Your name is Ignacia?" Rae asked.

She shook her head. "Only my mom calls me Ignacia. People who really know me call me Iggy, like Iggy Pop."

Rae shook her head.

"Iggy Pop? *Lust for Life*? He wrote 'China Girl' with David Bowie?"

Rae shook her head again.

"C'mon, he wrote the title track for *Repo Man*?"

"Is that a TV show?" she ventured.

Iggy groaned. "*Repo Man* is only one of the best movies ever made. And if you haven't heard *Let's Dance* yet, well, I don't really know what to say. We obviously have a lot of work to do."

She turned to her tower of cassettes and spun it until she spotted the one she was looking for. With the stern expression of a person intent on righting a terrible wrong, she passed the cassette to Rae.

The cover photograph featured a compact, muscular man with perfectly coiffed blond hair—David Bowie, she assumed—posing shirtless and wearing a pair of black boxing gloves. The name Bowie was printed in big turquoise letters in the upper right-hand corner, and the title *Let's Dance* was spelled out in a connect-the-dots pattern underneath. The whole aesthetic reeked of the eighties.

With one well-rehearsed motion, Iggy pulled the white cassette out of its acrylic case, flipped it upside down, and inserted it into the gaping mouth of her massive, silver boom box, raising one expectant eyebrow as she pressed the Play button. Her face twisted into an expression somewhere between torment and ecstasy as the first sharp notes of the piercing guitar burst out of the stereo's speakers. She nearly leaped out of her skin when the drums came in.

Rae could only stand there, shocked, at the sight of her mother—her self-conscious, introverted, uptight *mother*—gyrating her hips, shaking her shoulders, twisting her body, punching the air, flailing her head, and barking the lyrics of the song like an angry war cry. She knew every word.

"Rad, right?" Iggy shouted above the music.

Rae couldn't deny the tune was catchy, but she was disturbed by the lyrics almost as soon as the man with the arrogant voice opened his velvet mouth and started crooning.

The longer she listened, the more it bothered her. Dude was describing a toxic, codependent relationship between him—he was obviously a bigot—and his Asian girlfriend, a woman he clearly had no respect for and definitely didn't value as an equal. His feelings of racial and gender superiority and even ownership of her became more conspicuous as the song went on. Was he threatening racial violence against this nameless woman? Had she really just heard him say he was having visions of *swastikas* in his head? And mocking his girlfriend's speech patterns? David Bowie was a horrible person! She couldn't sit there and say nothing, not after she'd failed so hard to defend Hamia.

"Isn't this song a little racist?" she asked, crossing her arms over her chest.

Iggy stopped dancing as if Rae had smacked her on the head. "Excuse me?"

"For real. I mean, the title alone—'China Girl'—is objectifying and demeaning and blatantly racist. And the way he refers to her as 'his' little China girl is dehumanizing. He's putting the patriarchy on full display here. I mean, come on. These lyrics are menacing! Listen, right there." Rae pointed to imaginary music notes in the air above her head. "That stereotypical, Asian-sounding guitar riff right there? That's outright derision."

Iggy stomped over to the stereo and smashed the Stop button, then spun around with an expression of fury on her red face.

"This is blasphemy!" she screamed. "You don't know what you're talking about!"

She was so upset, Rae was afraid she might start crying.

"'China Girl' means exactly the opposite of what you're saying! Don't you get it? It's actually a commentary on Western civilization. He's playing the part of a racist womanizer to expose racism and the patriarchy! Don't you see? David Bowie is the least racist person alive!"

"Then why does he make fun of the way she talks?" Rae asked. "He's actively stereotyping and fetishizing Asian women. It's so obvious! I'm surprised *you* don't see it."

"You definitely don't get it," Iggy said, turning her back to Rae and staring out the curtainless window toward the Sangre de Cristo Mountains, which filled the horizon with their quiet, alpine splendor.

If Iggy was waiting for Rae to apologize, she would be standing at the window until the sun set and rose again a million times over. Why would Rae defend such a horrible song? David Bowie was obviously a racist and a misogynist. The eighties were more fucked up than she'd realized. And this girl was her mom!

Their awkward silence was broken when Younger Grandma returned with a bowl of dried fruit and a mason jar filled with water. She set the bowl down in front of Rae and sat cross-legged beside her.

"I'm Lydia," she said, taking a fat fig from the bowl and popping the whole thing in her mouth. Her grandma had once told her she had been named after a famous Mexican singer from Jalisco.

"I'm Andrea," Rae said. "But everyone calls me Rae."

"You have a nickname, too, like my little Ignacia."

Iggy grunted in disgust.

"What's wrong, Ignacia?" Lydia asked.

"I think I offended her," Rae explained. "I didn't like the song she played."

"Now, that *is* serious." Lydia laughed.

Rae helped herself to a handful of dried cranberries and took a long drink of cool water. She was so thirsty. How long had she been in 1984?

"May I use the restroom?" she asked.

Lydia opened the bedroom door and pointed to a room at the end of the hall. "If it's yellow, let it mellow," she said. "If it's brown, flush it down."

Confused, Rae walked down the hallway and closed the bathroom door behind her.

The toilet and bathtub were the exact same lilac as a purple Necco Wafer, which was funny. Rae only knew about Necco Wafers because her mom was one of the only people left on earth who actually enjoyed the hard, flavorless discs—even preferred them over other, actually delicious candies. They were always stale, and Rae would joke that they'd probably been sitting on the shelves since her mom was a kid.

Two thin, mismatched towels hung on a hook behind the bathroom door and another was crumpled on the floor where a bath mat should have been. An uncapped tube of toothpaste sat on the counter next to a Cabbage Patch Kids toothbrush.

Rae closed the toilet lid and sat. It was a good thing she didn't really have to pee because there were only a few thin squares of toilet paper left clinging to the cardboard tube on the wall. Lifting her hoodie, she flipped over the silver itinerary case and inspected the LED screen on the back. The numbers read 2:29. She couldn't remember what the numbers signified. Was the clock counting down how much time she had left or how much time had elapsed?

She closed her eyes and tried to empty her mind of everything but the memory of her last conversation with her grandma. She visualized the orange-and-pink butterfly pattern on the curtains above her grandma's sink and the glass mosaic tiles on her kitchen backsplash. When Rae saw those things clearly, she imagined herself sitting on one of her grandma's chrome-and-vinyl kitchen chairs. She remembered the way the seat cushions felt, the way they stuck to the back of her legs when it was hot outside and she was wearing shorts.

She opened her eyes—and found herself back in the yellow kitchen, sitting across from her grandma just as she bit into a mint Milano cookie. She watched as tiny crumbs fell from the cookie to the table as her grandma explained that ten hours in 1984 equaled approximately three hours in her real time.

She nodded and listened hard, then closed her eyes and opened them again.

Bam—she was back in 1984, sitting on Iggy's lavender toilet. She rubbed her eyes and shook her head. It really felt like she had gone back home for a couple minutes. Was that possible? She would have to remember to ask her grandma later.

For now, she had to figure her shit out in 1984.

If three hours back home equaled ten hours here, then every hour at home equaled approximately 3.3 hours here. The timer was obviously counting down the time back home. One half hour had passed on the clock, which meant she had been in 1984 for around an hour and a half.

She still had more than eight hours to go! How would she spend it? She'd only just met Iggy and she was already salty with her.

Rae reached for the phone in her back pocket and her heart sank as her fingers groped the edges of her empty pocket. If she could scroll TikTok for a little bit, she would feel so much better. Instead, she tightened the belt around her waist and returned to Iggy's room.

"Guess what?" Iggy screamed in her face as soon as she opened the bedroom door. "Rhody just called. There's a rager tonight!" Her mood had changed completely; she was laughing and bouncing around the room from one foot to another. Apparently, they were back on speaking terms.

"A rager?" Rae asked. She had only ever heard the term used ironically.

"A *rager*, you know! A big fucking party! Can you come? Please tell me you can come. Do you need to call your mom?"

"Um . . . "

Iggy picked up the phone and practically threw it at Rae, who lifted the handset to her ear and stared blankly at the rotary dial, wondering what to do next.

"I don't know how to use one of these," she admitted. She was afraid Iggy was going to think something was seriously wrong with her, but she just nodded.

"Do you have a cordless phone with, like, buttons?" she asked. "You're so lucky! I'm just glad we have any kind of phone at all. My mom won't let us have a TV. How messed up is that? She thinks the government uses them for mind control. And everyone at school is always talking about the latest episode of *Dallas*, and I'm standing there, like, totally clueless. It's so lame. At least Rhody has cable so I have a place to watch MTV, or else I might seriously die." She stopped talking for a second and took a deep breath. "Anyway, it's simple." She pointed to the clear plastic plate on the face of the telephone. "You stick your finger in one of these holes next to the number you want to dial and push it around in a circle—like this, see? The other phone will start to ring after you dial the last number."

Rae didn't know what to do. Her mother was actually sixteen years old and standing right in front of her while also somehow simultaneously existing forty years in the future. It was going to be impossible to reach her by phone. Should she say she couldn't remember the phone number? That happened to be true, but how would she explain not remembering her mom's phone number to someone who had never heard of a smartphone?

According to her real mom—the old, tired version of her—not having phone numbers memorized was one of the many tragic consequences of modern technology. *Back in the day*, she would say, *you kept all your important numbers stored in your head. What would you do if you ever lost your phone and found yourself in a dangerous situation? Who would you call?* Which, Rae thought, was a ridiculous question, because if it really was an emergency, how hard would it be to borrow someone else's phone and call 911? Rae was tired of the boomers and Gen Xers blaming all of the world's problems on technology and social media. They were the ones destroying the planet.

With Iggy watching her, Rae sat on the edge of the bed and—after recovering from her surprise at the blaring ringtone—dialed area code 505, followed by seven random numbers. As she was about to explain that there was no answer, someone picked up the line.

"Hello?" a man with a trembling voice said.

Rae gasped and hung up the phone.

"Who was that?" Iggy asked. "Why did you hang up?"

Rae grasped at the first believable lie. "Okay, it's time to spill the tea," she said. "That was my dad. I hung up on him because I ran away from home and I don't want my parents to know where I am."

Iggy's eyes widened. "You ran away? That explains why you're so secretive and uptight! Where did you run away from?"

"From Albuquerque," Rae replied. The fewer lies she told, the easier it would be to keep her story straight.

"That's so rad! There are so many awesome music stores in Albuquerque. Bow Wow Records is *so* bitchin'. And there's so much live music in Albuquerque. We don't get anyone big up here, just local bands. Do you go to a lot of shows? Have you ever been to the El Rey?"

"I've never been to a concert or show. My parents are, um, strict." They weren't really that strict, but it explained why she might run away.

"My mom doesn't care what I do," Iggy said. "But she hates the city, so I'm stuck here at the edge of the universe, where nobody ever visits. Did you know Thompson Twins played at Popejoy Hall last week?"

"Is music all you think about?" Rae asked.

"No, I actually think about boys a lot too." Iggy sighed and clutched her chest. "And guess what? The boy I'm totally in love with is in a band and they're going to be playing at the house party we're going to tonight. It's a punk band. We can slam dance!"

"I . . . don't really know how," Rae confessed.

"To slam dance? You are seriously sheltered! Are you religious or something?"

"I'm not, but my parents are super religious." Another lie. In fact, her parents didn't seem to believe too strongly in anything. Her dad took her to church during the holidays and sometimes her mom lit a candle and prayed, but they both told Rae she could believe whatever she wanted.

"Well, that explains it. They probably love Reagan, too, right?"

"They're on fire for Reagan!" Rae said, stifling a laugh. Her mom had always told her that Reagan's only enduring legacies were homelessness and poverty.

"I'm so sorry," Iggy said. She grabbed Rae by the shoulders and shook her. "Let's get my chores done fast, and then we're going to teach you how to live!"

Chapter Six

With the unwavering hope of one day either negotiating down her own chore list or increasing her pathetic allowance, Rae kept track of her friends' responsibilities. Cosima had the biggest allowance of anyone she knew—fifty dollars a week!—and she didn't have to do any chores at all, not even make her own bed. Sure, her parents accused her of being lazy and entitled, but they gave her the money anyway. Jordan and Madison had only had one or two simple chores that barely took any time or effort at all, and the only thing Alma had had to do was fold her laundry a couple times a week.

Rae, on the other hand, had to keep the bathroom clean, load the dishwasher, *and* take out the trash whenever her mom demanded, plus vacuum on the weekends. At one point, her mom had even tried to make it mandatory for her to wash and fold her own clothes, but Rae had complained so hard when it was time to do laundry that her mom had given up and gone back to washing everything herself. She couldn't admit defeat, though, so she would tiptoe into her room while Rae was at school and sneak away with her dirty clothes. They maintained an unspoken agreement to never talk about the mystery of the neatly folded clothes sitting outside Rae's bedroom door every Friday afternoon.

It had always seemed incredibly unfair that Rae had to work so much harder than all of her friends, but it finally made sense the day she had to help her sixteen-year old mother get through her to-do list.

After pinky swearing to try slam dancing at least once, Rae followed Iggy as she set off in search of her mom to determine which chores would have to be completed before they could attend the party. The grown-ups who'd been sitting on the floor were now standing around red-eyed, eating carrots with long, leafy tops that looked as if they'd just been pulled out of the ground. They didn't even notice when Iggy and Rae passed by, and Iggy just moved around them like they were pieces of furniture.

The vibe outside was livelier. A group of adults had gathered to watch the children play a game of capture the flag. A dozen or so ragged-looking people stood in circles by the campground and clapped or booed every time one of their ragged-looking kids got tagged and sent to jail, depending on which team they were rooting for. Lydia was cheering loudly and sharing a mug of red wine with the topless woman Rae had seen earlier. Rae tried hard not to stare at her boobs, which were big and tan with silver stretch marks that spread across the fleshiest parts, but they looked out of place and vulnerable in the bright sunlight. They practically demanded her attention.

Lydia took a big gulp of wine and told Iggy that yes, she could go to the party, but first she would have to make dinner for her brother, sister, and all the other kids at the gathering, then make sure they all ate before she cleaned the kitchen. She would also have to take down and fold all the clean clothes that were hanging outside on the long clothesline to dry.

Rae was shocked. It was hard to believe her grandma had ever been so strict about chores. Weren't hippies supposed to be laid-back and relaxed about everything?

"You're ruining my life, Lydia!" Iggy shouted as she stomped back inside to the kitchen.

Lydia just laughed.

The kitchen was an open room in the center of the house between the living room, which they'd entered from the back porch, and an informal dining area on the other side. The table in the dining room was so low to the ground, it didn't even have normal chairs. Instead, the three people at the table, who were passing a joint between them and flipping through a milk crate filled with vinyl records, sat directly on the carpet, some on cushions. The table was covered with mostly lit candles, and the wax dripped right onto the tabletop. No one seemed worried about it, so Rae tried not to dwell on the obvious fire hazard.

Every counter in the kitchen was crammed with stuff: empty wine bottles, dried flowers, packs of rolling papers, a wicker sewing basket filled with colored yarn, stacks of library books, and dozens of mason jars filled with dried herbs, spices, pasta, beans, rice, and all sorts of unidentified liquids and ointments. The jars reminded Rae of the storage jars in her mom's kitchen at home, only her jars had been purchased from Williams-Sonoma back when they had money, and her mom organized them alphabetically on counters so clean, it barely looked like anyone lived there at all.

As Rae wondered where they would find the space to prepare food, Iggy swept her forearm across one of the counters, shoving everything against the wall and knocking a bowl of almonds over in the process. A bunch of them spilled on the floor, but instead of picking them up, she kicked them one by one under the adorable Westinghouse refrigerator while she evaluated the food—vegetables, blocks of tofu, and a bowl of eggs with dirty shells—stacked inside precariously.

"I'll make spaghetti," she announced, removing mushrooms, green peppers, onions, garlic, carrots, spinach, and eggplant from the fridge and tossing them onto the counter she'd cleared.

The ingredients didn't exactly scream "spaghetti" to Rae, but she felt hungry enough to eat anything, so she helped Iggy wash the vegetables.

When Iggy finished chopping everything into surprisingly neat, even pieces and grated the big, lumpy carrots with a handheld grater, she added olive oil to a hot cast-iron pan and salted and sautéed the vegetables until they started to get soft. Then she added two jars of preserved tomatoes and a handful of fresh basil and oregano she picked from two of the plants growing on the windowsill above the sink. Rae's mouth watered.

The delicious smells must have caught the attention of the little kids running in and out of the house because they kept coming up to Iggy and asking when dinner would be ready. Every time they tugged on her jeans, Iggy stopped what she was doing and knelt to tell them everything would be ready soon. She was so damn nice.

"Are any of these kids related to you?" Rae asked.

"Just the two you saw before, Maria and Benny."

Rae felt beads of sweat pop up on her forehead as she realized that the two little kids she had seen playing on the porch were her aunt Maria and her uncle Benny, her mom's younger brother and sister. They were fraternal twins who had a different dad than her. Rae remembered her mom saying she'd been ten when they were born, so she'd been almost like a second mother to them. They'd only been six years old in 1984! In Rae's space-time, her auntie Maria was a criminal defense attorney who lived in Seattle and her uncle Benny worked at an organic dairy farm in upstate New York. Her mom always said they were as different as night and day and fought like cats and dogs, but they looked like the best of friends today.

"They're named after my mom's grandparents on her father's side, Maria and Benicio. I'm named after their son, who is her dad, Ignacio. He's a curandero."

Rae had heard all the family names and history before, of course, but she'd always half listened when her mom or grandma talked about what life had been like when they were younger. Their past hadn't interested her too much; it wasn't relevant to her life. Only now, as she stood beside this younger version of her mom and realized her great-grandpa was actually still alive in 1984 and she could maybe even meet him if she wanted to, did Rae experience an intense, never-before-felt curiosity about her family history. All the people she'd thought of as characters in a dull storybook suddenly felt very real.

Iggy left the spaghetti sauce simmering and dumped two packages of dried spaghetti into an enormous pot of boiling water. While the noodles cooked, she chopped romaine and cherry tomatoes for a salad and sliced open a loaf of crusty, brown bread, smearing it with a thick layer of butter and chopped garlic before putting it in the broiler. Rae had never seen anyone her age prepare such a complicated meal all by themselves before.

"Where did you learn to cook?" she asked. "You're so good at it."

"I taught myself," Iggy replied. "'Necessity is the mother of invention,' as they say." Rae had never heard that expression before and her face must have shown it. "In other words, my mom is a terrible cook."

Her grandma was not a terrible cook! It was true that she never made anything fancy like her mom—she stuck mainly to salads and sandwiches or little snack platters with cheese and crackers and sliced-up fruit—but it was always tasty.

"Maybe you'll be a famous chef one day," Rae said and was surprised by a sharp pain that shot up the side of her neck and into the muscles around her jaw.

"No way. Not me," Iggy said, shaking her head. She picked up the heavy pot of noodles and drained them with a colander before transferring them into a large serving bowl and covering them with the sauce. "I'm going to be in a new-wave band."

"Seriously? What instrument do you play?"

"None. I'm going to be the lead singer."

"You still need to play an instrument, though, right?"

Iggy looked up from the pasta and frowned. "Does Siouxsie Sioux play an instrument? Or Joey Ramone? Or Morrissey?"

Rae didn't know who any of those people were, so she shrugged and dropped the subject.

"Ha!" Iggy said and turned to the growing gang of kids surrounding her. "Are you ready to eat?"

They jumped up and down and cheered in one hungry voice. Rae counted nine kids, including aunt Maria and uncle Benny.

Iggy lined the kids up from shortest to tallest and served them each a small helping of pasta and salad on a plate or bowl she took from a mismatched stack in the cupboard. She led the little army into the dining room and helped them find places at the long table full of stoned hippies, who began shuffling over to the kitchen when they realized what was happening. Seeing this, Iggy raced ahead of them and grabbed two plates, hastily piling on most of what was left of the spaghetti and garlic bread.

"Let's eat outside," she said.

"We're not going to eat with everyone else?"

"I'd rather not."

Rae followed Iggy outside to the back porch, where they sat on upturned milk crates and ate with their plates in their laps. The bright flavors of the vegetables and the way they were sliced and seasoned reminded Rae of the food she ate at home. Her heart ached with every bite as she thought of how often she ate dinner directly across from her mom with her head in her phone. She hardly ever remembered to thank her.

"You truly slayed this meal," she said now.

"Thanks," Iggy replied, but she had withdrawn into herself again.

They ate in silence as they watched three dark red chickens hunting for bugs among the weeds in the backyard.

Rae reached for her phone to check the time. How many times was she going to search her empty back pocket before she realized it was gone? Not having her phone was so wack. She never knew what time it was, and the discomfort of not being able to check her socials was like an itch she couldn't scratch. Being deprived of a steady flow of updates on the state of the world and her friends in particular made her feel alone and adrift. It didn't help that she was floating in the weird, mysterious ocean that was 1984, with this pressed teenage version of her mother.

What if her mom tried to call her? Or her friends? How long would it take before they started to wonder why she wasn't responding to their Snaps or posts? Or posting any of her own? What about her Snap Map? Could it possibly pinpoint her phone's current location almost forty years in the past?

Had Andy responded to her last Snap? Was Cosima expecting an explanation for her disappearing act today? The unanswered questions created a pressure in her head that made her wonder if it might explode like in a cartoon. Shit, if time travel was possible, anything was possible.

Maybe the worst thing about being trapped in 1984 was that she couldn't even post any pictures of this amazing view of the mountains or her yummy dinner, or share any funny or interesting or ironic observations about her trip to 1984. It may as well not have been happening at all.

"What time is it?" she asked, scraping the last bits of food from her plate.

"Jeez, what is with your obsession with time?" Iggy stormed back into the house, leaving the unanswered question hanging in the air.

Rae stood and followed her inside.

There was no dishwasher in Lydia's kitchen. Iggy and Rae had to wash everything by hand, in a sink full of water that started out hot and sudsy but grew dirtier and more lukewarm with each pot and pan they'd used to make dinner, as well as every single plate, bowl, and piece of silverware that had been left lying around the house or piled on the sideboard by the hungry hippies. Funny how they'd conveniently ghosted now that dinner was over and it was time to clean up.

After Iggy and Rae finished washing, rinsing, and stacking the dishes on a bamboo rack, they brought in all the clothes from the clothesline in a big wicker basket and sat at the dining room table to fold them.

The cushions around the table were mostly empty now, except for a man with pigtails and a woman with a shaved head sitting at the furthest end from them, whispering and smoking from an old-fashioned pipe. Iggy didn't say a word as she dumped the basket of laundry on the table and began folding T-shirts with aggressive, exaggerated movements. It was like she was mad at the couple at the end of the table, though Rae couldn't imagine why. They seemed friendly enough—even glanced up at Iggy and smiled at her as she ragefully folded underwear.

They didn't speak to her, though. Maybe Iggy was so moody because the people in the house treated her like an employee who worked there instead of someone who lived there.

The socks and jeans from the clothesline weren't the warm, fluffy pile of Downy-scented softness Rae imagined when she thought of fresh, clean laundry. They were thick and stiff and omitted a strange mineral smell from being line dried in the open air.

While they scavenged for pairs in the mountain of socks on the table, Lydia sauntered into the living room and took a seat on the cushion next to Iggy. Her cheeks were flushed and her eyes were glassy and bloodshot, more or less confirming Rae's suspicions, resulting from the few times she'd picked her up from school red-eyed and acting weird, that her grandma dabbled in kush.

"Thank you for making dinner, Ignacia," Lydia said.

Iggy nodded but kept her eyes on the socks in her hand, moving her body almost imperceptibly away from her mom. Was she still pissed about the chores?

"It's getting late. Are you still going to your party?"

"Yes! Is that okay?" She turned and flashed her mom a fake smile.

"I think you deserve a night out with your friend. Here, this is from Abelino." Lydia pushed a folded bill across the table, gesturing with her shoulder toward a man leaning against the doorframe behind her. He had long, black hair that hung in a braid down his back and a thick, shaggy mustache. His chest was bare under his brown leather cowboy vest, and he was holding a wine bottle by its neck.

Iggy unfolded the five-dollar bill. "Thank you," she whispered, peering around her mom at Abelino.

Abelino took a big gulp of wine right out of the bottle and grinned at her. "De nada."

"Have fun and be safe, okay?" Lydia said.

"Totally."

"And call me tomorrow."

Rae glanced up from the tie-dyed T-shirt she was folding. *Call tomorrow?*

Lydia stood and grabbed Abelino's hand. "Let's watch the moon rise," she said in a flirty voice.

Abelino took another big drink of wine and followed her outside.

Rae wanted to ask Iggy why she was so upset with her mom and where she planned on sleeping tonight, but Iggy had apparently had enough of the silence between them. She started rambling about aliens in the trunk of a Chevy Malibu in *Repo Man*, and how beautiful Emilio Estevez was, and had Rae ever listened to the Circle Jerks?

The moment for real conversation was lost.

When they were finally finished with the sadistic number of chores, they went back to Iggy's room to get ready for the party.

Iggy plucked a cassette from her spinning tower and popped it in the boom box. "This will get us ready to rage!"

The song opened with the feverish strumming of an acoustic guitar contrasting with the spacey melody of a synthesizer, which were soon joined by a drum groove that rapidly built up speed until everything cascaded together and flooded the bedroom with one funky wave of sound.

"Hey, I know this song!" Rae exclaimed. It was "Burning Down the House," a song she had heard on at least one party playlist.

"We found something you like!" Iggy shouted, spinning around her room in celebratory circles, arms spread out.

She had been salty as hell when she was out in the house doing her chores and interacting with her mom and everyone else in the house, but the music had revived her. Rae watched in awe as Iggy morphed back into the wild girl from the desert, jerking her head in time with the music as she picked through the piles of clothes on her bedroom floor.

"I try things on and then leave them on the floor," she confessed.

Rae laughed out loud at hearing this bizarro version of her mom describe the habit that would make her almost cry with frustration when her daughter did the exact same thing some forty years later.

"I have a system!" Iggy insisted. "Dirty to the left, clean to the right."

"Trust me. Not judging."

Iggy scooped up a random armful of clothes from the clean side of her floor and stuffed them into her backpack. "You can borrow whatever you want," she said, pulling one white-leather Nike Cortez with a red swoosh from the pile.

Rae opened her mouth to say thanks but no thanks when she saw Iggy toss into the corner what appeared to be another pair of vintage Levi's. She approached the jeans slowly, as if they might jump up and run away, and picked them up for closer inspection.

The denim fabric was dark and slightly stiff, with an amazing white fade around the pockets and zipper. It was heavier than any other denim she'd ever touched before. Even the copper rivets looked special—substantial and old. She turned the jeans over and gasped aloud when she saw that the red tab on the back right pocket had the word Levi's printed in all capital letters.

"What is it?" Iggy asked her.

"These are Big E Levi's 501s!" she exclaimed. "Do you have any idea how rare these are?"

"Really? I paid two dollars for them at a thrift store and they don't even fit me. They're too short. I hate high waters. It's the curse of being tall—nothing fits right."

"Two dollars?" Rae was shocked. She turned the cuffs inside out and almost passed out when she saw the red-threaded edge on the inside of the denim seam. "These are honest-to-God, American-made, Levi's redline selvedge denim!" she exclaimed. "They're probably worth at least a G."

Iggy nodded her head absently as she continued her search for the other Nike Cortez.

They were the only pair of genuine Big E 501s Rae had ever seen in real life, though she had seen hundreds of photos on thrifting blogs and learned how to authenticate them on YouTube. She considered herself somewhat of an expert on vintage denim and spent hours in thrift stores, sifting through rack after rack of gross, moldy-smelling jeans, trying to make it easier for fate to choose her to be the first one there when some old man who didn't know the value of vintage denim brought a big sack of old clothes to Goodwill or the Salvation Army or some other lowbrow thrift store, where the employee on duty was a volunteer who maybe didn't know how much a really old pair of Levi's could sell for on Poshmark.

Unfortunately, most thrift-store employees were trained on how to identify valuable vintage items, so it was a rare occurrence for something as hot as a pair of Big E Levi's 501 selvedge redline denim to even make it to the retail floor. And if it did, a person would have to be there at just the right moment. Serious denim collectors hit the thrift stores several times a week, and they were all looking for the same thing.

Rae closed her eyes and stroked the fabric. It felt wonderful—totally different from the modern, mass-produced denim she was used to because it had been made on an old shuttle loom, back when people expected things to last and might own only one or two pairs of jeans in their entire lifetime. The pair she held in her hands was tightly woven, with a smooth, slick patina produced by age and wear. She could feel how exceptional the denim was.

"Oh my god, I've never seen anyone so in love with a pair of jeans." Iggy laughed, startling Rae out of her trance. "You can have them if you want."

"You can't be serious?"

"Like I said, I don't like the way they fit. They'll look better on you."

Rae jumped up and down and hugged the jeans to her chest. She was so happy, she wanted to cry.

"This is high-key the best gift anyone has ever given me," she gushed, wrapping Iggy in a spontaneous hug.

"Wow, okay. Well, I don't know what that means, but you're welcome."

Rae raced down the hall to the bathroom and changed into her unbelievably amazing vintage Levi's before Iggy could reconsider.

The jeans were baggy around Rae's waist and roomy in the thighs—exactly how she liked them to fit. She folded one wide cuff in each leg right above her ankles so the red line of thread on the inside of her pants leg was there for the whole world to see. Twirling in front of the mirror once—twice—three times, she ran her hands over and over across the glorious denim. They were absolutely perfect.

She reached for the bathroom door as Iggy barged in, wearing the same pants and boots as before, only now paired with an unbuttoned, oversized, white nylon trench coat over a bright orange T-shirt with the words FUCK THE MAN written in black marker across the chest. Between the T-shirt and the long coat, she'd layered a cropped, pink denim vest covered with band buttons and an inexplicable assortment of random objects. A book of matches, a concert ticket stub, a paper speeding ticket, and even a cigarette butt had all been attached to her vest with safety pins. She had accessorized the look with a leather dog collar and a chain of silver safety pins around her neck.

"You don't knock first?" Rae asked, putting her hands on her hips.

"I just need to redo my hair." She moved around Rae to the sink and turned on the tap, not even waiting for the stream of water to warm up before she jammed her head under it. When her whole head was soaked, she grabbed the towel hanging on the back of the bathroom door and rubbed her hair until it stuck up everywhere like a baby chick's.

"Hand me the Dippity-Do," she ordered.

Rae looked around the bathroom and located a big plastic jar filled with neon-green, extra-hold styling gel sitting on a stack of *Rolling Stone* magazines. She passed the gel to Iggy, who scooped up a sticky glob of the stuff and rubbed it between her palms before smearing it all over her wet hair. Next, she pulled up random sections of her hair and twisted them with her fingers until her whole head was covered in short, pointy spikes.

"I want to look like Sid Vicious," Iggy explained.

Rae had never heard of Sid Vicious, but the name pretty much said it all.

"Do you want to help me with my makeup?"

"I'm not very good at it," Rae admitted. She knew this from experience, having spent ridiculous hours watching makeup tutorials on TikTok when she should have been doing her homework, and trying a few of the techniques on herself—prism eyes, winged eyeliner, ombre lips. But they never looked right on her and she always ended up scrubbing her face until it was bare again.

"That's okay," Iggy replied, handing Rae a black Maybelline eyeliner pencil with a built-in sharpener. "I want to try something from a photo I saw in a punk zine. One eye lined all the way around in black and the other looking out from the middle of a big, black jester star, know what I mean? Like a disturbed clown."

"Got it," Rae said. She tried to recall the creepy clown looks she'd seen on Pinterest while researching Halloween costumes, but her brain still wasn't working right. Oh well. The worst that could happen was that Iggy would have to wash her face and start all over again. Rae could at least *try*.

Iggy dropped her head and closed her eyes. Standing as tall as she could, Rae grasped the eyeliner pencil and held her breath while she drew a five-pointed starfish shape around Iggy's right eye, adding a round dot to the end of each point for a jesterlike appearance. As she filled in the star shape, she studied Iggy's face and bone structure. Her face was full and firm and she didn't have any wrinkles, but up close like this, she could really see her mom in there. She had the same tan skin, high cheekbones, and arched brows. This teenage, emo version of her mom dressed in oversized clothes that hid her body and wore scary makeup that hid her face, but she was actually pretty.

"Why do you dress the way you do?" Rae asked.

Iggy kept her eyes closed and bit her lip while she thought about her answer. "I want the way I look on the outside to match the way I feel on the inside."

Yes! That made perfect sense. When Rae thought about putting on makeup and washing it off or changing her outfit fifty times until her ensemble finally clicked, this was exactly what she was aiming for, too, only she had never been able to articulate it.

"How do you feel on the inside?" she asked.

"I don't know. Different from everyone else. You know, like a new waver."

She didn't know. "I guess I don't really understand what new wave is."

"It's music more than anything else, of course." Iggy was biting her lip again. "But it's a way to be too. It's related to punk rock but not as angry or political, you know? New wave is, like, more fun, more colorful, but not in a United Colors of Benetton kind of way—not mainstream, no way! Maybe, when you think about it, new wave *is* political because it's experimental and anti-corporate and anti-status quo."

"That's a lot," Rae teased. "Are you sure *you* know what it means?"

Iggy's agitated eyeballs bounced back and forth behind her closed lids, and her voice got louder and shakier as she spoke. "Of *course* I know what it means, it's just hard to explain to a square like you. It's fashion, but at the same time, it's so much more than fashion because it's a way of being in the world. New wave is a new sound, a new feeling . . . Talking Heads, Siouxsie and the Banshees, New Order. It's not the same old conformist mentality everywhere you look. It's a community of people who don't feel like they belong, who don't *want* to belong. It's not Rah-Rah Ronald Reagan, not Van Halen, not The Gap, not killing yourself to look like a model in a magazine, not sacrificing your soul to get the approval of everyone else, not dying just to fit in. I don't want to look like everyone else! I want to be different. I want people to stop and stare at me and wonder what the fuck is wrong with me. I don't want to be a poser living her life just to make everyone else happy!"

It was hard to believe that this opinionated, emotional, oddball girl was going to grow up and—somehow, somewhere, someway—morph into her passive, accommodating, law-abiding mother. Even when she was drunk, her mom was mostly harmless, locking herself in her bedroom to listen to old music and cry.

"Okay," Rae said. "Open your eyes."

Iggy did as instructed. The white of her eye looked extra white staring out from the middle of the black jester star. As close as she was, Rae realized that what she'd always thought of as gold flecks in her mom's eyes were actually golden rings around her pupil.

"You look really cool," Rae said, proud of her work.

Iggy smiled at Rae's reflection in the mirror. "What are we going to do with you?"

Rae stared at her pale, ordinary face. The lip gloss she'd applied what was now an actual lifetime ago had disappeared, and her mascara was just tired-looking smudges under her eyes. She wasn't wearing any jewelry, and her hair had gone limp. Her whole vibe was blah.

"I look pretty gross, huh?"

"Oh no, I wouldn't say *that*." Iggy stepped back to evaluate her. "Your sweatshirt is rad, and I love your Cons. Those jeans are totally triumphant on you. We could rat your hair?"

Rae shook her head firmly. Whatever it was, it sounded bad.

"Maybe you just need some lipstick?" Iggy took a metal tube of L'Oréal lipstick from the breast pocket of her denim vest. "British Red Coat," she said, uncapping the tube. It was the same shade of vibrant red she'd been wearing earlier, when Rae had found her in the desert. "Pooch out your lips"," she commanded.

Rae closed her eyes and stuck out her lips while Iggy applied.

"There," she said. "Done."

Rae opened her eyes and looked in the mirror. The lipstick was way brighter than any other shade she'd ever worn before. It changed her whole vibe. She looked powerful and confident, like a Russian spy.

"So dope," Rae said, grinning.

As Iggy turned to the mirror to apply her own lipstick, Rae lifted her hoodie and peeked at the itinerary case. 01:36. Five hours left to go in 1984. Plenty of time for a party, and now she was ready.

Chapter Seven

They walked past the now-roaring fire pit where Lydia stood with the other adults, leaning into Abelino's chest and laughing at the little kids as they chased each other in circles around the warm, orange halo of light, spaghetti sauce still on their faces. The blazing fire lit up different parts of Lydia's face as it flickered and flared in the darkening sky, making her features appear familiar one second and strange the next. A tiny spider of panic crawled into Rae's head at the thought of leaving her behind. She'd felt safer knowing her grandma was around.

"Have fun," Lydia yelled at their retreating forms.

"Thanks!" Rae shouted back.

Iggy snorted in disgust and kept walking.

"Hold on a sec," Rae said. "We're not walking to this party, are we?" The thought of more activity made her feel panicky. Her body was exhausted from all the walking and washing and folding, not to mention traveling across space and time. The twinkling lights from the town of Taos looked very far away.

"We'll walk down to the main road and hitchhike from there," Iggy replied.

"Hitchhike? We can't hitchhike! We could be kidnapped! Or raped! And murdered!"

Iggy actually laughed at Rae and her completely justifiable concerns for their safety and well-being. "Take a chill pill, will you? Nothing is going to happen to us." She turned right onto a dirt road and kicked a rock in front of her forcefully.

The thought of doing something as stupid and dangerous as hitchhiking made Rae feel dizzy. The panic spider was laying eggs. How many soon-to-be-dead-and-dismembered characters in Hollywood movies had regretted the decision of climbing into the back of an unknown car? It had to be in the thousands. But it was not the most convenient time to have a panic attack, so she reminded herself that her mom had, in fact, survived her childhood, which meant that she and Iggy would not be murdered tonight. And her grandma had warned her not to resist anything too much, right? She breathed in slowly through her nose and out through her mouth—one, two, three times—until her racing heart slowed back down to normal.

The barest hint of diminishing sunlight lingered at the edge of the mountain range on the horizon, and the sky transitioned from azure to Prussian blue as they walked down the long road. The darker it got, the more stars revealed themselves until it seemed there were millions, billions, trillions of them spread out like a sparkling net before her, clean and bright against the velvety sky with no buildings or traffic lights to get in the way of their beauty. For a moment, Rae felt as if she were actually walking across the sky, as though she could reach out and touch a star. She almost forgot where she was when the crunch of Iggy's angry boots in the gravel brought her crashing back to Earth.

"That man with your mom," Rae said. "He's not your dad, is he?"

"Abelino? As if! He's my mom's latest boyfriend. My real dad is studying muralism and revolution in Mexico right now. He's lived there since I was nine—he had to find a way to make money outside of the Capitalist infrastructure. He lives on the beach and makes amazing sand sculptures. He's, like, the most awesome person on the planet."

"He makes money living on the beach and making sand sculptures?"

Iggy huffed. "He does other stuff too. I'm going to move to Mexico to live with him one day, whenever he gets settled."

Rae opened her mouth to say that if Iggy's dad wasn't settled after living in Mexico for seven years, he probably never would be. But that would be mean, so she stopped herself. She'd never met her grandpa and her mom never talked about him. The only thing her grandma had ever said was that he was a free spirit.

"My parents are divorced too," Rae said. "My dad lives in California with his new wife. My mom says they'll probably have a baby soon because his wife is young and she doesn't have any kids of her own. But I don't want to be some bratty kid's sister."

"It's not so bad." Iggy shrugged. "They're always happy to see me."

"I can get a dog for that."

"Harsh!" Iggy exclaimed.

It was, Rae had to admit. She was so preoccupied by how angry she was with her mom that she sometimes surprised herself by how angry she was with her dad.

"I might be going to California pretty soon myself," Iggy said.

"On vacation?"

"Ha ha. No, there's this boy. His name is Simon and he's the lead singer of the band we're going to see tonight, Liquid Squid. They're going to tour the entire United States in a converted school bus, and he asked me to come with them! They're going to California first. Rad, right?"

That did not sound rad. It sounded terrifying.

"How old is he?" Rae asked. "How long will you be gone? Did your mom really say it was okay?" As open-minded as Lydia seemed, it would be pretty irresponsible to let her sixteen-year-old daughter drive to California in a school bus with a bunch of boys in a punk rock band.

"He's eighteen and a senior. He has the most beautiful brown eyes I've ever seen, like truly hypnotic. Wait until you see him—you're going to die! He's major. Don't get any ideas, though, okay?" She laughed and kicked another rock down the road, where it bounced and landed on the blacktop of the highway. "I can't tell my mom. She would never let me go. Who would do my chores and watch

Benny and Maria when she wanted to go away on one of her little *adventures*?" Her voice was hard with sarcasm.

"So you're going to run away from home?" Rae was alarmed that her mom had ever considered doing anything so reckless.

"Why do you sound so surprised? You ran away from home, didn't you? I thought you of all people would understand."

She had totally forgotten about her made-up backstory. "Well, my parents are super strict. Your mom seems cool."

"Yeah. I guess." Iggy opened her mouth to say something else but closed it again when they reached the highway. She turned around and started walking backward so she was facing Rae and the oncoming traffic.

"This is a bad idea," Rae protested. "It's so dark out here. What if we get hit by a car?"

"Hopefully I die quickly and don't suffer too much."

"I'm not kidding!"

"Relax. I do it all the time."

"Famous last words."

A pair of white headlights loomed on the highway, and Iggy stuck out her thumb as the vehicle approached. Rather than slow down when it passed, the driver of the car sped up and veered toward the shoulder of the road, pressing down hard on the horn as he whizzed by.

Rae screamed in terror.

"Fuck you!" Iggy shouted, picking up a handful of gravel from the side of the road and throwing it at the receding car. Undeterred by their brush with death, she resumed her backward walk and stuck out her thumb again as the next pair of headlights rounded the corner.

Rae ran into the sagebrush that lined the highway and watched as a classic car riding low to the ground slowed down and came to a complete stop about a hundred yards ahead of them.

"Oh, hell yeah!" Iggy cheered, running toward the car. "Cholos!"

"I'm pretty sure that's a derogatory word!" Rae yelled after her.

Rae knew what a lowrider was, of course. She'd seen the tough-looking drivers of these customized cars showing off their hydraulics in car shows and parades all over northern and central New Mexico. But if she lived her whole life without getting inside one, that would be okay. The people who drove them seemed like they were from a totally different world than hers. She couldn't imagine one thing she might have in common with them. What would they talk about if she got inside?

Yet she watched herself leave the safety of the bushes and run toward the menacing vehicle.

The lowrider's passenger door slowly opened, spilling out warm air and light from the inside. The car was a vintage, Jolly Rancher-green Monte Carlo with red, sparkly flames painted along its entire length, whitewall tires, spinning spokes, and an engine that purred like a predatory animal attempting to reassure its prey.

"This is crazy, really crazy," Rae protested.

The man in the front passenger seat, whose face she couldn't see, leaned forward and adjusted his seat so they had enough room to crawl inside. Iggy bent over and disappeared into the back seat. With a growing sense that something awful was about to happen, Rae realized the car only had two doors. There would be no way out if they were attacked.

"Get in!" Iggy shouted from the back.

Rae rubbed the itinerary case for good luck and followed her inside.

The back seat was not at all what she was expecting. The seats were large, comfy, and covered in some kind of luxe material. Rae looked around and realized the whole car was upholstered in red velvet, including the dashboard and door panels. Everything was immaculate—not a stray candy wrapper or speck of dust anywhere in sight. A small statue of the Virgin Mary was mounted on the dashboard, and a school photo of a young child with slicked-back hair and glasses was tucked into the speedometer. A pair of big, fuzzy dice hung from the rearview mirror.

"Nice, huh?" Iggy said as the passenger door slammed shut and they pulled back onto the highway.

The man in the passenger seat, whose hair was slicked back like the kid in the photo and covered with the kind of hairnet lunch ladies wore, turned to look at them. His creaseless, brown flannel shirt was fastened by a single button at the collar, and he wore a white tank top underneath.

"Where are you headed, güeritas?" he asked in a soft voice.

The driver, who was older than the passenger, stared straight ahead with a stern expression that made Rae nervous.

"Just to the Plaza would be awesome," Iggy said. "And I'm not a güera. I'm Hispanic too."

Rae kicked her in the leg so she would stop talking. While it was technically true, she didn't exactly present as Hispanic, and anyway, how could she be sure that he identified as Hispanic? Maybe he thought of himself as a Latino. Maybe he was Mexican American and proud of his Indigenous ancestry; maybe he identified as a Chicano.

But the passenger laughed. "Well, you look pretty white to me."

The driver turned up the volume on his fancy audio system and Rae almost jumped out of her seat as a fusion of Latin and rock music blasted from multiple speakers. With her hands over her ears, she counted two speakers on the ceiling, one on the inside of each door, and one installed between the back-seat headrests.

Iggy started shaking her shoulders and clapping her hands in time to the beat. "I like this song!" she yelled.

The guy in the passenger seat turned again. "You like Santana?" he asked.

"Yeah!" she shouted. "*Abraxas*! My mom has this album."

The passenger and driver looked at each other and nodded in approval. Even though the music hurt Rae's ears, it did relieve some of the awkwardness she felt from being confined in such a small space with two scary strangers. She was so close to them, she could smell their laundry detergent, but the vibe was okay. She turned her attention to the passing scenery.

They'd left behind the long stretch of sagebrush between the southern canyon and the edge of Taos and were now driving past small adobe houses, yellow streetlights, and, as they approached the center of town, gas stations and businesses whose lights were already turned off for the night.

The lowrider cruised down the road well below the speed limit, so Rae was able to scrutinize the few pedestrians they passed, looking for any sign to confirm the unbelievable truth that she was visiting Taos in the year 1984. She kept forgetting it *was* 1984; things didn't feel as different as she thought they would. The people outside all looked pretty ordinary, wearing basic outfits and jackets in boring, neutral colors and normal hair. Where were all the leg warmers, satin bomber jackets, and acid-washed jeans that supposedly had been so popular in the eighties? Where was the feathered hair?

At least the cars cruising beside them looked like they were out of another decade—big, boxy, ugly Buicks, Pontiacs, Lincolns, and Volvos in weird colors like chalk white, navy and pea green, probably sucking up as much natural gas as a small country. There wasn't one Tesla or Toyota Prius among them and no SUVs either. It was funny that the car that seemed the least out of place to her was the one she was riding in. A restored, customized, vintage Monte Carlo lowrider from 1971 stood out almost as much in 1984 as it would in 2024.

Traffic slowed as they approached the stoplight south of the Taos Plaza, a quadrangle of connected adobe buildings that housed souvenir shops, New Mexican restaurants, jewelry stores, and art galleries, all of which surrounded a small central park with benches, monuments, and a raised gazebo.

Rae knew from her seventh-grade New Mexico History class that the square was once the central meeting place of the whole valley, but the area felt to her more like a stage set designed to appeal to tourists from Texas and New York. These tourists came to Taos in drones, to take photos of the Tiwa natives who lived at the Taos Pueblo, one of the oldest continuously inhabited pueblos in the United States, to buy their beautiful handcrafted silver-and-turquoise jewelry or take home a piece of the Southwestern art made famous by R.C. Gorman and Ansel Adams and Georgia O'Keefe. They came in the winter to ski at the world-class alpine ski resort, and they came in the warmer months to raft and fish in the Rio Grande or to hike the Wheeler Peak trail.

Rae had read online that New Mexicans had a love-hate relationship with the tourism industry, which brought a steady flow of much-needed cash to one of the poorest states in the nation, along with the often culturally ignorant and insensitive out-of-towners who were there to spend it. She was surprised to see that Taos had been dependent on tourism as far back as the eighties. All the shops and galleries looked sort of corny and kitschy, and everything felt manipulated to meet the expectations of the tourist gaze. One shop had even set up a big wooden sculpture of a Native American person wearing a traditional headdress outside with a sign advertising a sale on moccasins. The obvious racial stereotyping and exploitation horrified Rae. Even the McDonald's outside her window—which was advertising a Big Mac Value Pack for $2.59!—blended into the Southwestern decor of the rest of the town, with fake adobe walls and wooden latillas that clashed with the golden arches and bright, primary colors of the kids' play area visible through the glass windows.

As Rae fantasized about pulling up to the McDonald's drive-thru for some fries, Iggy leaned forward and stuck her head in between the two men.

"Hey," she said, grinning.

Oh god. What now?

The passenger turned around with an amused smirk on his face. Rae could see him more clearly now. He was younger than she had originally thought—maybe not even twenty years old—with smooth skin and sparkly eyes. Her heart pounded as he glanced from Iggy to her.

"Does your car bounce or what?" Iggy asked.

The older man turned to the younger one with a deadpan expression on his face, and for a second, Rae thought Iggy had said something offensive. But then they both laughed, and the driver flipped a series of silver switches from a box mounted below the cassette deck.

Rae shrieked as the back of the car rose off the ground and began to jump up and down, getting a little higher off the ground with each bounce.

"Higher!" Iggy yelled. "Higher!"

"You're crazy, girl." The driver laughed, flipping more switches until they were bouncing so high, Rae was afraid they might flip over.

But she couldn't stop herself from laughing, too, as she turned to see the people in the car behind them pointing and staring with their mouths hanging open in awe.

When the light turned green, the driver flipped the switches again so the car stopped bouncing and the chassis lowered to its normal height a few inches off the ground.

"Thank you so much!" Iggy screamed. "That was so rad!"

The driver looked at her in the rearview mirror. "Normally, I wouldn't be flexing like that with so many pinche hura in the area, but this one's for you."

As he turned into the plaza, the driver rolled down his window and turned up the volume on his stereo until it blasted so loud, the entire car vibrated. He circled the Plaza three times, and all the tourists walking around outside stared at the fantastic, green lowrider as they crept by.

Just as Rae was actually beginning to enjoy being part of such a spectacle, the driver pulled into a parking spot and the handsome younger lowrider tilted his seat forward again so she and Iggy could get out. Rae climbed out of the car and noticed the words *Mi Novia Celosa* airbrushed in dark green cursive beneath the flames on the side of the Monte Carlo's apple-green paint job, which glimmered with flecks of gold under the streetlamps.

"Cuidado, chica," the young lowrider said, and then he looked directly at Rae and winked. Her stomach fluttered as she watched him drive away.

Iggy stretched her arms toward the sky and then turned and ran toward the plaza square. Rae followed her as she climbed up to the top step of the gazebo and sat.

"We're meeting Rhody here," Iggy said.

"Who's Rhody?"

"The coolest person in the whole world."

Well, shit.

Rae didn't feel like sitting down. She was too excited about the party and now about meeting this new person, Rhody. Instead, she walked around the gazebo, down the steps, and across the square, which was partially illuminated by the warm, golden splotches cast by old-fashioned streetlamps.

The square was made of red brick interspersed with patches of dried grass and one large, crooked cottonwood tree, with wrought-iron benches placed here and there for people to sit. A Native American man wrapped in a light blue blanket was sitting on one of the benches in the corner across from her. When he noticed her gaze in his direction, he gestured for her to come near him. But Rae didn't know what the strange man wanted or what she would say to him, so she pretended to be interested in the huge iron cross in the middle of the square.

She walked up to the metal plaque beneath the cross, but it was too dark to read most of what was written. It was a war memorial, that much was clear, and she could feel beneath her fingertips the raised letters of the names of the people from Taos who had died in what she was pretty sure was the Bataan Death March of 1942.

As she slowly traced each name, it struck her that these people had been alive once, really alive, as alive as she was. They might've eaten eggs in the morning and worn their favorite shirt on repeat, they'd had hair on their arms that stood on end when they were frightened or cold, and they might've even walked around this same square and bought candy or nuts at the five-and-dime on the corner. Now they were gone.

It was hard to comprehend how something so alive could be totally obliterated from the world.

When it seemed the man had lost interest in her, Rae left the memorial and crossed the street to the rows of shops surrounding the square. She walked past art galleries and jewelry stores, a trading post with woven rugs and moccasins displayed in the window, a store that sold hiking and camping gear, and a candy store that sold piñon fudge and brittle. They were all closed for the night, except for one restaurant that still buzzed with the hum of diners sitting on the patio, talking and laughing and clinking their wine glasses as they scooped up what was left of the green chile on their plates with hot sopapillas and honey butter.

Stomach growling, she walked back to the gazebo. Iggy was still sitting on the steps but with a cigarette dangling between her lips.

"Oh my god!" Rae shrieked. "What are you doing?"

"Uh, smoking?"

"That is beyond disgusting."

"You are such a square," Iggy said, exhaling in Rae's direction.

"Yuck!" Rae coughed and waved the smoke away from her face. "Do you want me to list all the reasons why cigarettes are a terrible idea?" She held up her fingers. "One, they smell disgusting, and people who smoke them smell like garbage. Two—"

"You didn't even know I smoked, so I can't smell that bad. So there."

Rae ignored her. "*Two.* Your lungs will fill with fluid and you will fight for every breath you take before you eventually die from lung cancer. Three—"

As she scoured her brain in search of every repulsive, antisocial thing she had ever heard about smoking cigarettes, Rae remembered the mom she knew was not a smoker—which meant Iggy was going to quit at some point, and it was probably a waste of time to argue with her now. But it was hard for Rae to accept the fact that this younger version of her mother was smoking a cigarette right in front of her as if it was a perfectly legit pastime. And after the thousands of lectures she had given Rae about how terrible cigarettes and vaping were and how she'd better not ever try it unless she wanted to be grounded for life. Her suspicions that her mother was a huge hypocrite had certainly been confirmed today.

"Are you done?" Iggy asked.

"Yes."

"God, I hope you're not going to be this uptight at the party. Because there's going to be some stuff going on, you know what I mean?" Iggy stamped out the cigarette beneath her boot and kicked it away from her.

"What kind of stuff?" Rae asked. "Bad stuff?"

"Not *bad*, but you know, not strictly legal. Underage drinking, that kind of stuff."

Despite what Iggy thought, Rae wasn't a total square. She'd been to two unsupervised house parties in her lifetime, one during her freshman year at her old school and one this year, just over a month ago, when Cosima's parents decided she was responsible enough to be left alone with their million-dollar mansion in Altura Park *and* her annoying thirteen-year-old brother Caelin while they celebrated their twentieth wedding anniversary at Ten Thousand Waves in Santa Fe.

Cosima had bribed Caelin with two hundred dollars of her saved allowance to stay at a friend's house while she threw a pool party in her backyard. She'd invited mainly juniors and seniors Rae had never met before, most of whom had fake IDs and brought six-packs of beer, hard seltzer, and bottles of Fireball. Stefan, who was a pretty big deal on the varsity soccer team and whose dad owned a dispensary, had brought a bunch of THC gummies and a packet of prerolls he'd shared with Cosima and Rae while they sat on the edge of the pool in their bathing suits, legs dangling in the water. Rae had been afraid of the gummy bears, but she'd puffed on the joint and drank an entire Water-Melon-Rita and let a tall senior named Jayden pressure her into taking a shot of vodka before she knew he was going to try to jam his tongue down her throat. She'd told Jayden she was feeling sick, which was pretty much true, and passed out on the tufted leather couch in the living room, where she dreamed she was standing in front of an open fridge, drinking ice-cold cranberry juice all night. She'd woken up thirsty as hell with a button imprint on her face and a pounding headache that stayed with her the whole next day, while they cleaned the house and skimmed trash out of the swimming pool with a long telescope pole. Rae definitely wasn't a stranger to parties.

"No, I get it," she responded. "It's all gucci."

"Gucci?" Iggy cocked her head and raised an eyebrow, but before Rae could explain what the expression meant, she yelled at someone behind Rae, frantically waving her arms over her head. "Over here!"

Rae turned and watched as Iggy sprinted over to a tall, thin boy with an absolutely epic black mohawk. She jumped into his arms, hugging him like she hadn't seen him in years. She didn't care that people were staring. On their way back to the gazebo, they stopped to visit the Native American man on the bench—Iggy took a drag off his cigarette—while Rae stood there, feeling stupid. For some reason, she'd thought Rhody was going to be a girl.

"This"—Iggy waved her arms like she was introducing the next president of the United States—"is my best friend, Rhody."

Rhody was a lot, wearing jeans covered with chains, zippers, band patches, and strips of black cloth and leather sewn on with heavy, white thread in an overlapping patchwork pattern that was intricate and beautiful in a raw sort of way. His pants were tucked into a pair of tall Doc Martens with the words NO CONTROL painted across one toe and RIOT across the other, held up just below his hip bones by a three-row, pyramid-studded belt. Black metal spikes protruded from the shoulders of his leather motorcycle jacket, which had the anarchy symbol spray-painted on the back. His eyes were smudged with black eyeliner.

Rhody bent for a hug. Rae stood on her toes and wrapped her arms around his stiff, squeaky jacket.

"Let's motor," Iggy said, grabbing Rhody's hand. Rae groaned aloud. "Don't worry. We're just walking across the street, over to the park, then across an alfalfa field and down a dirt road, and we're there!"

Rae tried to keep up with Iggy and Rhody, but they had long legs and were walking fast and talking faster. They weren't including her in their conversation, anyway, which was fine because they were taking about a band named Black Flag and Rae had never heard of them. She fell two steps behind them and studied the construction of Rhody's mohawk as she walked.

It was made up of eight individual spikes extending at least twelve inches from his scalp, which was shaved bald everywhere except for the mohawk part. The spikes were rigid; they stuck straight up in the air and didn't move one millimeter as he walked. It was like he'd made a weapon out of his hair. What kind of product did they have in the eighties that would literally freeze hair? It looked like too big a job for Dippity-Do.

Rae wasn't the only one fascinated by Rhody's appearance. Traffic at the four-way stoplight was even more congested than when they had passed through in the lowrider, and many of the people cruising the main strip in cars or on foot were openly staring at Rhody. Most of them seemed harmless, but some of the gawkers were pointing and giving off a hostile vibe, and Rae began to feel less than safe. Iggy and Rhody seemed oblivious to the attention. Just as Rae was about to voice her concern, someone inside a purple Nissan Z rolled down their window and threw a half-empty Sonic cup at Rhody.

The Styrofoam cup bounced off his chest and burst open on the ground in front of him, spraying both him and Iggy with crushed ice and neon-blue liquid.

"Fucking faggot!" a male voice yelled. The other people in the car laughed.

Rhody stepped over the Sonic cup and continued walking down the street with his head held high, not even glancing at the carload of scary bullies. Rae was relieved that even though he looked like he might be all about confrontation, he was evidently not the type of person to be lured into a fight. Good. She didn't really want to find out what would happen if he publicly challenged this particular group of homophobes. Most bigots probably weren't worthy of a response anyway. It wasn't like confronting their ignorance was going to change their opinion, right? It was better to ignore them. Safer too.

Just as it seemed the awkward moment would pass without further drama, Iggy ran over to the Nissan as it crept forward in traffic and started banging on the hood of the car with her fists.

"Hey, fuckwad," she yelled. "Get out of the car!"

A clean-cut jock type with big arms and a mean face stuck his head out of the passenger window while the people inside hissed like a basket of snakes.

"Are you crazy, bitch?" he snapped. "I'm going to get out of this car and kick your fucking ass!"

Rhody raced toward the car and grabbed Iggy by the waist, attempting to pull her off the car. Everyone on the street stopped to watch the action.

"Let me go, dammit!" she screamed, squirming away from Rhody's grasp. "C'mon, you fucking coward, get out and fight!"

She kicked the car with one of her boots, leaving a black scuff and a big dent on the passenger-side door. The bully's expression changed from rage to confusion to alarm and then back to rage again as he weighed how to respond to this out-of-control girl. As he made up his mind and opened the door to confront her, Rae's feet came unglued from the sidewalk and she ran over to help Rhody pull Iggy away from the car.

They pried her fingers from the hood and pulled her across the street while she kicked and cursed at them. Rhody led them down a dark alley, and Rae refused to let go of Iggy's arm until it felt safe enough to stop and catch their breath.

"What the actual *fuck*," Rae said, her hands trembling. That was by far the most TikTok-worthy moment she'd ever witnessed.

Iggy laughed. At first she tried to repress it, but then her laughter grew louder and more hysterical until Rhody joined in and they were both bent over laughing and slapping their knees and gasping for air. Rae couldn't resist. Even though she was worried the bullies might have followed them down the alleyway and she was super pissed at Iggy for putting them in such a dangerous situation to begin with, she was laughing right along with them. It felt good to release her nervous energy.

"Does that happen to you a lot?" she asked when she could speak again.

"All the time," Rhody said. "Especially when I'm wearing my liberty spikes." He touched the tip of one of his mohawk spikes.

"Liberty spikes," Rae repeated, trying the phrase out. "How do you get your hair to stay up like that anyway?"

"Knox gelatin and a blow-dryer."

"Yeah, and, like, three hours," Iggy said, rolling her eyes.

"But I don't do it every day. Only when I feel like getting my ass kicked." He laughed, but his voice was shaky.

"Do you get in a lot of fights?" Rae asked.

"At least once a week. More if I don't have my bodyguard with me."

Iggy flexed her biceps.

"Do they pick on you because of the way you look or because you're gay?"

Iggy and Rhody both stepped back and stared at her with their mouths open, as if she had said something horrible.

Iggy grabbed her by the shoulders. "Take that back!" she yelled, shaking her.

"I'm not *gay*!" Rhody said, wringing his hands. "Do you think I'm gay?"

"I don't think you're gay or straight or pansexual or whatever," Rae said, twisting away from Iggy's grasp. "I don't even know you. But it's okay if you *are* gay. You know that, right?"

"Whatever you say," Iggy mumbled as she started walking back down the alley.

Rhody stared at Rae for a long moment before he, too, continued walking. Rae wasn't sure what had just happened, but she had no choice but to follow them.

The alley led to a side entrance into Kit Carson Park via a wrought-iron gate that Iggy unlatched in the dark. Only after they were walking single file down the trail did Rae realize with a flash of terror that they were actually passing through a small cemetery. Actual graves and headstones lined the path, all of them old and some of them crooked, with names she couldn't read by the light of a nearby lamppost.

"Oh my god, where are we?" she yelped.

Rhody answered in a fake tour-guide voice, "We are currently entering Kit Carson Park through the historic memorial cemetery, originally established in 1847."

Iggy snickered.

"There's a cemetery in the park?" Rae asked. "Isn't that weird?" She thought of cemeteries as solemn, isolated places you would have to make a special trip to visit, not places you would stumble upon in the middle of the community's main recreational gathering space.

"Is it?" Iggy asked, holding her hands out like claws and laughing like a vampire.

"Stop it," Rae pleaded.

Iggy dropped her teasing as they toured the rest of the cemetery, pausing at a few of the more ornate gravestones. While they walked, Rhody told her that the body of the famous frontiersman Kit Carson was buried there, along with a bunch of soldiers, early Taos traders and merchants, and the wealthy art patron Mabel Dodge Luhan. He was a good storyteller, and Rae was surprised that someone who looked like him would know so much about local history.

The fact that nobody had been freshly buried underneath them made the cemetery seem a little less scary. The longer they walked, the more peaceful Rae felt, until she could begin to understand how locating an eternal resting place right beside the normal activities of life might inspire a person to relax and reflect on how things once were. Walking through Kit Carson Cemetery with Iggy and Rhody made death feel less terrifying.

When they reached the end of the path, Rhody opened the gate and walked up to a rough, white gravestone that was situated outside of the main cemetery for some reason.

"Hello, Arthur," he said, saluting the pale gravestone. He and Iggy plopped down and sat cross-legged right on top of the man's grave.

"Who's Arthur?" Rae asked.

"Arthur Manby," Rhody replied. "He planted the trees in this park and on Pueblo Road."

Iggy laughed like Rhody had said the funniest thing in the world, but Rae didn't get it.

Rhody patted the spot in the grass next to him. "Sit."

"I don't know," she said. "Isn't that disrespectful to the dead?"

"Don't worry about disrespecting this dude," he said, pulling a curved, silver flask out of his back pocket and unscrewing the cap. "Let me tell you about Arthur. Arthur Manby was an evil fortune hunter from England who became, like, totally obsessed by the beauty of Taos after his first visit in 1883. From the moment he first cast his eyes on this magical valley, he could not sleep until he possessed everything he saw. And he stopped at nothing to get what he wanted—he even created a secret society of rich people whose sole mission was to double-cross local people out of their land. Little did these scumbags know that once they joined Manby's secret society, this freakazoid would kill them all before he would let them leave. Yep, Arthur Manby was one of the most heinous people who ever lived. Some even say he was into the black arts—a dark sorcerer. By the time he was an old geezer, he'd murdered, lied, stole, and cheated hundreds of people out of their family homes and property." Rhody paused to take a big swig of whatever was in his flask before passing it to Iggy.

"Yikes!" Rae said, fascinated by his tale. "He sounds really awful."

"He was awful, all right," Rhody agreed. "But he finally got his karma. Of the hundreds of people he betrayed and cheated during his lifetime, one of them finally had enough. Monster Manby was found murdered in his own home in 1929 when he was almost seventy years old."

Rae gasped and clutched Rhody's arm. This monster was buried right underneath them!

"But that's not everything. Are you ready for this? The sheriff discovered his headless, maggot-infested corpse in one room and found his head in another—whatever his hungry dogs had left of it, that is."

"No way!" Rae screamed.

"Yes way," Iggy insisted. "I swear to God and hope to die, he is not lying! That's why the epitaph on his gravestone is so choice. The only decent thing they could come up with was that he planted the trees in this park."

"And on Pueblo Road," Rhody added. "Don't forget about Pueblo Road."

They were both laughing so hard, they could barely speak. Rae wasn't sure if she could believe this crazy Manby story, so she reached for the phone in her back pocket.

It still wasn't there. The fact checking would have to wait.

Iggy finally stopped laughing and passed her the silver flask. Rae held it up to her nose and sniffed.

"It's Malibu rum," Iggy said.

"Is this where you usually do your pregaming?" Rae asked, taking a bigger drink of the syrupy liquid than she meant to. She'd expected the rum to taste like a Tropical Blue Coconut from Bahama Buck's, which was what it smelled like, but it was strong and burned her throat. She coughed a little bit after swallowing.

"What's pregaming?" Rhody asked.

"You know," she said. "The party before the party?"

"Yep." Iggy laughed, patting Arthur Manby's headstone. "This is our spot."

Iggy and Rhody took turns drinking from the flask, but Rae shook her head the next time her turn came around. She already had a warm sensation in the pit of her empty stomach, and her face felt like it was on fire.

When the flask was empty, Iggy led them across the park and through an adjacent plot of knee-high alfalfa. It hadn't taken them long to reach this greener, more rural part of town, and as they lifted their knees and tromped single file through the quiet field, Rae realized she didn't feel anxious about anything. She wasn't worried about what kind of people were going to be at this party or how her hair looked or even how much time she had left before the time portal opened to take her back home. Instead, she let the hum of conversation between Iggy and Rhody wash over her like a waterfall. Moving through the crisp mountain air made the skin on the back of her neck tingle in pleasant waves.

Arthur Manby was right about one thing: Taos *was* beautiful. The night air smelled of pine and wet rocks, and the Sangre de Cristo Mountains sprawled in every direction, purple-blue and ominous in the dark sky. The mountains looked close enough to touch, even though she knew it was a trick of her mind. In reality, it would take them days to reach the top of even the nearest peak.

Rae kept her eyes focused on the biggest, highest mountain as she walked. As weird as it seemed, she felt like the mountain was exuding some kind of mysterious, magnetic energy that made her forget all about her tired legs as it pulled her into the unknown.

Chapter Eight

The party was located in a run-down ranch-style home at the end of a winding dirt road, hidden from view of the neighbors by a thicket of wild shrubs and red willow trees. The first thing Rae saw as they neared the house was a bunch of kids hanging around outside, some of them standing in clusters and smoking, some sitting on top of an old school bus parked behind the house, and some hovering over a girl as she puked in a lilac bush by the front porch. They all looked sort of cool and edgy.

She was nervous about fitting in until she noticed everyone was drinking out of red Solo cups. How different could they be?

"Let's get fucking wasted!" Iggy yelled, pumping her fists in the air as she moved through the crowd of kids on the porch. The kids hollered back their approval.

The screen door opened to a wave of people jumping up and down in front of a three-man band playing shockingly loud punk rock music in a cramped corner of the room. Rae froze in place, mesmerized by the lead singer as he screamed profanities and thrashed his body with the microphone stand, whipping his long hair up and down and spraying the crowd with his sweat. Next to him was a short, pudgy guy who was shirtless and sweating profusely as he banged out distorted chords on a bass guitar held together by duct tape, bobbing his shaved head in time with the frantic beat. Behind them both, a wispy girl with red hair beat her drum kit with a power and intensity that defied her small frame. The gruesome image of a bloody squid in a blender was stenciled on her bass drumhead, with the name of the band in large, capital letters: LIQUID SQUID.

Every so often, one of the people jumping in a messy, chaotic sort of pogo dance would break away from the throng, climb one of the two couches on opposite sides of the room, and fling their clammy bodies so they slammed full force into the crowd. Aside from the sad, broken-down couches, the room was bare—no paintings on the walls, no houseplants, no coffee tables, no carpet or rugs, just crushed beer cans and cigarette butts littering the floor.

Iggy leaned in and shouted directly into Rae's ear, "Welcome to Scum House!"

"Um . . . thanks, I guess," Rae replied. She was having a hard time peeling her eyes away from the lead singer.

Iggy noticed. "That's him," she yelled. "That's Simon!"

On her other side, Rhody rolled his eyes. "I need a drink!" he announced, leaving them.

So *this* was the guy Iggy was ready to run away with. He wasn't exactly Rae's type, but she had to admit he was pretty damn snacky with his high cheekbones and extreme physicality. She noticed Iggy wasn't the only person in the room obsessed with him. Almost every other girl and a few of the guys were fixated on him as he screamed and twisted and writhed. When he abruptly stopped singing and gestured for his bandmates to stop the set, he either didn't see or didn't care to acknowledge the intensity of the adoring eyes that watched him while he messed with the knobs on his amp. He let his long hair hang in front of his face and avoided eye contact with the crowd.

When it became obvious that Liquid Squid was on a break, virtually everyone lit a cigarette at the same moment, and the room quickly filled with the stench of burning tobacco.

"God, can we please get out of here?" Rae asked in between fits of coughing. "I'm dying."

"Yeah, let's grab some jungle juice before the next set."

Rae followed Iggy into a filthy kitchen that was nearly buried under crushed beer cans and half-empty bottles of booze. The single-compartment sink was filled with moldy dishes sitting in stagnant water. It smelled like a rotten corpse, but no one seemed to care—the small space was packed with people grabbing cans of Budweiser and Pabst Blue Ribbon from a battered fridge, laughing and yelling over each other to be heard.

Iggy headed straight for a galvanized steel tub sitting on a sticky countertop, filled with some kind of scary-looking punch with a layer of lemons and oranges floating on top. The fruit's formerly white pith had turned bright pink from soaking up the artificial coloring and now looked like fruit from another planet. Iggy grabbed two plastic Solo cups from the open pack on the counter and handed one to Rae before dipping hers directly into the toxic-looking liquid.

"What's in it?" Rae asked, crinkling up her nose and saying a silent prayer that Red Dye No. 2 had been banned by 1984.

"Hawaiian Punch and Everclear," Iggy replied. "It's awesome. You can't even taste the alcohol."

Rae used another cup to pour punch into hers, avoiding the lemons and oranges.

"Oh no, you have to get the fruit!" Iggy insisted. She scooped out a couple of orange slices with her bare hands and dropped them into Rae's cup. "They soak up extra alcohol."

She had already guzzled her first cup and was pouring herself another by the time Rae took her first sip of the lukewarm punch. All she could taste was fake tropical sweetness mixed with citrus, so she took another, bigger drink. She still couldn't taste any alcohol, but the tissue in her mouth tingled and a metallic numbness slid down her throat.

The sounds of the band tuning their instruments for the next set suddenly filled the kitchen.

"Let's go!" Iggy shouted as everyone jostled to get back into the living room.

"I have to go to the bathroom!" Rae shouted back.

"What?"

"THE BATHROOM!"

Iggy pointed to a door down a narrow hallway where a half dozen others were lined up, waiting. When Rae turned around again, Iggy was already gone. It was the perfect opportunity to ditch her cup of jungle juice on the kitchen counter. The alcohol didn't feel right when it reached her stomach, and what would her grandma say if she came back drunk?

She got in line for the bathroom right behind a boy and girl who were making out so hard, it was a miracle they could even breathe. The girl had short, blonde hair with black tips, and she had her hands in the boy's back pockets and was pressing her crotch into his while they kissed.

The furthest Rae had ever gone with a guy was kissing with some tongue, and she couldn't help but wonder if these two had had sex. They weren't much older than her, but it looked like they probably had. She felt a rush of sensation between her thighs just as the girl opened her eyes and saw her watching them.

The girl laughed in her boyfriend's mouth and, in a deep state of unbearable cringe, Rae turned her attention to the bathroom door and counted the holes someone had punched in the door. Thankfully, none of them went all the way through.

An older guy exited the bathroom, still buttoning up his pants, and the couple went inside together. She could hear them laughing and kissing. It didn't even sound like they were peeing. They stumbled out nearly ten minutes later, wiping their noses as they pushed past her toward the music.

Rae checked to make sure the door was locked three times before she felt secure enough to pull down her pants. You couldn't see through the holes in the bathroom door but you could definitely hear through them, and she felt like she was peeing right in the middle of the party. To make matters worse, the toilet had gross stains and a slimy, green ring inside the bowl. She did her best to pee without sitting all the way on the toilet seat, and it was only after she'd started that she realized there was no toilet paper. She had to hover there and air dry for a minute, unsteady from the half cup of jungle juice. The bathroom also lacked soap, so she held her hands under hot water until she was certain any germs she'd picked up had been destroyed.

Her reflection in the mirror was shocking. The British Red Coat lipstick was mostly smudged off, and her eyes were bloodshot from the smoke in the house. Oh well. It didn't matter, since no one was paying much attention to her anyway. She wiped off what remained of the lipstick and checked the itinerary case.

One hour left.

She flushed the toilet and left the bathroom to find Iggy.

The mood in the living room had become more extreme in a short amount of time. The punk music sounded harder, faster, and louder, and the throng of people surrounding the band were squished together skin on skin, many of them actually shirtless. Bare-chested boys and girls in their bras hopped in time to the accelerating tempo of the music like one giant, gyrating beast. Every few minutes, someone would peel away from the group, get some distance, and run back and hurl themselves into the wall of flesh with what looked like bone-jarring impact.

She spotted Iggy and Rhody near the front of the throng by the band, punching the air, gnashing their teeth, and jumping next to each other like angry lunatics. Rhody had removed his jacket and they were both sweating profusely, so much so that the jester star was sliding down Iggy's face in a disturbing, black puddle.

Rae took a deep breath and pushed her body into the overheated crowd. The sea of human flesh yielded slightly to her body before she was once again shoved outside of the circle by someone's massive shoulder. At first she was upset that a big guy with silver spikes in his ears was trying to keep her out, but she realized quickly that it was all part of the dance. The key to making it further into the mob was letting her body go limp against the crush of other bodies, allowing the wavelike motion of the crowd to suck her in and pull her slowly inward. The added benefit was that the less she resisted the elbow jabs and foot stomps, the less they hurt.

When she finally reached Iggy and Rhody, she was so excited, she threw her arms around them in a three-way hug. They laughed and screamed in her ears as they dragged her into their crazy pogo-dance circle. The music was so fast and loud, it was impossible to talk or even think, so Rae let the bass and drums vibrate through her body and show her what to do, jumping higher and faster with every two-minute song.

Before long, she found herself joining the push and shove of the crowd. She, too, was leaning on the people next to her with her shoulders and forearms. She, too, was punching the air in time with the beat. It was exciting to be this close to the source of the music, like she was dancing in the middle of an electrical storm. When she glanced at the band to see if they were feeling it, too, Simon was looking right at her. She turned away quickly, closed her eyes, and danced even harder, hoping he was still watching her.

When the band stopped playing and threw their instruments on the ground for another break, Rae was not ready to stop.

Iggy grabbed one of the dozen plastic cups that had been left on top of the tall amp and began weaving her way outside with Rhody and Rae following her like always. She stopped to hug or high-five every single person she knew on the way out. She was slurring and cursing more than usual and didn't seem to notice or care if Rhody and Rae were still with her.

It was like she'd totally forgotten they were even there. Rae looked at Rhody and raised her eyebrows. He shrugged as if the whole situation was normal—just part of hanging out with Iggy.

With that shrug, Rae realized Iggy's dismissive attitude felt familiar to her too. The way she looked at her without actually seeing her, the way she brushed past her like she wasn't there, made Rae want to scream, *Hey, asshole! Look at me! I'm right here!*

As they emerged from the smoke-filled house into the fresh, cool air outside, Rae stared up at the indigo sky and silently counted the stars, trying to calm the panic rising in her chest. It was the same panic she'd felt as a young girl when her mom would lock herself in her room and her dad would pound on the door and demand that she come out *right fucking now*, and Rae's heart would slam against her chest because her mom was drunk again.

Sometime during the night, she had allowed herself to forget Iggy *was* her mom. For a minute, she'd believed she was just hanging with friends.

Iggy took two cigarettes from the pack in her jacket pocket and handed one to Rhody. She swayed as she struck a wooden match across the bottom of her boot and struggled to line up the flame with the tip of her cigarette. When she closed one eye to improve her focus, Rae felt a secret fury building inside her.

"Here, let me," Rhody said. He grabbed the cigarette out of Iggy's mouth and put it next to the one in his, lighting them both with a silver Zippo before passing hers back. They both inhaled and exhaled, spewing repulsive clouds of smoke everywhere.

"That was fucking rad," Iggy said. Her words were slow and awkwardly enunciated, even though she was making extra effort to speak clearly. Rae fought the urge to tell her she looked ridiculous with her black makeup smeared down her face. Everything in her wanted to lash out at her mom right now, but no one would understand.

"Fucking hellacious," Rhody agreed. He didn't seem nearly as drunk as Iggy. In fact, Rae hadn't seen him drink anything since they'd shared the flask at the cemetery.

"I hate that word. *Rad*," Rae blurted. "It's stupid."

"Rad," Rhody said, which made Iggy cough and laugh.

"Oh, damn, I have to pee," she shrieked, jamming her hands between her legs as she ran toward the house.

"Wait, I'll come with you!" Rhody shouted, and Rae was suddenly alone in the crowd of kids—just her and her rage.

She walked backward slowly until she was partially hidden by a large elm tree.

She'd been having such a good time before Iggy got drunk. Why didn't Iggy stop after a drink or two? Why did she keep going until she was stupid? Why did her mom have to open another bottle of wine? Wasn't one bottle enough? Being drunk never made her feel good. It made her miserable—especially the next day, when she had to drag her puffy, parched self out of bed and drive Rae to school. She wouldn't say a word the whole way, just moan when they went over a speed bump. The car would smell like a bus station bathroom by the time they got there.

Whatever pain or shame her mom felt, it had never been enough to stop her from doing it again the next night. Only the accident had stopped her. At least for now.

Rae peeked under her sweatshirt to check the time on her itinerary case. She had fifteen minutes left in 1984. Should she wait in the bathroom for the portal to open? Or hide here in the trees? She wasn't sure how bright the portal was or how obvious it would be to other people.

As she pondered her options, Rae realized someone was watching her from across the front yard. By the silhouette, she was pretty sure it was a boy.

He noticed her noticing him and started walking across the yard toward her. Hopefully whatever he had to say would take less than fifteen minutes.

When he emerged from the shadows, Rae was startled to see the boy was Simon.

"Hey," he said.

"Hey," she replied. Up close like this, she realized he wasn't much taller than her. He had seemed so much larger when he was performing.

"I saw you in the mosh pit," he said. "Dancing with Rhody and what's-her-name."

"Iggy!" Rae blurted. *What's-her-name?* The guy Iggy was ready to abandon her entire life for thought of her as *what's-her-name?*

"Yeah, her. She's okay. I mean, she's a little too stoked on the new ro shit," he said, shaking his head. "I mean, who doesn't love The Cure, but fuck Visage! Fuck Spandau Ballet, you know what I mean?" Simon curled his lip in disgust. "Fucking sellout synth-pop music with no soul, if you ask me."

"I'm pretty sure she's into punk music too." To be honest, Rae didn't have a clear understanding of the difference between punk and post-punk and new wave or new ro or any of it, but she was so offended on Iggy's behalf, it didn't matter.

"What about you? Are you into punk?" Simon asked, moving closer to her.

"I'm just now getting into it," she heard herself saying, which was definitely not true. The dancing had been fun, but she could not imagine listening to that spastic, angry music on the reg. Why did she say that?

Simon nodded in approval. "I'm really inspired by Minor Threat and Ian MacKay. I'm actually thinking about going straight edge—no beer, no pot, nothing. I'm also really into Dead Kennedys. Jello Biafra is a genius, you know what I'm saying? The name of our band is sort of an homage to his record label, Alternative Tentacles. Tentacles, squid . . . get it? We're going to California to play some shows with them in the Bay Area and hopefully get into the punk scene that's happening out there. LA too. Nothing but hardcore, man. Real, burly shit. Fuck all the posers out here in New Mexico."

"Uh-huh," Rae agreed, hoping Simon would find her responses boring enough that he would go back inside for another set before the portal came and sucked her up right in front of him—or, worse, accidentally swept him up with it. Was that even a thing?

But instead of losing interest, he was inching nearer.

"You should come with us," Simon said, so close to her now that he only had to whisper to be heard. She could smell the sweat drying on his skin, warm and woodsy.

"Come with you?" she asked, flustered. His transformation from the screaming maniac of twenty minutes earlier to this smooth, flirty boy with a silky voice was alarming . . . yet fascinating.

"Yeah, dude, come to California! We're trying to get a bunch of people to come with us, like, on the bus or in a caravan. You know, people who follow us on tour and come to all our shows."

"You mean, like, groupies?" Rae asked, embarrassed that she had believed for a minute that he was actually interested in her. Did he really think he was so special or talented that she would actually ghost her life and follow him around the country? Was he for real? Iggy seriously fell for this bullshit?

"Everyone else would be groupies," he said, staring into her eyes, "but you would be . . . something else."

Rae put her hand over her mouth to hide her laughter as Simon turned his head to kiss her. It was like she was watching in slow motion as his face moved toward hers, and she had time to wonder if his lips would feel as soft as they looked—and then she felt her head moving forward to meet his, as if someone else were controlling it.

Just as their lips were about to touch, Rae sensed a vibrational shift in the atmosphere. A strong breeze blew through the leaves in the tree above her head. The hair on her arms stood up.

"I have to go!" she yelled, pushing Simon away from her.

"Whoa, what the fuck?" he said as he stumbled backward.

Rae scanned the big yard for any hidden spot, but there were clusters of people everywhere, smoking, talking, making out. She moved further away from Simon.

"Where are you going?" he asked.

There wasn't time for explanations. She had to get as far away from this party as she possibly could before the portal opened to take her back home. She raced out of the yard, down the long, dirt driveway, and back down the road she and Iggy and Rhody had walked hours earlier.

She almost made it to the end of the road before the air around her started to crackle with pops of static and shimmering waves of heat crept into her peripheral vision. She ran to the nearest tree and leaned over, hands on her knees, to catch her breath in the dark. As the subtle vibration in the air morphed into a high-pitched scream worse than the screeching of seventeen-year cicadas, Rae closed her eyes and concentrated on breathing in and out, getting as much oxygen as she could. Clinging to the tree, she braced herself for the terrifying sensation of endless falling as the portal opened around her and she struggled to hold on to consciousness.

And then there was nothing.

Chapter Nine

Rae opened her eyes as she landed hard on her feet. Weak from her unbeliev-ably long day in 1984, her knees buckled on impact and she collapsed in a heap on the floor, hitting the side of her head on the ceramic tile in her grandma's kitchen.

"Oh dear," her grandma said, rushing to her side. "I'm so sorry! I should have put a blanket down. I forgot how hard it is to stick the landing when you're beginning."

Rae sat up in a daze and rubbed the knot already forming on the side of her skull.

"At least I didn't pass out this time," she said. "I don't think I did, anyway. It felt like I left my body but I was still awake somewhere else."

"Don't think about that too much, dear," her grandma said, pulling her up by both hands and helping her steady herself on her feet. "I want to hear all about your trip."

"I'm so tired, Grandma. Can I take a nap first?"

"It's better not to," her grandma replied, pushing her toward one of the kitchen chairs. "The whole experience will start to feel like a dream if you fall asleep right afterward. It's better to stay awake and talk about it. How about I make you a grilled cheese sandwich and some coffee with lots of cream and sugar, the way you like it?"

"Sure," she said, her stomach growling at the thought of food.

As her grandma rummaged through the fridge, Rae studied the shape of her head and her wrinkled face, trying to get her brain to accept the fact that this was the same person she had met only a few hours ago. This was Lydia.

"You were there, Grandma," she said. "I saw you."

"Oh really?" her grandma asked, slicing cheddar cheese.

"Yes. I ran into Iggy—my mom—ditching class in the middle of the desert and she brought me to your house. There were a bunch of people there hanging out. You were with your boyfriend, Abelino."

"Of course. Yes, I remember Abelino," her grandma said, trying to hide her smile in her shoulder as she spread butter on pumpernickel bread.

"You were . . . you were different."

Her grandma dropped the butter knife and turned, frowning. "I was a different person back then, Rae."

"You didn't know I was your granddaughter," Rae said, changing the subject. She didn't want to upset her. "Did you even know about time travel back then?"

"Of course. In fact, I met Abelino day tripping in France in 1926. He was a time traveler, too, and we were both at the Folies Bergère to watch Josephine Baker perform. My god, what a woman."

Well, that explained Abelino's weird vibe. He'd seemed like he was hiding something or knew things he shouldn't know.

"I started time traveling when I was a child," her grandma explained, "like everyone else."

The buttered bread sizzled as it hit the hot frying pan.

"If that's true, then why doesn't my mom know about time travel?"

"Your mom ran away from home before I had a chance to teach her. We didn't speak for a few years and by the time we were communicating again, it was too late."

Rae was shocked. She left her mouth hanging open so her grandma could see exactly how shocked she was. This was the first she'd ever heard of her mom running away from home. She'd known her mom and her grandma didn't always get along—but not speaking to each other for years? It didn't make any sense.

"When did she run away? And why? How long was she gone?"

Her grandma sat next to Rae and grabbed her hand. The wet, popping sounds of the coffeemaker filled the small kitchen.

"She left when she was sixteen. She doesn't like to talk about her reasons why and frankly, that's okay with me. I respect that. People waste so much of their time trying to understand their past, don't you think?"

Rae was too busy processing this information to respond.

"We spoke on the phone every now and then, but we didn't see each other again until she was pregnant with you."

"Oh. My. GOD!" Rae yelled, pulling her hand away. "You didn't see your own daughter for over *twenty years*?"

Her grandma nodded, lost in thought, and stood to pour the coffee.

Rae couldn't believe it. Her mom and grandma complained about each other constantly, but she had always thought of it as their unique, sort of funny way of communicating with one another, like a comedy routine they had been developing for decades. The fact that they could go more than twenty years without seeing each other meant they probably just did not like each other. Why had no one told her? It made her feel exactly the way she did when her parents split up—like her entire life was a lie.

"Give me my cell phone," she demanded. The last thing she wanted to do was sit there and obsess about her mom's screwed-up life. She needed to scroll some random shit immediately.

"Honey, I think we need to talk about this."

"Give me my phone," she repeated.

Her grandma sighed in defeat and took the phone out of her sweater pocket. She slid it across the kitchen table until it was close enough for Rae to grab. It felt solid and reassuring in her hands as she stroked her special-edition, rose-gold glitter case with its Good Vibes Only sticker. She tapped the phone lightly to wake it up. Her heart swelled with anticipation as the screen lit up and she saw the familiar lock-screen photo of her and Cosima throwing peace signs by one of the bronze lobo statues on University of New Mexico's campus.

She swiped down to scan the dozens of notifications requiring her immediate attention—Snaps from friends, texts from her mom, replies to posts, unseen Stories, TikTok videos, new likes on her lame selfie—the list went on. She had a lot of work to do.

With her phone in one hand and a mug of strong, sweet coffee in the other, Rae trudged into the living room and sank into the overstuffed couch. Her grandma followed her, holding a grilled cheese sandwich cut into four small squares.

"Are you going to bury your head in that phone of yours?" she asked, setting the plate on the coffee table in front of Rae.

Without taking her eyes off her screen, Rae picked up one of the sandwich quarters and stuffed the whole thing in her mouth. Her grandma had cooked it low and slow until the cheese got gooey and the outside of the bread was crispy. She'd also tucked tomato jam into the layers of cheese before cooking, which was a sweet, smoky complement to the sharp cheddar.

"You're not a terrible cook," Rae said, switching from Snapchat to Instagram.

"I beg your pardon?" her grandma replied.

"Iggy—my mom—said she taught herself to cook because you didn't know how."

"She said that, did she?"

"I bet you didn't know your lousy cooking would inspire her whole career."

Her grandma laughed, but it was a sad laugh.

Rae finished her sandwich and looked around for something to wipe her greasy hands on. She was about to wipe them on her jeans when she realized that she was still wearing the Big E Levi's Iggy had freely handed over like it was no big deal.

And to repay her for being such a nice person, Rae had nearly kissed the guy she was in love with. She was a horrible person.

Her grandma was watching her like she knew she was going to start talking any second.

"Did she run away with Simon?" Rae asked.

"I don't think I ever knew his name," her grandma replied.

Rae could feel her heart hurting, a real pain in her chest right where her heart was. It wasn't that Simon had seemed like a bad person, because he hadn't. He'd had a beautiful face and he'd been passionate about music and he hadn't acted like everyone else, and she could understand how it would be fun for someone like Iggy to take a road trip to California with a bunch of rowdy people in a punk rock party bus. But she couldn't stop thinking about how Simon had referred to Iggy as *what's-her-name*. He hadn't even known her name! Had the trip been fun for her? And what about Rhody? He and Iggy had seemed inseparable. Had he gone too?

"I don't know any of the details," her grandma continued. "She doesn't like to talk about it, like I said. She had a hard life for a long time. She got into drinking. Drugs too."

"Oh my god, that *sucks*," Rae said, resisting the tears that stung her nose on their way up to her eyes.

"I'm sorry, honey. You know your mom struggled with alcohol."

"Yeah, like, a couple years ago. Not when she was sixteen!"

"Well, she's been sober for almost two years now. Thank god for that."

What if Rae had been able to talk to Iggy before the portal opened and told her that Simon didn't even know her name—that he'd tried to kiss Rae under the tree ten minutes after meeting her? Would Iggy have changed her mind about running away with him? Would her life have been any different?

"You said you want me to go back to 1984, right, Grandma?"

"Yes, but only to persuade your grandpa to make another travel card for me, not to hang out with your mom. Don't get any ideas about how things could be different, Rae."

"But if I could convince my mom not to run away with Simon, maybe she would end up having a better life."

"You can't convince her of that, Rae. It already happened."

"But what if I could make it not happen?"

Her grandma closed her eyes and rubbed her temples with a pained expression on her face.

"Now, I know you've watched enough time-travel stuff on TV to understand that you can't change the past without changing the present and future. Running away like she did placed your mom on a path that led to your dad and, ultimately, to having you. Do you want to create a world where you don't exist?"

"No."

"Then listen up! As time travelers, we have a responsibility to explore the Block as observers only. My goodness, when I was a girl we had to take an oath that we would never attempt to alter history before we were even allowed to travel. That's why so many time travelers are Taoists. Eventually you learn that it's easier to exist in harmony with the universe. Go with the flow. Accept what is. Don't interfere."

"But what if I do interfere?" Rae persisted. "You said before that it was pretty much impossible to change the way things happen anyway."

"And that is true. But under certain circumstances, the past can be altered. And you don't want to fool around with that. The entire fabric of the universe would be affected and the world as we know it would be obliterated. Do you want to be responsible for that?"

Rae tried to imagine what an obliterated world would feel like while her grandma laced up her boots.

"I can't explain everything to you now, Rae, I'm sorry. It's after nine o'clock and we need to get you home. You have to trust me. Constantly trying to change things is what got time travel banned for private citizens in the first place."

"Wait, other people know about time travel? Like, it's a thing? And it's banned?"

"Of course it's a thing! Of course people know about it! Haven't you heard 'Day Tripper' or 'Iron Man'? John Lennon and Ozzy Osbourne were both travelers. Lots of artists are and many philosophers, too—and, unfortunately, plenty of entrepreneurs and government bigwigs. Ever wonder how Jeff Bezos came up with Amazon? He's no soothsayer, believe me. But under current ITTOC guidelines, only licensed government officials can legally skim time and all of that is on the hush-hush. If anyone found out what we were up to, we could be fined or jailed or worse. Lucky for us, no one pays too much attention to two little birds like you and me."

Rae's head was spinning with all the new facts her grandma was throwing down. "The ITTOC?"

"The International Time Travel Oversight Committee. An intergovernmental organization established in 1948 around the same time as NATO, when so many people were traveling back in time trying to kill Hitler."

"I didn't believe you." Rae shook her head. "I thought you had Alzheimer's."

Her grandma winced.

Rae unbuckled the belt around her waist to get a better look at the silver itinerary case. The LED countdown had stopped and the mysterious black screen was giving away no clues. If she hadn't experienced it for herself, she would've never believed this harmless belt buckle had been somehow responsible for propelling her body forty years across time and space and back again.

"We'll have to continue this conversation later," her grandma said, ripping the belt out of Rae's hands.

"But I have so many questions!"

"Let's get together Sunday. We'll plan your next trip and I'll answer whatever questions about time travel I'm capable of answering. Be warned, though, I'm no physicist."

"So in the meantime I'm supposed to go home and act as if I didn't spend a whole day and night with my sixteen-year old mom?"

"Exactly." Her grandma nodded. "Now, let's get you back before she stops speaking to me for another twenty years."

Chapter Ten

Rae unlocked the front door and turned to wave at her grandma before stepping inside the house, which was dark except for the familiar light from the television flickering in the entryway. Her mom had a habit of falling asleep in the den while watching cooking competition shows on TV. Normally, Rae would have been happy for the opportunity to avoid her. Tonight, though, she had to at least look at her.

She was curled up on the sectional with her bare feet and ankles sticking out from under an old orange-and-brown afghan. Her eyes snapped open the same moment Rae stuck her head in the room.

"Hi," she said. Her hair was sticking up on one side from being smushed on the pillow, the only echo of her former self.

"Oh, uh, I'm sorry," Rae said. "I didn't know you were sleeping."

"I was waiting for you. I wanted to apologize for this morning."

Rae sat at the end of the couch by her mom's feet. "How was work?" she asked, steering the conversation away from this morning. She was the one who should be apologizing, but she wasn't quite ready for that.

"Oh, fine. I had three jobs. The continental breakfast and two late-afternoon deliveries at UNM. No service, just prep and drop."

"Cool."

Her mom's face was illuminated by the creepy glow of the TV, and it was obvious that she was exhausted. She never wore makeup or did anything else to make herself look nice, just washed her face in the morning and slapped on some basic face cream. If she was scheduled for full-service catering she might put on some lip tint and a coat of mascara, but most of the time, she didn't.

It hadn't always been that way. When Rae was a little girl, she used to love to hang out in the bathroom with her mom while she got ready for a night out. She would perch on the edge of the bathtub, transfixed by her mom as she stood in front of the mirror with her collection of colored pots and shadow palettes and tiny brushes and pencils, making her eyes wider and her lips fuller with a few thoughtfully placed strokes. Rae had been mesmerized by the ritual of transformation, convinced her mother was the most beautiful woman who had ever lived. In the morning, when she would find her mom cooking breakfast in her plain old chef whites again, Rae would cry and beg her to put on some lipstick. Her mom would laugh and promise her there would be another date night, but date nights became less and less frequent, from once a week to once a month to a couple times a year. By the time they divorced, her mom and dad hadn't been on a date in years.

Rae hadn't given much thought to her mom's relationship with clothes and makeup until she met Iggy, who obviously had her own style and enjoyed picking out outfits and wearing makeup and being noticed by others, even if the attention was sometimes negative. She was unpredictable and obnoxious, sure, but she was also confident and outgoing and friendly. She loved music and dancing. It seemed like all her mom wanted to do now was blend into the background and disappear.

Rae couldn't even remember the last time her mom had listened to music or painted her nails or had lunch with a friend. All she did was work, sleep, eat, and watch TV. When she compared the person her mom used to be with the person she was now, she saw her from a whole different perspective. For the first time in her life, Rae looked at her mom and saw what a sad person she was.

She wasn't emotionally withdrawn because she was an introvert or because she didn't enjoy spending time with Rae. The reason it was so hard to connect with her mom was because her mom was broken inside.

What had happened to her? Where had Iggy gone?

"Did you have a good time with your grandma?"

"Oh yeah. We played, uh, Texas hold 'em with nickels. I won two dollars and thirty-five cents," Rae replied, surprised at her own ability to lie on the fly like this.

"Is that old hustler losing her touch or what?"

Before Rae could answer, the commercial break ended and the cooking show her mom had been watching came back on.

"Hold on," her mom said. "I want to see who they chop."

Rae turned to the two chefs and the panel of judges on TV. The show's host had his hand poised over a silver cloche, which he would soon lift to reveal to the audience which of the two chefs had been eliminated and which had won the ten-thousand-dollar cash prize. Her mom's gaze was riveted to the screen, although Rae was pretty sure they had watched this episode together at least once before.

The host lifted the cloche to unveil blackberry-and-freeze-dried-cricket cobbler sitting on a sad-looking plate of melted ice cream. The chef with long dreadlocks and full-sleeve tattoos had been eliminated.

As she put her hand up to her face in a gesture of dismay, Rae could see part of a word tattooed across her knuckles. What was it? *Feed*? *Need*? Definitely two *ee*'s in the middle. She could remember having this exact same sequence of thoughts once or twice before. They had definitely watched this episode together.

"Damn," her mom exclaimed as if for the first time. "I wanted her to win!"

"You should try out for *Chopped*, Mom," Rae said like she always did. "I bet you could win the ten thousand dollars."

"Oh, no way." Her mom shook her head, her standard response. "I couldn't think straight with all that pressure. If I don't have a clear plan going into things, I'm a mess. I would definitely regret my choices." She stood and arranged the afghan blanket across the back of the couch, then fluffed the pillows and straight-ened the remote control on the coffee table. "Well, I'm off to bed," she said, leaning down to kiss Rae's head in a gesture so familiar, Rae barely registered it was happening.

"Sweet dreams," she said, absentmindedly massaging the area around her heart as she watched this shadow of her mom shuffle out of the den and down the hallway.

Chapter Eleven

The chemistry paper that had seemed monumentally important only twenty-four hours ago now felt totally irrelevant, so Rae spent most of Saturday afternoon in bed researching time travel instead.

She wasn't at all sure what the scope of her powers were. Could she travel to the year 3000 with the right card? Could she go back as far as the dinosaurs? She wasn't even sure if the ability to travel through space-time could be characterized as a power at all. Did only a few people possess this ability, or could anybody with a special belt and deck of cards skim time?

Armed with her laptop and a Costco-sized bag of Pirate's Booty, she Googled "time travel" and quickly scanned through a bunch of boring articles about the theory of relativity and ring wormholes and that kind of stuff, and a loooong list of popular movies and TV shows with time-travel plots. She decided to start her research on a lighter note by streaming episodes of *Doctor Who*, a TV show from the UK that revolved around a mysterious Time Lord known as the Doctor who used a time machine called the TARDIS—Time and Relative Dimension In Space—to travel through space-time. Rae was surprised to learn the Doctor's actions were governed by Laws of Time that were almost identical to the rules her grandma had mentioned: Time Lords were not supposed to interfere in the history of others, and they were banned from crossing over into their own time stream.

Rae watched a few random episodes from different seasons until one in which the characters met their greatest fear in a hotel room scared her so badly, she decided to switch to reading articles about time travel instead.

The articles didn't answer any of her specific questions, but their theories helped Rae understand how time travel worked. Most physicists seemed to agree that time travel was at least theoretically possible if humans could figure out a way to move faster than the speed of light and not get killed in the process.

One theory that grabbed her attention said that time travel was plausible because the past, present, and future were all equally real and all existed together at the same time in the sort of block universe her grandma had talked about. Unlike the common perception of time as something that moved in one direction from the past toward a future that people were in the process of creating, the block universe theory suggested that time was actually directionally neutral, like a book sitting on a table that people were accustomed to reading first page to last but could theoretically be as easily read starting with the last page and jumping around wherever one wanted.

The question of why human beings tended to experience time as moving forward instead of backward was complicated and had to do with the second law of thermodynamics. It turned out time travel violated the second law of thermodynamics, which stated that everything moved from an ordered to a disordered state. This limitation made it seem like the past was always behind people and the future was always ahead. Humans' perception of time, then, was like a cup of coffee with cream—once mixed together, it couldn't be unmixed. You couldn't go back.

Except, Rae now knew, you could. People with the ability to travel through time were somehow free from the dictates of the second law, of the limitations of the arrow of time that moved relentlessly from the past to the present to the future, and were somehow able to access any part of the book whenever they wanted. Rather than being limited to reading the story in one direction, one page at a time, time travelers were like earthworms tunneling out shortcuts wherever they wanted in the big book of time—backward, forward, maybe even sideways.

This strange way of thinking about time made sense to Rae on an intuitive level, although she couldn't help but wonder how free will fit into this concept. If the book was already written, did personal choices really matter that much? If the future was already happening, did it matter if Rae decided to go to college or if she was a good person or if she even got out of bed in the morning?

Reading about time travel made her head hurt, and the more she tried to understand how it all worked, the more eager she was to see her grandma again.

They decided to have their planning session at the Frontier Restaurant, which was a high-key legit restaurant on the corner of Central and Cornell that sat over three hundred people in five dining rooms and was so big it took up half a city block. The Frontier was famous for New Mexican diner food like breakfast burritos, green-chile-and-cheese-smothered hash browns, and homemade tortillas, but they also served greasy burgers, fries, and these huge, legendary sweet rolls. The restaurant was always packed with every kind of person you could ever imagine, no matter what time of day it was—college students, working people, street people, families, cops, criminals, the young and the old—so it was easy to have a conversation there without anyone listening in. They probably wouldn't even be the only people at the Frontier talking about time travel.

Her grandma picked her up at ten in the morning on Sunday and they drove to the Frontier Restaurant without saying much. They waited in line and each ordered a breakfast burrito and a sweet roll to share before scoring a booth by the front door, next to one of the big windows overlooking the busy college campus across the street.

Rae had written down all her most pressing questions about time travel in a spiral notebook she now placed on the table in front of her, along with a zip-up pouch of pens and neon highlighters. Since she didn't want to interrupt the interview once she got going, she waited until after their number had been called and they'd collected their plates of food at the counter and smothered their burritos with ladles of fresh green-chile sauce from the bubbly cauldron at the silverware station before she began.

"Are you ready for my questions?" she asked after they had taken a few bites of their burritos. She flipped her notebook open to a page marked with a bright purple tab.

"Ready when you are," her grandma replied.

"Question number one: How does time travel work?"

Her grandma put down her fork and pushed her plate aside. "Out of the gate running, are we? Okay. I've done my best to piece together my knowledge of time travel, which I got from my father, who learned from his father, who learned from his. I'll explain it like he explained it to me when I was around your age."

Rae was tempted to express her disappointment that the passing-down of tradition in their family had been apparently almost exclusively handled by the men, but she decided to save her speech about crushing the patriarchy for another day. Right now, she needed answers.

After taking a deep breath, her grandma continued, "Imagine that from the moment you are born and begin your journey through space-time, which is the three coordinates of space—height, width, and depth—along with the fourth dimension of time . . . are you with me here?"

"Yes," Rae replied, writing furiously in her notebook.

"Okay, imagine that as you move through space-time, you're creating a path, much as you would if you were walking through a dense forest or jungle. The path one would create while walking through the tangled plants of a jungle would be visible so that another person might be able to come along later and use the path to get to the same place, right? Only faster than the person who originally made the path."

"Okay, I get it," Rae said, remembering the path she and Iggy had walked along in the desert, which had been cleared by Iggy in her dozens—maybe hundreds—of trips back and forth through the sagebrush.

"Well, it turns out that you create a path as you move through your life as well, a path that starts the day you were born and stretches along behind you, wherever you go, throughout your entire life until the day you die. The path isn't visible to the human eye, but it's there nevertheless. And just like the path through the jungle, it turns out other people can come along later and use the path you made."

Rae stopped writing and looked up at her grandma. "Wait, what?"

"Yes. Our life paths can be accessed by others. Isn't it far-out?" Her grandma picked up her fork and dug into her burrito once again, apparently satisfied with this incredibly inadequate explanation of time travel.

"So when I traveled from Albuquerque to Taos in 1984, I was using someone else's life path?"

"More like multiple paths. Because of the billions of people constantly moving through spacetime, all the paths end up crisscrossing. When you skim time, there is no real way of knowing whose life path you are using at any given moment or where it's going unless you have specific physical coordinates for a particular destination point. A destination card, in other words. It is hypothetically possible to travel with unidentified paths, but who knows where you will end up? You might land in the mouth of an active volcano or in the middle of a war or in outer space with no space suit. The destination cards enable us to move through space-time with relative safety."

"Can anyone travel through space-time if they have the cards?"

"No, no, no. You have to be born into it. It's in your blood. Legend has it there are forty-eight thousand time-traveling families spread across human history, but I don't know if that's true or just a story. And you need access to the technology, of course—the belt, the case, the cards."

"But how do they actually work?"

"The silver case holds exotic matter, dark crystals that combine with the special type of muscovite mica that the cards are painted on to produce a negative energy density, which allows access to the life paths—or wormholes, as they are also known."

"But how?" Rae asked.

"I can't explain that," her grandma said, taking a bite of the sweet roll. "I can't even explain how electricity works. All I know is that at this point in space-time, there is no more dark crystal and no more special mica. All the mines have run dry."

Rae was writing so fast, her wrist ached. She had taken two pages of notes on her first question alone, and there was so much more she wanted to know.

"My next question," she said, "is why do you have to be a certain age to learn to time travel? Why can't you learn later in life?" She was thinking of her mother, of course. It seemed unfair that everyone in the family could time travel except her.

"Well, Rae, it turns out that time travel is hard on the ole noggin. It's confusing to our sense of reality. If you start too young, it's harder to accept the normal passage of time and you grow up restless and easily bored with the day-to-day tasks of human life. Most people who start too young become drifters, never settling down in any one place or time, never committing to anyone or anything. On the other hand, if you take it up later in life when your brain is less malleable, it can cause a mental breakdown. The process of reconciling the reality of space-time with what one previously believed to be true about time and space is so profound, it can cause a brittle mind to shatter. It turns out sixteen is the ideal age to introduce time travel. The brain will have already adapted to the everyday flow of time but is not so rigid that the experience will cause it to unravel."

"So you could still learn if you were older. It just wouldn't be the best idea," Rae clarified.

"It is said that no one past the age of twenty-five has successfully taken up time travel."

Rae chewed on the end of her pen. Maybe it was an urban legend. "My next question is, why can't you travel to a time when you already exist?"

Her grandma let out a deep sigh and crossed her arms over her chest. "That's a big question, Rae. Can't you take my word for it?"

Rae twirled her pen and thought about it. "I could, I guess. And I will if you want me to. But I'd rather know why."

Her grandma leaned across the table until her face was an inch away from Rae's. "If you travel to a time where you already exist," she whispered, "you risk losing your very soul."

A chill ran up Rae's spine. She put her pen down and stared at her grandma, unblinking.

"Let's say you travel to 2014 and accidentally bump into yourself when you were an adorable little girl," she continued. "It won't end well for one of you. When the two versions of yourself meet, your consciousness will split for a nanosecond. But your soul—your spirit, psyche, whatever you want to call it—is not capable of splitting. It can only remain with one version of you, which usually ends up being the stronger, healthier version. Once the soul decides, consciousness will follow. The less robust version of you will still be technically alive but with no life force—no memories, no vitality, no drive. Just enough electricity left in the brain to keep you alive, and sometimes not even that. If both versions do make it through the confrontation, you better believe one version will be a blithering idiot."

"Grandma, that is so not cool to say."

"Well, it's true, Rae. Do you know how many of the mentally ill people you see walking down the street are actually time travelers who ran into themselves at another point in their life? It's a tragedy. But there's more."

"More?" Rae whispered. The thought of interacting with a past or future version of herself had already been transformed from a crazy, fun possibility to the stuff of nightmares.

"Yes. Depending on which version of you your soul stays with, there is also the risk of contributing substantially to the already fragile and overcrowded multiverse."

"The multiverse?"

"Yes. You could end up creating an entirely separate yet parallel universe superimposed on the one we currently inhabit, different in certain crucial ways."

"Are you for real right now?"

"You know it! Let's say you run into your six-year old self during a visit to 2014. Your soul would most likely remain with the younger version of yourself because—let's be honest here—younger usually equals healthier and stronger."

"But I'm only sixteen!" Rae protested. It wasn't like she was an old lady.

"Sorry, but the moment we're born into this world, the dying begins." Her grandma reached over and patted her hand. "So sixteen-year-old Rae either drops dead on the spot when her soul departs or the body survives, condemned to live out the rest of its unfortunate existence as an empty shell with nothing much happening on the inside. Sucks for her, but at least there's no time paradox there because nothing will have changed for six-year old Rae. She'll be stuck in a dreadful time loop when she turns sixteen and goes back to meet her six-year old self again, but that's another story. Now, imagine you decide to visit 2032 and meet yourself when you are . . . um . . . "

"Twenty-four," Rae interjected.

"Twenty-four! Ah, what a lovely age. Let's say you're twenty-four and you've devoted yourself to self-actualization and staying physically strong, and you've tended to your emotional health too. You're in good shape all around. Maybe you're a cello player for the orchestra playing at Popejoy, and one night during intermission you head for the bathroom and boom! You bump into your six-teen-year old time-traveling self right there in the lobby, and just like that, your consciousness is forced to choose. It's unlikely this would ever happen, but let's imagine twenty-four-year-old Rae keeps the soul and sixteen-year old Rae has to live out the rest of her life as a zombie."

"Oh no!" Rae exclaimed.

"Oh yes! But think about it now. If sixteen-year-old Rae travels to 2032 and becomes a zombie, how will she ever become a cello player? The portal will bring you back home to your original life path, but you'll be too incapacitated to live the life that would have led you to the point where you'd meet yourself when you're sixteen. Your life spark will have been snuffed out. You'd be a shell of a person. A carapace. A sack of meat with no animating principle."

Rae could barely contain the fear and panic rising in her chest. "Grandma, stop it!" she whispered.

"Stay with me now," her grandma replied, dragging the last bite of sweet roll through the pool of butter and icing congealing on her plate. "How is this contradiction remedied? Your travel to 2032 has effectively created two versions of your life story, one in which you are a grown-up cello player and one in which you become catatonic at the tender age of sixteen."

"Grandma!"

"I'll tell you how!" her grandma shouted, lifting her fork. "An entire alternate universe has to be created to contain this paradox, a universe in which you never grow up to become a functioning, productive adult, a universe in which your mom gets a call from the Albuquerque Police Department telling her that her daughter was found wandering around UNM, unresponsive and confused. A universe in which you have to wear adult diapers and never grow up and learn to play the cello and fall in love or have babies or go to college—"

"Stop it, Grandma!" Rae yelled. The line to order food was now so long, it snaked past their booth, and several people turned to see what the commotion was all about. Embarrassed, Rae hid her face in her hands.

Her grandma reached out and squeezed her forearm.

"I know it's a scary thought," she said. "But you need to keep this possibility in your mind at all times when you travel through time. And there's more too."

Rae spread her hands and stared at her grandma from between her fingers. "More?" she asked in a muffled voice.

"Yes. Listen. The multiverse is not infinite. It can only grow so much before it collapses completely and space-time itself tears apart. The Big Rip, they call it." Her grandma drew her hand slowly across her neck for emphasis.

"The Big Rip," Rae mumbled.

"And then it's game over for everyone and everything that ever was or ever will be. Time itself will stop. So we don't want to create any more parallel universes, now, do we?"

"Definitely not." Rae picked up her fork and poked at her cold food with all the enthusiasm of a robot, hoping everyone in line would go back to what they were doing before they started staring at her.

Just outside the plate-glass window, an unhoused man walked by, pushing a shopping cart piled high with aluminum cans, scrap metal, and dirty, crusty clothes. His pale blue eyes stared out from behind a mask of skin that was wrinkled and brown from walking around every day in the New Mexican sun with no sunscreen.

Whenever Rae saw a destitute person up close like this, she usually found herself wondering about their family. Didn't they have a mom or dad or daughter somewhere, someone they could stay with, someone who would care about them and make them a sandwich and listen to them talk about their day? She looked at the blue-eyed man and tried to imagine what had happened in his life to bring him to where he was now. Maybe he had met himself while time traveling and lost his soul. What a horrible fate.

She didn't bother wiping away the tears that slid down her cheeks.

"What does it feel like?" she asked her grandma, who was watching her watch the man.

"What does what feel like?"

"To have your consciousness split like that," Rae said. "To lose your soul."

"It doesn't feel like anything to the person who retains consciousness and keeps their soul. It happens too fast. Nothing changes for them. But for the one who loses their soul? Well, no one really knows, but I imagine it must feel like dying." Her grandma shivered.

Rae slammed her notebook closed. "Oh no," she said. "No, thank you. I don't think I'll be doing any more time traveling."

Her grandma's eyes grew huge and she sat up ramrod straight in the booth. "Oh, Rae, please. I need your help! I need another card if I'm ever going to travel again. I promise there's absolutely no danger if you stay away from places where you already exist. It's why the cards come with little color-coded symbols, so you know when to avoid."

Rae shook her head. No way. No thank you. No siree.

"Help me, Obi-Wan Kenobi," her grandma pleaded. "You're my only hope."

With this one reference to *Star Wars*, Rae's resolve softened like her grandma must've known it would. The weekend after Rae learned her parents were splitting up, they had watched the first two *Star Wars* trilogies in release order, staying in their jammies for two days straight and living off of Cap'n Crunch's Crunch

Berries and popcorn topped with nutritional yeast. Rae had been convinced she would not survive her parents' breakup when they started *A New Hope,* but by the time they finished *Revenge of the Sith,* she knew she had to.

Was she really the only person who could help her grandma get her card back? It didn't seem fair to put so much pressure on her. "Why is time traveling so important to you?" she asked. "Can't you be happy where you are?"

Her grandma looked surprised at her question. She opened her mouth to speak, shut it, then opened it again. "There are a few things I need to do before I can settle down," she said.

Rae sighed. "How am I supposed to find your dad?"

"That shouldn't be a problem, right? We'll send you back to 1984 and you can get your mom to introduce you."

"You want me to casually ask Iggy if I can meet her grandpa?" Rae asked. "That's beyond cringe."

"Hmm. Well, he was a famous curandero. Maybe pretend you're sick?"

As half-baked as her plan was, the thought of going back to 1984 was appealing. She hadn't been able to stop thinking about how Iggy turned into her mom. Another trip was sure to provide more clues. And 1984 had been so much fun! There was a vibe at that party that Rae had never experienced before, a freedom to say what she wanted and look how she wanted and dance how she wanted without worrying if she looked all right or if she was doing it right or if someone might post an embarrassing picture of her on their socials. She'd felt less exposed in 1984; she'd felt hidden and safe. That world had felt smaller somehow. And, if she was honest with herself, it had felt liberating to not have to check her phone 24/7.

"I'll do it," she said, holding up her hands in surrender. "I'll go back to 1984."

"Oh honey, thank you," her grandma said, grabbing one of her hands and exhaling a long sigh of relief.

Rae glanced up and made accidental eye contact with a young mom sitting at the booth behind theirs, who quickly averted her eyes and grasped her toddler-aged son. Someone had been listening in on their conversation, after all.

As far as this lady was concerned, Rae and her grandma were two more crazy people hanging out at the Frontier Restaurant. Rae shuddered and pushed away the slimy thought.

What if it were true?

Chapter Twelve

They spent the rest of the afternoon in her grandma's storage unit, looking through plastic bins for a destination card with a date not too long after the day Rae first met Iggy, with coordinates that would land her near Taos High School in the middle of a school day. If Iggy decided to go to school that day—and that was a big *if*—it should be pretty easy to track her down. Finding the right card, not so much.

The masking-tape labels across the front of the bins suggested that they had at one time been categorized by dates and parts of the world, but the cards had become totally disorganized since then. It looked as though her grandma had been removing travel cards from their proper container and then replacing them wherever, like she wasn't even *trying* to put them back in the right place. The more time they wasted looking for a good card, the more frustrated Rae felt with her grandma. How could she be so careless with something so important?

"Whoever originally organized these cards would be pretty heated to see how you keep them now," she said. The box she was currently going through was labeled *New Mexico—1940-1990*, but there were a lot of other years and parts of the world mixed in. She held up a card from Argentina, 1918, for her grandma to see.

"Oh, that was me," her grandma replied. "I reorganized the cards after my dad died and named me Keeper of the Cards."

Rae was surprised. "Then what happened?"

"Oh, I don't know." Her grandma gestured toward a rickety frame loom and broken-down beach cruiser propped against one wall, then toward the cardboard boxes filled with mismatched china and smelly books and other old, forgotten things that surrounded the spot they had cleared for themselves in the middle of the unit. "I got overwhelmed with everything, I guess. But you're right—my past self would definitely be disappointed to see the mess I've made of these cards. And my dad? Oh boy, would he bawl me out!"

"Did he paint all of these cards?"

"Oh no, there are at least five generations represented by the cards here, painted by the more creative members of our family. Some of them are initialed in the corner, but if you spend a lot of time with them, you'll start to recognize each artist by their unique style." She held up a card with a picture of a sandy beach in Borneo, overlooking a stormy sea. "See how this painting is made up of a bunch of tiny little dots? That was my brother, Alejandro—Alex. He spent some time in France, studying pointillism with Georges Seurat."

As she looked at the cards again, Rae could begin to recognize some of the more distinctive artistic styles among them. Some of the cards were realistic and natural looking while others were dreamy and surreal. There were abstract cards, black-and-white cards, and bold, bright, graphic cards. She could tell by looking for the dots which ones were made by her great-uncle Alex, and she noticed her great-grandpa Ignacio used thick brush strokes.

"They're all so beautiful and different," she said. Her grandma nodded. "Have you been to all of these places?"

"Oh, heavens no. Very few, actually. It's funny how you tell yourself you're going to travel to new places and meet new people, but you always find yourself going back to your favorite spots."

"Where are your favorite spots?"

"When I was younger, I used to love hanging out at the speakeasies in Chicago in the 1920s. My favorite was a jazz club called the Green Mill. I had this gorgeous, sequined red dress that belonged to my grandma, and I used to wear it every time I went. That dress was the real reason I first visited a speakeasy to begin with—I was looking for a place to wear it. Oh, but how I loved to stay up all night dancing with the boys and drinking gin out of teacups. I can still visit the Green Mill, of course, but it's not as much fun when you're my age. No one wants to dance with me now."

"Oh, grandma."

"It's okay, honey. Another of my favorite places is Waikiki Beach in 1901, right after the Moana Hotel opened and the sacred wetlands of Waikiki were just beginning to be transformed into the famous tourist destination it is today. The hotel is gorgeous, but I love to just sit on the beach and watch the local surfers and think about how things change. Waikiki was so lovely and pure back then. No high-rises yet."

"You sound sad. Does Waikiki make you sad?"

Her grandma shook her head. "Not sad exactly," she replied, but she didn't elaborate.

"Do you ever go to the future?"

"I sort of lost faith in the future after I had my first meal made entirely of synthetic products. Nothing grown in the ground, no fruit, no animal prod-ucts—100 percent man-made. It smelled delicious but tasted like nothing. I was at a fancy five-star restaurant and everyone else kept talking like it was the best meal they'd ever had. And there's no cash in the future, so it's almost impossible to visit for more than a few hours. Everything is rationed and distributed among the populus on their microchip implants—food, energy, clean air, free time, everything. For people like us, anyway. Rich people can still do whatever they want. The older I get, the closer I have to stay to my own space-time, anyway. Remember that the further forward or backward you travel, the more you age relative to where you live."

"How does that work again?" Rae asked.

"Add five minutes to every hour for every year you're away. It helps to memorize the formula, 5MHY. When I visit Waikiki in 1901, every hour I'm gone from this space-time zone equals ten hours over there, which has its perks! You can duck out to take a long nap after Thanksgiving dinner and spend a day or two in Hawaii if you want. The problem is your body ages in accordance with whatever space-time zone you're in, so if I spent a day of our time in 1901, I would actually age ten days by the time I returned. It's nothing you'd notice after a short trip, but the time dilation starts to accumulate. You start to age more quickly than the people around you. People start to notice. *You'd* start to notice."

"Did that happen to you?"

Her grandma jumped up, holding a card with a picture of the now-familiar Taos skyline painted in vivid colors in the background. "Look what I found!" she shouted. The card depicted a parking lot somewhere in Taos, New Mexico, 11:45 a.m., June 4, 1984.

"Our work here is finished," her grandma said, turning her back to Rae and putting cards back in their plastic storage containers.

Apparently, their conversation was also finished. It was almost like her grandma had been hiding that card up her sleeve until the moment she was asked a question she didn't want to answer. There was a lot about her life that Rae didn't know, and unless she was imagining things, her grandma definitely wanted to keep it that way.

Chapter Thirteen

It made sense to wait until the following weekend to take her next trip to 1984. Why should she miss any of her classes if she didn't have to? But all Rae could think about as her mom drove her to school on Monday was how much she dreaded going back.

"Are you okay, Rae?" her mom asked. "You're so quiet. And no phone? What's up?"

It had been awkward keeping all this time-travel stuff from her mom, so Rae had spent most of her time at home hiding out in her room. When she did bump into her mom on her way to the bathroom, or when she sat across from her at the kitchen table, eating the food she'd made while Rae was living a secret life that intersected unbelievably with her mom's own private past, she felt like she must be going crazy. Like she had to be making this whole situation up in her head. Maybe her grandma's delusion was so powerful, Rae had fallen into a shared psychosis! It was a terrifying thought, but thankfully all she had to do was open her closet and rub her face on the Big E's hanging inside and she knew once again that it was all for real. She was a time traveler.

The problem was her mom wouldn't stop asking her what was wrong.

"Cosima and I are having issues," Rae replied in the car. "And I guess I'm feeling anxious about seeing her."

Which was true. Rae had sent Cosima a Snap of her open science textbook as soon as she'd gotten home from her trip to 1984, hoping Cosima would believe she'd been involved in homework all weekend and that was why she'd ghosted her. But not only did Cosima never Snap back, she'd actually gone further and blocked her on all the socials.

It had now been two whole days since she had seen or heard anything from Cosima, and she was beyond anxious about it. She was scared.

The trip to 1984 had warped Rae's perception of time, and the whole food-shaming incident felt like it had happened three years ago instead of three days ago. But for Cosima, the injury of being avoided and ignored by an inferior human being like Rae probably still stung like a fresh wound. She would probably ask Rae right to her face why she had snuck out of school on Friday, forcing her into a conversation she did not want to have. How would she casually point out to someone like Cosima that the way she treated Hamia at lunch on Friday was not okay? She wouldn't, that was how. Not if she wanted to survive high school.

"What's going on with Cosima?" her mom asked.

Rae suddenly felt too tired to deflect her mom, so she relayed the entire Cosima/Hamia incident exactly as it happened. Her mom listened with a thoughtful expression on her face.

"How are you feeling about everything now that you've had the weekend to think about it?" her mom asked when she had finished.

"I feel bad that I didn't stick up for Hamia," Rae replied. "But I also feel like I betrayed Cosima somehow. She's my best friend and I didn't give her a chance to explain or defend herself."

"It's impossible to know for sure what a person's true intentions are," her mom said as she pulled up to the drop-off zone. "You have to trust your intuition. And remember that real friends take care of each other, Rae. It's a two-way street."

"Oh jeez," Rae said, rolling her eyes.

"What did I say?" her mom asked, looking hurt.

"Nothing! That's the problem!" Rae said. "I could get the same advice from a bumper sticker!" She opened the car door and got out, intent on slamming the door behind her for emphasis.

For some reason, she changed her mind and leaned back in the car.

"What should I do?" she asked.

Her mom's face brightened when she realized she had been given another chance. "Do the right thing, Rae."

Rae groaned and slammed the car door.

On her way to the cafeteria for lunch, Rae stopped in the girls' bathroom to inspect herself in the mirror. She was experimenting with an emo look inspired by her trip to 1984, so she'd applied black liner on her upper and lower lids this morning, along with dark purple lipstick and a pale finishing powder. For her outfit, she had chosen a black turtleneck and a black skirt. Her hair had a sticky, grubby texture since she had intentionally gone without washing it all weekend. She'd hoped this fit would give her courage, but she was so nervous about seeing Cosima, she felt like throwing up. She decided to act like everything was normal and leave it up to Cosima to decide how the drama would play out today.

Her first clue that things were going to be rough was Cosima's absence at the cafeteria entrance.

Ignoring the butterflies in her stomach, Rae got in the food line all by herself. It felt like the first day of school all over again. At least she could take advantage of the fact that Cosima wasn't there to influence her food choices and treat herself to the school hot lunch—a gooey square of cheese pizza with apple slices and a cup of vanilla yogurt.

Zigzagging through the maze of tables on her way outside, Rae ran into Olivia and Evani sitting at a table in the middle of the cafeteria with two other people she'd never met.

"Oh hey," she said. "Why aren't you outside?"

Evani scowled and shook their head in disgust. "I can't even," they said.

"What?"

"There's a situation out there," Olivia explained. "I'm pretty sure we will no longer be invited to dine at Cosima's table."

"Like I would ever eat lunch with her again!" Evani spat.

"What do you mean?" Rae asked.

"Go see for yourself," Olivia answered.

Rae turned reluctantly toward the glass doors.

"See you back here in a minute!" Evani yelled in a hysterical tone.

Cosima's back was toward Rae as she approached their usual table under the sycamore tree. She, too, was sitting with a new group—an unidentified boy on her right and a dark-haired girl wearing mirrored sunglasses sitting across from her.

The girl looked up when she noticed Rae walking toward them and Rae almost dropped her lunch tray. Hamia. What was happening here?

"Oh hi," Hamia said with an awkward half smile.

Cosima turned around to see who Hamia was talking to and her eyes narrowed when she saw Rae. She looked mean but excited, like a hungry predator who had spotted its prey. Today, the predator was wearing a cool vintage green-and-brown sweater coat with an embroidered owl on the front that Rae had never seen before. Clearly a thrift-store find, which was really more Rae's style and made her wish she had decided to wear something special today—like her new Big E's—instead of waiting until she and Cosima were on better terms to unveil them. She would have dominated this particular battle of thrift-store finds, that was for sure.

She couldn't stand there forever, grasping her lunch tray and gawking like a stan, so she moved casually around the table and sat next to Hamia, who didn't scoot over to make room for her but instead sat there like she was invisible. Rae heard herself hum a fake-happy tune as she squeezed herself into the available space, resolving to move ahead with her plan of pretending everything was okay.

A quick glance at Hamia's lunch tray confirmed what she already suspected: Hamia had ditched her delicious falafel for a tasteless, fat-free salad. The transformation had happened so quickly! She either had Stockholm syndrome or suffered from acute internalized self-loathing. Either way, it was gross.

Rae finally got the nerve to look across the table while she was adjusting her tray. Her hand froze on her carton of milk as she processed what she was seeing.

The boy across the table was Andy.

Cosima was sitting next to Andy.

Cosima was sitting next to Andy.

Cosima was sitting next to Andy.

Cosima was, in fact, sitting so close to Andy, their thighs must have been rubbing against each other.

Rae felt like she had been punched in the heart. What was worse, though, was being forced to watch Cosima watch her reaction to this nauseating spectacle. She was taking visible pleasure in her pain.

If there was ever a time to play it cool, that time was now.

"'Sup, Andy," Rae said in what she hoped was a casual voice. "I didn't know you guys were friends." She gestured with her chin toward the invisible bubble enveloping Andy and Cosima and took a big bite of her congealing pizza to show that everything was all right in her world.

"Rae!" Andy sounded happy to see her, but he was licking his lips like he was nervous. "We aren't friends," he said. "I mean . . . um . . . we are now, obviously. We officially met this weekend."

"Really? This weekend?" What a strange coincidence.

"Yeah, Cosima DMed me after we took that game in Cruces. Right?" he asked, turning toward Cosima.

Cosima looked a little flustered at having her strategy so thoroughly exposed. She knew Rae had a mad crush on Andy, but she probably hadn't believed they were actually friends who talked.

"So you guys won?" Rae asked. She had forgotten all about his game.

"Yeah, we crushed it. Forty-nine to zero. Total blowout."

"How were your stats?"

"Seventy-four yards, one touchdown."

"Dope!"

Cosima cleared her throat. "Pardon me for interrupting this riveting conversation, but what is going on with your aesthetic, Rae? Since when did you become such a goth girl? If you don't mind me saying, you look like shit."

Hamia, who had been observing the group dynamic in silence, snorted appreciatively.

"You do look different," Andy said. "But not bad or anything," he added when he saw Rae's crestfallen face.

Cosima threw her an icy smile from across the table.

"I guess it's not enough for me to look basic anymore," Rae replied, raising her eyebrows in the direction of Cosima's outfit as she drank her milk. She knew she was crossing a line into dangerous territory, but she had to defend herself, right? Especially with Andy and Hamia listening.

"Excuse me?" Cosima leaned across the table. "Did you just call me basic? Did I hear that right?"

Rae shrugged.

"Okay, look, I don't know if Andy being here has suddenly turned you into a little bitch or if you've inherited your mom's drinking problem, but—"

"Whoa, whoa, whoa!" Andy said, getting up from the bench. "Don't drag me into this. I don't know what's going on here, and I'm not trying to hear about anyone's problems."

"Oh, my bad. You guys seem like such good friends, I thought for sure you knew that her mom was a drunk fresh out of rehab."

Hamia turned her head away like she couldn't bear to watch the scene unfolding in front of her. Poor Andy scrambled to gather his belongings and get away from the table as fast as he possibly could.

This awkward situation would leave a permanent mark on their friendship, Rae realized. It wouldn't be light and fun and easy anymore. It would be forever weighed down by this weirdness.

Everything felt like it was happening in slow motion, so much so that Rae wondered if her sense of time had been damaged by her trip across space-time. Mere seconds had passed since Cosima opted to publicly humiliate her, but it felt like hours were passing as she considered how to respond. She felt like she was eleven years old again, learning to play chess with her dad, who would have her evaluate the chessboard before every turn and say out loud all her possible moves, along with all the ways her dad might respond, to better understand the risks. According to her dad, life was exactly like a chess game.

Her first instinct was to throw shade right back at Cosima, to make her feel as terrible as she did now. Rae knew personal things about her that would be embarrassing if she said them out loud. She could reveal that Cosima ate her boogers while she slept, or that she still used pads because she was afraid tampons hurt. She could tell Andy that one time, she woke up in the middle of the night and found her friend in the bathroom, binging on a package of Oreos.

But her mom had said real friends took care of each other. Just because Cosima had thrown her under the bus didn't mean she had to behave the same way. As satisfying as it would feel to humiliate Cosima in front of Andy right now, it would probably actually make her feel worse about herself in the long run—the same way she felt after saying something mean to her mom.

Would it be better to act like it didn't bother her if everyone knew her mom was a drunk who had lost her marriage, her business, and even their home? Rae would look like the stronger person if she continued to act like nothing mattered. Cosima didn't matter, Andy didn't matter, Hamia didn't matter. It didn't matter what anyone thought of her; it meant nothing to her. She was completely secure in who she was and didn't need anyone's validation to feel okay about herself.

But she knew she couldn't pull it off. Just thinking about going to see her mom when she'd been in rehab made her want to cry. Rae used to have to wait for weeks to see her; she would spend the time in between visits drawing her pictures and writing her letters and weaving her friendship bracelets she'd learned to make from tutorials on YouTube. And then when the time finally did come to see her, Rae had only been allowed to visit for a few hours at a picnic table in a grassy courtyard, surrounded by a bunch of other families visiting their alcoholic loved ones. What she'd really wanted to do was crawl onto her mom's lap and bury her face in her neck and lose herself for one minute in the comforting smell of her hair and the softness of her skin. But she'd been almost fourteen years old, not a baby. What would everyone think? Instead, she'd sat next to her grandma with her hands in her lap, answering her mom's questions about school in as few words as possible. When she'd gotten in bed those nights, she would cry herself to sleep, wishing so much that she'd hugged her harder.

The memory made Rae's sinuses ache with the pressure of tears on the brink of spilling over. She realized that her dad was wrong. Life wasn't at all like a chess game. Because unlike chess, you couldn't tip the board over and start a new game if you made a few bad moves. You had to live with the consequences of your actions forever.

Everyone at the table was staring at her, waiting for a reaction. She didn't bother to wipe away the tears when they finally leaked out of her eyes and ran down her cheeks—making a mess of her experimental makeup, no doubt. Cosima had stolen her crush, one of the few people she'd felt a genuine connection with, right out from under her, and then before Rae could even recover from the shock, she'd exposed the most shameful, painful part of her private life. What could Rae possibly say to come back from that?

What if she refused to play? What if she didn't try to explain anything or defend herself or pretend like nothing mattered? What if she accepted what she was at that moment—vulnerable, embarrassed, hurt—and didn't do a thing to change it?

The idea was liberating. Cosima, Andy, and Hamia couldn't make her feel small if she didn't let them. They couldn't force a reaction out of her. They couldn't rob her of herself.

Rae picked up her backpack and stood to leave. She left her lunch tray where it was.

"Hey, are you okay?" Andy asked her.

Even Cosima looked concerned.

Rae couldn't hear them. Their voices were small and muffled and far away, as if she were underwater, as if she were a shadow of a person who existed in another dimension. As if she were listening to new-wave music through a pair of headphones only she knew was there.

She turned and walked back inside without saying a word.

Chapter Fourteen

In the span of one school week, Rae fell from a rung somewhere in the middle of the social ladder all the way to the bottom. No one was beneath her. She went from eating lunch every day with one of the school's most popular girls to sneaking through the hallways, looking for an empty classroom where she could be alone.

She joined Olivia and Evani's table on Tuesday, but they weren't very friendly when she sat and they didn't make any effort to include her in their conversation about whether an ethical vegetarian would be violating their beliefs if they ate meat cultivated from animal cells in a laboratory. Olivia argued that since cultured meat didn't produce any suffering, a vegetarian could consume it in good conscience. Evani maintained that because lab-grown meat was made from cells harvested from real, living animals, it was technically meat and absolutely could not be considered vegetarian, ethical or otherwise. Their friend Rhianna chimed in that taking even one cell from an animal against their will was exploitative. No one asked what Rae thought.

On Wednesday, she sat alone under the shade of a bushy elm tree wearing earbuds and watching TikTok videos about lucky girl syndrome, trying to manifest positive vibes as she worked her way through a big plastic tub of pineapple and blueberries left over from one of her mom's catering gigs the day before. It wasn't so bad. She felt like she did on the first day of school when she didn't know anyone yet. Sure, it was a little lonely, but at the same time, it was exciting because at any moment something new could happen.

Then Cosima and Andy walked by holding hands, pretending they didn't see her. Cosima was wearing a pink, pleated Barbiecore skirt and she had done her hair in a four-strand braid like Rae sometimes wore before she'd chopped her hair off. She used to tell Rae she looked like a little girl when she wore her hair like that.

The sight of Andy holding hands with such a spoiled, cruel, superficial hypocrite was almost unbearable. How could she have been so wrong about him? She'd really believed that he was smart and sensitive and interesting and that they'd shared a special connection, a secret understanding of one another that didn't need to be put into words. But someone like that wouldn't have fallen prey to Cosima's manipulations—at least, not so fast.

It occurred to Rae on Thursday that she could potentially avoid seeing anyone and spend her lunch period in peace if she could find an empty classroom to hide in, and she was surprised when the second classroom she checked was unlocked and unused. It was eerie with the overhead lights off, eerie but peaceful. She sat at a desk in the back of the large room and arranged her water bottle, pear, and peanut-butter-and-honey sandwich on the desk in front of her, ignoring the talking and laughing that floated in from the small window overlooking the courtyard outside. She read the study questions written on the chalkboard in front of the classroom as she ate her sandwich. *What role does the past play in* Long Day's Journey into Night? the English teacher had written in large block letters across the board. Beneath that was: *Was it bad luck or fate that turned Mary into an addict?*

Rae felt a shiver down her spine. Was it bad luck or fate that had turned her mom into an addict?

She hadn't known anything about her mom's childhood before her trip to 1984. Her mom never talked about her past, and Rae had really never been that interested. She'd never wondered what her mom was like when she was younger. She hadn't been curious about the life her mom had led before she'd met Rae's dad and started a family. Rae didn't know when she started drinking or why. She had been furious at her mom for fucking up her entire life, but until now, she had never wondered why she had made the choices she did.

Now all she wanted was to learn more about her mom. About Iggy. Maybe she should stay in 1984 and never come back to this lousy time. Why should she? She didn't have any friends, and the idea of eating lunch alone in a dark classroom for the rest of her life was beyond depressing.

Or maybe she should try to change the way her mom's life had turned out. It could end up changing her own life for the better too. Maybe persuading her mom not to run away with Simon wouldn't make Rae vanish into thin air because maybe Iggy would end up meeting her dad, anyway, but under different circumstances, when they were both younger and happier, instead of when her mom was already old and wrecked.

If her mom hadn't run away from home when she was sixteen, maybe she would have grown up to be a less self-destructive person. Maybe she would have pursued a career as a music producer or graphic designer—something stable and creative. Maybe she and Rae's dad would still meet somewhere, somewhere wholesome instead of some bar in Las Vegas. They'd still fall in love and have a baby and they'd still name her Andrea, only this time they would be enough for each other and her mom wouldn't become an alcoholic and her dad wouldn't leave them for some skank thirty years younger than him. Instead of erasing her own existence, Rae would return home from 1984 to a reality in which her mom and dad were still married and all three of them still lived together in their old house, and she still went to Ponderosa Prep with all her old friends, and Cosima wasn't even in the picture. If time travel was a thing, couldn't anything be possible?

There was no way her grandma could know for certain what would happen if she messed with the past. Her warnings reminded Rae of the horrible stories in *Der Struwwelpeter*, an illustrated book from her dad's childhood that he'd insisted on reading to her when she was only five years old. The stories were creepy German fables about the terrible things that would happen to children if they misbehaved. In one, a girl who played with matches burned herself to death, and in another, a little boy who wouldn't stop sucking his thumb got them both cut off by a crazy tailor with enormous scissors. The stories had terrified Rae, but as young as she'd been, she'd still understood they weren't real. They were meant to frighten children into obedience, just like her grandma's stories about the potential risks of time travel.

Chapter Fifteen

Before school on Friday, Rae removed the books and folders from her back-pack and replaced them with a change of clothes, her personal hygiene kit, a Hydro Flask filled with filtered water, and a half dozen energy bars. She picked her outfit based on what would help her blend in with everyone else while still being comfortable and ended up in her Big E's and lucky hoodie again, along with navy-blue Nike Cortez shoes with a white swoosh.

School reached a new level of cringe during fifth period, when Andy held up his hand and asked Mr. Quintana if he could change lab partners in front of the whole classroom.

"Absolutely not," Mr. Quintana replied. "Whatever lovers' quarrel you two have going on, work it out. Now."

Rae felt herself turning fifty shades of red as everyone turned to look at them.

"What did I ever do to you?" she asked under her breath.

Andy shook his head. "Cosima," was all he said. He didn't need to say anything else.

She and her grandma went out to eat at the Flying Star after school, where they had dirty chais and split a Greek salad before going to the bank to withdraw one hundred dollars' worth of one-dollar bills. Dollar bills were the only money Rae could safely use on her trip, her grandma explained, because it was the only bill that hadn't been redesigned since the 1980s. If she tried using an updated bill to purchase something, people from 1984 would probably think that the money was counterfeit and she could end up in jail. Lack of appropriate funds was a real problem for travelers, since credit cards obviously didn't work when you traveled back and forth in time and having the wrong cash could get you in trouble. One option was to buy vintage bills on eBay, but you could end up paying a lot more for the money than the money was worth.

"Or you could always try to get your hands on some cash when you arrive at your destination." Her grandma winked.

Rae wasn't sure what she was meant. Dollar bills would have to do.

At her grandma's house, Rae brushed her teeth, peed, and performed a five-minute stretch routine. When she was ready, she strapped on her backpack and stood in the middle of the living room while her grandma fastened the travel belt around her waist. The destination and duration cards were already locked and loaded into the itinerary case. The portal that would take her to some random parking lot in Taos on June 4, 1984, would open as soon as she inserted her personal travel card.

Her grandma pulled her hood over her head and placed her wrinkled hands on her shoulders while she looked into her eyes. Rae returned her gaze without blinking.

"What is your mission?" her grandma asked.

"Find Iggy—uh, my mom, and casually suggest she take me to your dad's house, where I will figure out a way to talk to him alone and reveal that I'm his granddaughter from the future who has come for a new personal travel card for his daughter Lydia. Collect said card, then get back home."

"When you put it that way, it does sound a little farfetched."

"It's totally farfetched, Grandma!" Rae laughed. She didn't mention anything about her own agenda.

"C'mon, Rae, you could sell honey to a bee! Now I want you to try out a new starting pose when you teleport."

Her grandma breathed heavily as she crouched and positioned herself with her chin on her left knee and her right knee on the floor, both hands touching the ground at her sides.

"I saw this in a science-fiction movie a long time ago," she said. "It's helped me stick the landing ever since."

Rae knelt and stretched one leg behind her like she was about to run a race. Her grandma stood and adjusted Rae's back so it aligned with her hips.

"Do you feel stable? Solid?"

"Yes."

"All right. Now, focus on your breathing, the same way you do when you feel an anxiety attack coming on. Relax and breathe. Let it happen."

"I know, Grandma."

"There's nothing left to do but put your card in the belt."

Rae hugged her grandma one last time. With her arms around her, her grandma slipped a sealed envelope into the small pocket of her backpack.

"Give that letter to my dad," she said.

Rae nodded and pushed her travel card into the empty slot, kneeling quickly as the case sucked and whirled. She breathed in through her nose and out through her mouth as the air grew thick around her, then heard the high-pitched scream of the cicadas and felt her grandma's hand dig into her shoulder as she pushed the thought of what was happening to her body out of her head.

The vibrations and sensation of falling engulfed her, but this time, she kept her hands planted firmly on the ground until the cicadas and falling gave way to a deep stillness that seemed to stretch on and on until it felt like there was no time anymore and no space either. It was hard to remember where and who she was for a minute, but it wasn't scary anymore.

S he knew she had landed when she heard the sounds of daytime traffic and the back-and-forth chatter of birds filling the air around her. Her grandma's traveling position worked pretty well—she landed steady and hadn't lost consciousness. Or had she? It was kind of hard to tell. She felt different this time, for sure.

The destination card they had picked showed a concrete curb in a parking lot with a crumpled piece of chewing-gum foil on the ground next to a clump of foxtail growing out of the cracks in the asphalt. While studying the card, Rae had wondered why the artist had bothered to put so much detail into such a mundane parking-lot scene. Now here she was, and there was the chewing-gum wrapper just inches away from her hand, sparkling in the sun like a diamond.

She was behind what she could safely guess was a grocery store, based on the stacks of broken cardboard boxes and blue dumpster bins filled with expired bread and overripe fruit and other edible stuff. The dumpsters were a visual reminder that Americans threw away more than half of the food they produced. Apparently, they had been doing so since at least 1984.

Rae felt as if she were seeing through the eyes of the relative who painted the destination card as she followed the source of the birdsong to the tallest birch among a row of trees to her left. Even from where she stood some twenty feet away, she could see the delicate veins on each individual leaf and a line of ants marching up the white trunk toward a single drop of sap.

As she stood there, a winged songstress hopped to a lower branch and released a string of urgent chirps. Rae could swear the bluebird's little black eyes were staring directly into hers, as if she were trying to tell her something.

She walked around to the front of the store and recognized the big sign advertising Furr's Supermarket and TG&Y from her and Iggy's ride into town with the lowriders. As fate or luck would have it, she had landed at a strip mall on the main road through Taos, just a couple of miles south of the plaza.

A man wearing a baseball cap too small for his head walked by, pushing an empty shopping cart toward the grocery store.

"Excuse me," she said, stepping into his path. "Can you tell me how to get to the high school?"

The man stopped and pointed directly across the busy street. "It's right there. Down Cervantes." He moved his cart closer to get a better look at her, frowning. "Are you okay? Don't you know where you are?"

Rae realized too late that, as a high-school-aged person in the middle of the day, it would seem sketch that she didn't know where the high school was.

"I, uh—I'm not from around here, actually," she stammered.

The look of concern on the man's face continued to grow. As he took his hands off the grocery cart and started walking toward her, Rae saw something dark move across his features. Whether it was worry for her or something more sinister, she couldn't tell.

She took a few rapid steps backward.

"Come here, girl," the man said, reaching for her with his thick hands.

"Hey!" someone yelled behind her, and she turned around to find Simon standing there.

He had a can of Pringles in one hand and two bananas in the other. His long, black hair was pulled back in a ponytail, and he was wearing jeans and a light blue T-shirt with the name Redbone printed above a faded image of four band members.

Relief flooded her body as the creepy man spun toward the store again.

"Thank you," Rae said. She had to stop herself from hugging him. "That guy was seriously sus."

"You want a banana?" he offered, peeling one for himself.

She shook her head. "What are you doing here?"

"What are *you* doing here is a better question," he replied, biting off half the banana and chewing slowly. "The last time I saw you, you were running away from the party. Like, you totally freaked out! Your friends couldn't find you. Everyone was worried. Why were you trippin' so hard?"

How embarrassing. And difficult to explain.

"I was, uh, dealing with some personal issues. Sorry I worried you."

"Oh, I wasn't worried. I don't even know you. But your friends were pretty upset." Simon finished the banana and threw the peel over his shoulder as he turned and headed in the direction of the high school.

"Hey!" Rae yelled after him.

"What?" he said, turning and walking backward across the parking lot.

"That's littering! What's wrong with you?" She ran to catch up with him.

"The crows will eat it," he replied, turning his back on her again.

"Are you going to the high school?" she asked.

"Yeah, lunch is almost over. Where are you going?"

"The high school, I guess. I'm looking for Iggy."

"I saw her on my way to the store. She's hanging out up there." He gestured toward the road across the street.

When they reached the traffic light, Simon used the side of his fist to pound on the crossing button. As they waited for the light to change, they were joined by other high-school kids on their way back to campus. He raised his chin to a few of them, but he didn't seem to be in a talkative mood today. In fact, he seemed like a far less friendly person than he had at the party. Why was she so disappointed?

"You're lucky you have an open campus," she said after a high-key awkward silence.

"You don't?"

"No. We can't leave campus at all during school hours, not even for lunch. We're prisoners."

"We're prisoners, too, believe me," he scoffed. "Just because they let you out to walk the yard doesn't make you free."

As Rae tried to think of a witty comeback, the crosswalk light changed from the flashing, red DON'T WALK to the flashing, white WALK instead of the combination of the red hand and the little walking man from her space-time zone.

Back in the eighties, you had better speak English if you wanted to cross a busy road.

As the group of high schoolers crossed the street together, Rae thought about how easy it would be to forget she was in 1984 if it weren't for little differences like the crosswalk light. People didn't look or speak like she thought they would when she'd imagined what life had been like before she was born. She had expected 1984 to have a musty, old-fashioned vibe that permeated everything, but it felt pretty much the same to be alive here as it did in her real life. And it didn't look the way it did in old photographs either. Fashion had changed, but a lot of the hair and clothes she saw looked pretty normal when you were right in the middle of it.

She had always thought of herself as having been born during the most important time in human history, with a special position at the forefront of what was happening—part of a generation of progressive iconoclasts who would finally bring about real change. Now she wondered if every person who had ever lived felt the same way, like their time to be alive was the only time that mattered. After all, wasn't the world she thought of as the "real" world also destined to become nothing more than a collection of old memories and digital photographs no one looked at anymore? The idea astounded her.

"You're quiet," Simon said, startling her.

She felt exposed, as if he could possibly know the strangeness of her private thoughts, and grasped at the first normal thing she could think of to talk about while they walked.

"Is Redbone a punk band?" she asked, nodding at his T-shirt.

Simon laughed. "No way! They're a classic rock band from the seventies. My dad was into them. They sang 'Come and Get Your Love'."

Rae shook her head.

"C'mon, you've heard it," he urged, and then broke into song. Using the Pringles can as a microphone, he looked her right in the eyes as he sang the part of a man trying to convince his girlfriend there was nothing wrong with her mind or her sign or anything else about her. All she had to do was come and get her love.

"Oh yeah, I know that one," Rae lied. He sounded good, much better than when he had been screaming punk-rock songs at the party. His voice was deep and clear, and each word flowed into the next without hesitation. He made a funny little curtsy when he finished, and a couple of the girls walking next to them started clapping.

"Two members of Redbone were Yaqui and Shoshone Indians," Simon said. "They were the first Indian band to ever have a gold record."

His use of the word *Indian* to refer to Indigenous people made Rae cringe. "You mean Native American, right?"

Simon scoffed. "*Native American* is just another name given to us by you people. It's no better than being called Indian. It's still a phrase that groups everybody together as if we're all the same. Do you know how many hundreds of different Indian tribes there are in this country, each with a unique history?"

Rae was surprised to hear that the term Native American was offensive to him. She had been taught in elementary school that the term Native American was appropriate because it acknowledged that they had been here first, not to mention the fact that *Indian* was a name that resulted from the butcher Christopher Columbus believing he'd sailed to the West Indies.

Why did Simon have to say *you people*?

"So you're, uh, Indigenous? Um—Indian? American Indian?" This boy flustered her. She cleared her throat. "What exactly are you?"

"I'm Navajo'," he replied, jabbing his chest with his thumb. "I'm Diné. Call me by my tribal name." He sounded proud but angry.

As she formulated her response, Rae spotted a group of people standing in an empty lot on the side of the road, smoking cigarettes and listening to music from a portable cassette player on the ground. She recognized Rhody right away since he was so much taller than everyone else, even without his mohawk standing up. Next to him stood Iggy, leaning into the music with an intense expression on her face and wearing a men's suit jacket, baggy jeans, and a black bowler hat tipped back to reveal bangs plastered to her forehead in little black spikes. She looked up when she noticed Simon, and her expression transformed from curious to surprised to furious as she realized the girl he was walking with was Rae.

"I'm so fucking mad at you!" she screamed, running toward them.

Rae froze, but Simon continued his casual stroll to the school as if nothing out of the ordinary was happening. Iggy briefly paused her march of fury to admire him as he walked by.

"I'm sorry!" Rae yelled at her. "Don't be mad at me!"

She hadn't considered how Iggy and Rhody would respond when she disappeared from the party. If she had, she would have made up a story beforehand to explain that she might have to leave early, although she couldn't imagine now what that story would've been. This life of deception took a lot of careful planning.

Iggy came to a halt in front of her. "Why are you with Simon? How do you even know him?" She took a drag from her cigarette and exhaled the smoke in Rae's face.

"I *don't* know him." Rae coughed. "I mean, just from the party. I'm sorry about leaving like that. I should have told you—"

"Oh, fuck that. Are you into him or what?" She was wearing round, mirrored sunglasses, so Rae couldn't see her eyes.

"Simon? No way! You like him, right?"

Iggy leaped forward and covered Rae's mouth with her hands. "What's wrong with you? Don't announce it to the whole world!"

"Stop it!" Rae shrieked, pulling away. "Ugh, disgusting! Your hands smell like smoke."

Iggy dropped her hands. "Shut up, then."

"Why? Is it, like, some big secret that you like him? He doesn't know?"

"No!" Iggy snapped, lowering her sunglasses so Rae could see her death stare. "And don't you tell him."

"C'mon!" Rhody shouted from up the street. He turned off the cassette player and shoved it in his backpack. "We're going to be late!" Their friends were already walking back.

Iggy grabbed her by the hand and they ran toward the school. Never in her life had Rae met someone whose mood could change so quickly.

"I'm happy you're alive," Rhody said when they caught up with him. His fit was giving rock star on a Sunday: dark jeans folded with a sharp three-inch cuff, brown Chelsea boots, and an open, blue-and-gray flannel shirt with a black T-shirt underneath. He had smudged eyeliner on his bottom lids but overall, he looked a lot less menacing than the night they had met, especially with his mohawk hanging in waves on one side of his face. His eyes looked sad, though, and Rae returned his hug with both arms.

"Are you okay?" she asked.

"He's okay," Iggy answered. "Just trying to survive this hellhole like the rest of us." She punched Rhody hard in the arm as if to prove how okay he was.

"Fuck!" Rubbing his shoulder, he glanced back at Rae like he had something more to say before he turned and merged with the stream of kids moving through the gate in the chain link fence surrounding the high school. Rae ducked behind Rhody's towering silhouette as they passed the school security guard leaning against a white booth, smoking a cigarette and scowling at them.

"One more minute and I would have closed the gate," he said.

"Fuck you," Iggy mumbled.

"What happens if he closes the gate?" Rae asked as they rushed past him.

"We can't come back in and we're marked officially truant, that's what," Rhody said. "Too many truants and you're held back a year."

"Not that it matters," Iggy said. "I'm pretty sure I'm going to fail this year anyway."

"Not that it matters to *you*," Rhody clarified. "Some of us want to graduate from high school."

Iggy scowled. "You're no fun anymore."

Taos High School consisted of a cluster of plain, concrete buildings across from a row of prefabricated portable classrooms and a small athletic field. The entryway to the main building was as unfriendly as the security guard—just three sets of glass-and-metal doors under a concrete canopy held up by large cement columns, unadorned by trees or potted plants or anything aesthetically pleasing. If it weren't for the wooden sign with a pouncing tiger on it that announced they were entering the *Home of the Taos Tigers*, Rae could have easily mistaken the campus for a prison compound.

Iggy kicked open one of the doors with a scuffed-up Doc Marten, leading them into a lobby swirling with a kaleidoscope of kids with books and backpacks, hurrying to their classrooms. The orange walls of the lobby were lined with glass cabinets displaying old sports trophies and photos of student athletes, and a large banner hung on the wall above the cabinets announcing an end-of-year dance. The vibe inside was very school spirit, very rah-rah-rah.

Acid-washed denim was heavily represented among the crowd, along with crimped hair and headbands, pastel paisley, scrunchies, plastic jewelry, shoulder pads, leg warmers, and color-blocked Benetton crop tops. In addition to the stereotypical eighties fashion Rae had been dying for, there were a few punk kids dressed more like Iggy, with spiked hair and chains, safety pins, ripped jeans, black T-shirts, flannel, and plaid. She recognized from the party a blonde girl with a pierced lip who walked by and threw them the peace sign, and an angry-looking guy with a buzz cut passed by and nodded like they were part of a secret society.

Another visual pattern Rae became aware of in the crowd was the predominance of brown skin and dark, straight hair. The majority of kids were obviously Latine, descendants of the earliest New Mexican settlers from Spain and Mexico, with only a few Anglo and Native kids mixed in. And no Black people.

"Where are all the Black people?" she asked aloud.

Rae had learned in her US history class that thousands of Black families had relocated to the Southwest after the Homestead Act of 1862, seeking to build a new life for themselves far from the racial discrimination of the South. These families had even started a homesteader colony named Blackdom outside of Roswell in the early 1900s. From their lack of representation in the high-school lobby, the homesteaders obviously hadn't made it up to Taos. The complete absence of Black people felt wrong to Rae.

Iggy shrugged. "It's New Mexico, right?"

Rae had also learned that the concept of land ownership the way it was described by the Homestead Act of 1862 had been a foreign concept to Native people, who did not think of land as a commodity that could be owned by anyone. As a result of the Act, thousands of Native people had been pushed out of their tribal lands and forced onto crowded reservations.

Trying to appear casual, she looked around the lobby for Simon but didn't see him. He would definitely have an opinion about the Homestead Act, and she felt a strong desire to know what it was.

As the first bell rang, Iggy ran for the stairs while Rhody turned right toward the gymnasium.

"Later," he said. Rae waved, but he didn't seem to notice.

They climbed the stairs to the second floor and turned down a long hallway where a bunch of older kids were leaning against the walls in groups, telling each other stories about their weekend and waiting for the final bell to ring. As they passed, each person stopped and turned to stare at them with cold, unblinking eyes. Anxiety banged around Rae's stomach like a leaden butterfly.

"Hey, Boy George!" a boy yelled to get Iggy's attention before tossing a balled-up piece of notebook paper at her head. She looked up right as the ball bounced off her bowler hat and rolled down the hallway.

Everyone in the hall burst out laughing, pointing their fingers and chanting, "Boy George, Boy George, Boy George," in creepy villain voices. Rae braced herself for a violent reaction from Iggy, but she kept walking down the hallway as if nothing had happened.

"Why did he call you Boy George?" Rae asked.

"Because I wear men's clothes and don't look the way they think I should. These squares have no imagination."

"Is Boy George nonbinary? I've never heard of them."

"Okay, now I *know* you're kidding."

Rae wasn't kidding. She added the name "Boy George" to her mental list of things she needed to Google.

They made it to their destination as the tardy bell rang and slid into two empty desks at the very back of the classroom. From the equations written on the chalkboard, it was obvious they were in an algebra class.

A few of the students sitting nearby glanced at Rae when she sat, but the teacher didn't look up once as he took roll call. Iggy slouched deep in her desk and barely grunted when he called her name.

The teacher, who was identified as Mr. Garcia by the name plate on his desk, moved to the blackboard to begin his lecture. He had thick, dandruff-y hair that had left a pile of greasy flakes on his shoulders so big Rae could see it from way back where she was sitting. His glasses kept sliding down his nose as he spoke in a singsong voice about radical and rational exponents.

Rae had aced algebra in ninth grade, and she had to fight the urge to raise her hand when Mr. Garcia asked for a volunteer to come up to the chalkboard and work through an equation. Everyone shrank in their seats as he waited for a volunteer—everyone except a tall girl with feathered hair and a bright yellow fanny pack who stretched her hand high and practically ran when he called her name. As she watched the girl work through the problem, Rae wondered if they would've been friends if she lived here.

"Brownnoser," Iggy snorted as the girl walked back to her desk.

Rae turned to look at her. Everyone else had their textbooks open, but she was writing something in a spiral notebook she must have kept folded in her bottomless jacket pocket, along with everything else she owned.

When Iggy finished whatever she was writing, she put down her pen and carefully removed the sheet of paper along its perforated edge, instead of tearing it off the coil as Rae would have done. She folded the page in half horizontally before she folded each corner inward and then flipped it over and continued making folds until she had an adorable little envelope with a triangular pull tab. She wrote Rae's name on the tab in large capital letters before passing it across the aisle.

Rae took the note from Iggy and pulled the tab. So this was life before text messages!

Dear Ray,

I'm glad you're OK and I forgive you for leaving the party without saying anything. I'm sure you have your reasons.

There's going to be another rager tonight at the river. You can come with me if you promise not to disappear. Ha ha.

P.S. Did Simon say anything about me?

P.P.S. Hands OFF! Ha ha.

XOXO, Iggy

Rae reached across the aisle and grabbed Iggy's pen off her desk. She flattened the page down as best as she could before she began her reply.

Dear Iggy,

I would love to attend the rager with you and I promise not to disappear.

Simon didn't talk about you exactly, but he told me where you were hanging out. Which means you're on his radar.

XOXO, Rae

Rae drew a smiley face next to her name. The original emoji. She tried to refold the note before giving up and passing it back to Iggy, who read the note and mouthed, *Really?* with a dorky grin on her face.

Rae laughed and nodded. Everything Iggy did was so passionate and exaggerated, you couldn't help but get sucked into it. She realized too late that in her eagerness to make Iggy smile, she had forgotten about her plan to sabotage Simon.

This is your mom, she reminded herself for the millionth time. *This is who you came from.*

That made her think of her grandma, which reminded her that she had to figure out a way to talk to her grandpa. Suddenly, she had a brilliant idea. She gestured for the note frantically until Iggy passed it back to her.

She wrote:

P.S. My grandma has a mysterious stomach problem and she asked me to look for some herbal medicine while I'm in Taos. Do you know where I can find some?

Iggy wrote back quickly:

My grandpa knows a LOT about herbs and stuff. Maybe we can hitch a ride to his house tomorrow.

For the win! Rae couldn't believe how easy that was. Everything was working out exactly as she had planned. She would be going to a super lit party tonight, and then tomorrow she would meet up with her great-grandpa and hopefully he would give her another travel card for her grandma. Once she completed her mission, she could focus on figuring out why her mom had decided to run away and hopefully find a way to change her mind.

The dismissal bell rang as Mr. Garcia was starting to show some emotion about raising exponential expressions. Iggy stood with a jerk and accidentally brought her whole desk up with her before it clattered back to the ground. She and Rae both started laughing.

Mr. Garcia stopped talking and peered at the ruckus in the back of the classroom, making eye contact with Rae for the first time. His eyebrows shot up in surprise.

"Who are you?" he asked.

But it was too late. The entire classroom of students was scrambling for the exit, including Iggy, who had untangled herself from the desk.

"I'm sorry!" Rae blurted as she ran past Mr. Garcia. His look of utter confusion was priceless. She and Iggy laughed so hard, they would have collapsed in the hallway if they weren't in such a hurry to get away.

Chapter Sixteen

After coming so close to being busted as an intruder, Rae was nervous to tag along with Iggy for her last two classes. She didn't want to risk getting caught and being held in the office while the principal tried calling her parents, who were both forty years away. But when she suggested waiting for Iggy off campus, her plan was immediately rejected.

"Trust me," she said, "no one gives a flying fuck."

Which seemed to be true. In her social studies class, where they once again sat in the very last row of desks with all the other kids who were missing their homework or had forgotten their books, the teacher either didn't notice or wasn't interested in the presence of a new student in her classroom. She also didn't seem to mind that Iggy spent the entire period doodling in her notebook instead of paying attention to her lecture about the hundreds and thousands of immigrants who had fought and died for the Union Army during the Civil War.

Rae nearly had a full-blown panic attack during Iggy's final class of the day, when the art teacher toured the room to evaluate his students' work and paused for a minute behind her seat. He turned quickly and walked to his desk, and she thought he was going to call the police for sure, but then she remembered cell phones weren't even a thing here. He came back with drawing paper and a box of colored pencils and set them on the table in front of her without even asking her name or what she was doing there. She took a black graphite pencil from the box and began sketching one of her design ideas for a wide-legged pantsuit constructed from sweatshirt fleece, but it was hard to focus when she was so much more interested in what Iggy was doing.

Everyone in the class was working on an individual design for a screen print, which was a process Rae had never seen before. Iggy was using an X-Acto knife to cut out a portrait of a punk-rock girl on a Mylar sheet. She held the knife with steady hands as she moved the blade across the transparent film she'd placed over her original drawing. She told Rae that after she was finished cutting, she would tape the Mylar to a silk-screen frame and use a squeegee to transfer the design onto paper or cloth with whatever color paints she selected. She was a good artist. Rae was flooded with ASMR tingles on the back of her neck and scalp as she watched Iggy hold her breath and slowly drag the blade across the Mylar. She could have watched her all day.

"Is that you?" she asked, pointing to the picture of the spiky-haired girl.

"No! It's Siouxsie Sioux. Can't you tell?"

"Oh yeah. I see it now," she said, adding the name to her list.

As soon as the dismissal bell rang, Iggy stuffed her supplies back into her cubby and rushed out of the classroom ahead of everyone else, leaving Rae to sprint after her to the double row of metal lockers in the lobby outside of the cafeteria. Rhody was waiting for them there, looking stiff and salty with his backpack strapped to both shoulders. He frowned at his feet.

"What's the plan?" Iggy asked, ignoring his obvious mood.

"My mom is picking me up," he replied.

"But what about the party?"

"I have some things I have to do first. I might meet up with you later." He turned and walked outside without a backward glance at either of them.

"What's up with him?" Rae asked. Was he upset because she had shown up again? He had seemed genuinely happy to see her.

"He's been acting bogus lately," was all Iggy said. She opened one of the lockers on the bottom row and threw her notebook on top of a stack of dusty textbooks before slamming the door shut again. "The bummer is I was counting on him to get us to the party. He was supposed to borrow his uncle's car. Now how are we going to get there?"

"Walk?" Rae suggested, following Iggy outside.

"No way, it's too far. There'd be no beer left by the time we got there. We could hitch a ride."

"Ugh, no. How would we get home?"

"Rhody, maybe?"

"But what if he doesn't show up? I don't think he's feeling it."

"We could ask someone at the party for a lift. Or we could sleep there."

"Outside? By the river?"

"Yeah, so? You've been camping before, right?"

"Yes, but we don't have a tent or sleeping bag or any camping gear or food or anything. Do we?"

Iggy laughed. "You've got your hoodie. We could find a soft spot."

"That sounds dangerous. I'm not doing it."

"Figures," Iggy said. But she didn't argue.

They walked in silence as Iggy chewed her bottom lip.

"What about all your other friends?" Rae asked. "Aren't they going to the party?"

"They're not the kind of friends I would ask for a ride to a party, you know? Not this late, anyway. That would make me feel like a loser. Desperate. Like I don't have any other options."

"Well, do you?"

Iggy shot her a dirty look.

"So . . . is Rhody your only real friend?"

"Wow. Maybe I am a loser."

"I didn't mean it that way," Rae said. "One of my mom's favorite quotes is 'If you have one true friend, you have more than your fair share.'" She didn't think before she said it and was surprised when Iggy's eyes lit up.

"I love that," she exclaimed, clutching her heart. "I'm going to remember it forever."

Rae felt a painful burning sensation on the back of her neck and the left side of her face, like her nerves were on fire.

"Who said that?" Iggy asked.

"Hmm?" Rae rubbed the back of her neck, hoping to massage the pain away.

"The quote. Who said it?"

The tingling moved up the side of her face to her left temple and crossed her skull to the right temple, slithering under her skin like a water snake, gaining intensity as it traveled.

"I . . . uh . . . I don't remember."

As the pain crawled down the right side of her face toward her chest, Rae was overcome with the sensation that she was walking in two places at the same time. She was still walking away from the school with Iggy, but she was also somehow walking on a dock toward the sparkling, blue sea on her way to jump into the water. She looked down and saw she was wearing a plain, navy-blue swimsuit, the same kind she'd worn when she was on the swim team at Ponderosa Prep.

She stopped in the middle of both walks and shook her head. She had never been to the ocean before. But the experience of being in two places at once felt overwhelmingly real. She was in Taos and she was at the ocean, yet at the same time, she was somehow outside both of these experiences looking in, watching herself glitch back and forth between her hoodie self in Taos and her swimsuit self by the ocean. She could do nothing but stand in the middle of the road and dock, waiting for the episode to pass and for the dock to evaporate—maybe Taos too.

Maybe the whole time-travel thing was an illusion and she was going to snap out of it and wake up back home in Albuquerque. She told herself this, but she knew in her bones that all *three* worlds were real. The asphalt beneath her sneakers was solid, and she could taste the salt from the spray of the ocean in her mouth.

She suddenly understood what had happened.

The universe had cracked open like an egg the moment she accidentally told Iggy what her mom's favorite friendship quote was and another world had leaked out—another world where she existed.

Without meaning to, she had created a time-travel paradox, the kind the Internet had warned her about. She had introduced the quote to Iggy, who would later grow up and become her mom and introduce the quote to her, who would then travel back in time and introduce it to Iggy again, and the scenario would repeat itself over and over again for infinity, worlds inside of worlds. Rae had fucked with the multiverse, and in so doing, she had opened up the door to another version of herself. Saying the quote out loud had been a tiny error, but the painful tingling was the multiverse's way of letting her know she had put her current self in danger. Or maybe the pain was a preview of what it felt like to have your soul ripped from your body.

She stood for a moment, transfixed by terror, as sweat leaked from her pores.

As the burning sensation in her face and neck dissipated and the dock on the ocean slowly receded, all Rae could think about was that she had to be much, much more careful about what she said to Iggy than she had been. She had to reveal as little about herself and her past as she possibly could without seeming sus. The pain in her face and the nauseating sensation of being in two places at once was not an experience she ever wanted to repeat.

"Hey," Iggy said, hopping back and forth from one leg to the other in an effort to contain her excitement. "If you're done spazzing out, I have a plan for how we can get to this party!"

It took them almost two full hours to walk to the pile of salvaged lumber on the land behind Iggy's house. She had to admit her mom hadn't been exaggerating when she claimed to have walked everywhere when she was younger. Rae's feet hurt and her brain ached from having to listen to Iggy's ninety-minute analysis of the album *Combat Rock* by the Clash.

"Joe Strummer is God," Iggy concluded.

"I thought David Bowie was God."

"David Bowie *is* God."

"And Siouxsie Sioux—what is she? Just part of the choir?"

"No, she's God too."

As they approached the enormous pile of dry, splintery wood a quarter mile behind Iggy's house—a pile that had to be a fire hazard, out here under the desert sun—Iggy explained that the hippies at her house collected the wood from construction sites around town. Someday they would clean it up and sell it, but in the meantime, Iggy hung out there when she didn't feel like being at home with her family. There was a blanket folded and tucked between two planks of wood in case it rained, and a Folgers coffee can filled with nasty cigarette butts.

Iggy pulled herself up on one of the long pieces of wood sticking out from the disorganized pile and removed a pack of cigarettes and a box of wooden matches from her jacket pocket. Striking a match on the crease of her boot where the sole met the leather, she cupped her hands around the flame to protect it from the breeze and lit her cigarette.

Rae searched the pile of wood until she found an entry point that appeared relatively free from the rusty nails protruding from the boards at all angles. Splinters were clearly an unavoidable issue, so she pulled the cuffs of her hoodie over the palms of her hands and carefully hoisted herself up onto the pile beside Iggy.

"I'm starving," Iggy said. Smoke came out in little puffs as she spoke.

Rae remembered the protein bars in her backpack and pulled out two—one chocolate mint and one crunchy peanut butter. "Which one do you want?" she asked, offering both.

"You have candy?"

"No, they're protein bars."

"What's a protein bar?" Iggy asked, grabbing the peanut butter one and examining the wrapper intensely.

"You know, energy bars? Sort of like candy bars but with protein and vitamins so they give you energy. Like for when you're working out."

Iggy shrugged and opened the wrapper, sniffing the bar suspiciously before taking a small bite. She chewed for a while and took another bite.

"It's not very good."

"That's because it's supposed to be healthy."

Iggy finished the protein bar and threw the balled-up wrapper on top of the enormous pile of wood. Hoping to grab the wrapper before it was snatched up by the light breeze blowing from the foothills, Rae stood and made her way cautiously across the wobbly boards, grabbing the wrapper before it could be strewn somewhere in the pristine desert. She folded the wrapper neatly and put it back in the small pocket of her backpack, biting her tongue. If she wasn't suddenly afraid of revealing too much about her personality, she would have definitely told Iggy what a slob she thought she was.

"Damn, now I'm thirsty," Iggy grumbled.

"I also have water." Rae pulled out the thirty-two-ounce yellow-and-pink-ombre Hydro Flask her dad had given her last Christmas.

"Oh my god, is that a water bottle? It's so beautiful! Let me see that!" Iggy grabbed the multicolored flask out of Rae's hands right as she was taking a drink, which made her spill water down her chin and neck. Iggy didn't care. She turned the flask round and round, studying the lid, its built-in straw, and the stickers Rae had added.

Oh boy. She hadn't given any thought to how out of place the items she packed would look in 1984, and now she had to prepare herself for questions that would take lies to answer.

Lucky for her, Iggy seemed more interested in the stickers on the side of the bottle than the bottle itself. She traced the iridescent Alexandra Savior sticker with her finger, the big red Beach House *Depression Cherry* sticker, a sticker of the Little Bear Coffee logo—her and her grandma's spot to get coffee—and her new favorite, a "Destroy the patriarchy not the planet" sticker she had found on Etsy.

"Are these the bands you like?" Iggy asked.

"Some of them, yeah."

"I don't know who any of these groups are! How do you know about all this cool stuff I've never even heard of?" She sighed and shook her head. "I guess that's what you get when you live in the middle of Bumfuck, Egypt, without a TV." She stood as she spoke and waved her arms in annoyed circles toward the piñon trees, the sagebrush, and even the magnificent mountain radiating the golden pink light of the setting sun. When she was through being extra, she sat again and reached into her jacket pocket for her Walkman.

"But have you heard *this*?" She pressed Play and held one of the spongy Styrofoam earpieces to her left ear and offered Rae the other. Rae scooted next to her and put the earpiece up to her right ear.

She was so close to Iggy, their heads were touching. She smelled clean but not perfumey, like the line-dried clothes they had folded together. For some reason, being this close to her made Rae's heart hurt. She closed her eyes and tried to focus on the song seeping out of the crappy eighties headphones. The man's voice was mysterious and low, and the strings in the song had a haunting quality. The lyrics suggested something was about to happen—something terrible or wonderful, Rae wasn't sure.

"It's good, right?" Iggy asked when the song was over.

"It's so good. What is it?"

"'The Killing Moon' by Echo and the Bunnymen." She looked like she was going to say more about the song, but the silence around them was suddenly interrupted by rock 'n' roll music blasting from her house. Iggy leaped to her feet. "That's our cue!" she said, jumping off of the woodpile and jamming the Walkman back into her magic pocket. "That music means the party is *on*. They'll be too faded to notice us."

She ran toward the circle of cottonwood trees surrounding the compound with Rae close behind her, gasping and stretching her legs to keep up. When they reached the trees, Iggy stopped and crouched low to the ground, observing the area. Rae copied all her moves.

A group of people was gathered around a bonfire in roughly the same place they had been the last time Rae visited, in a big, open patch of land across from the main house. They were all talking and laughing as they piled more logs on the fire, making the flames lick the sky higher and higher. Someone inside the house turned up the volume on the stereo, and a couple of people moved away from the fire and started dancing in slow, hypnotic movements that didn't match the propulsive rhythm of the blaring music.

The sun had started its final descent below the horizon and the first visible stars twinkled faintly in the massive sky. The party was ramping up.

"You stay here," Iggy whispered over her shoulder before she took off running toward the house, zigzagging between the trees as if she were avoiding a sniper in a war movie.

"Bring me an apple or something," Rae called after her.

She kept her eyes on the people around the bonfire while she finished the protein bar from earlier. A figure she instantly recognized as her grandma broke away from the circle and started rounding up the half dozen or so kids chasing each other around the garden, then led them to a blanket she'd spread on the ground a safe distance away from the fire. A few of the younger kids—Rae was pretty sure she recognized Maria and Benny among them—lay down on the blanket right away, obviously tired, but the older ones sat up and leaned on each other as they shared what Rae imagined was grapes or popcorn with nutritional yeast from a big bowl her grandma handed them before she returned to her place around the fire. Her hair was worn loose and floated around her back, mimicking the way her skirt floated around her ankles. She moved like a magical being, a wood nymph or fairy queen or something equally feminine and mysterious.

As she studied her grandma, Rae noticed another figure hidden in the trees on the other side of the bonfire, watching the people around the fire like she was. It was Iggy. She watched for a while before she disappeared, emerging minutes later from a tree right beside Rae, who stifled her startled gasp.

"I found them!" Iggy whispered, dangling a set of keys from a macrame rope.

She had changed her outfit and was now wearing an Army surplus messenger bag slung across her body over an oversized blazer and pegged jeans. In the few minutes she had been inside the house, she had also taken off her hat, rewet and gelled her hair, and put on lipstick, which didn't exactly seem fair.

"I brought you this," she said, handing Rae a limp article of black clothing.

"You want me to wear a beanie?"

"It's a beret! To jazz up your outfit a little bit. You'll look rad!"

Rae stared at the hat in her hand, unconvinced.

"Johnny Rotten wears a black beret."

Rae had no clue who Johnny Rotten was, but his name sounded cool so she pulled the beret over her head. Laughing, Iggy reached over and readjusted the beret so it was above her ears and slanted to one side.

"Perfect," she said. "C'mon."

They crept quietly to the center of the circular driveway, where the station wagon sat covered in dust and cottonwood fluff. Up close like this, the pea-green Chrysler Town & Country seemed cartoonishly large. It was as long as four people stretched head to toe and had to weigh at least two tons. You could probably cram fifteen fully grown adults inside if you had to. It was hard to imagine Iggy controlling this big, ugly beast.

"So you took driver's ed?" Rae asked.

Iggy scooted into the driver's seat and unlocked the passenger door.

"Not exactly. My mom and Abelino took me to the Piggly Wiggly parking lot and we drove around there for a while."

"You can't be serious?"

"Shhh! Do you want them to hear you?" Iggy released the parking brake and shifted the car into neutral before leaping out again and leaning her weight into the doorjamb. "Okay, get ready to push as hard as you can. Just to the end of the driveway, and then I'll jump in and start it while it's rolling."

"This is crazy," Rae protested, but she got into position and waited for Iggy to count to three before pushing on the doorjamb as hard as she could. They pushed and grunted until beads of sweat sprang up on Rae's forehead, but the car only rocked forward slightly before swinging heavily back into its original spot.

"There's no way we're getting this to the end of the driveway," Rae gasped.

"Thanks so much for that information," Iggy snapped. "Then I'll have to start the engine here and hope my mom doesn't hear us."

"What will she do if she catches us?"

"I'm not sure. This is my first time stealing the car."

"I honestly don't think we're meant to go to this party." Rae sat in the passenger seat and leaned her head on the enormous dashboard. The car smelled stale, as if it hadn't been driven in a while, and there were potato-chip bags and Styrofoam coffee cups strewn all over the floor.

"What do you mean, we're not *meant* to go to this party? We are the captains of our own destiny! Stop talking like that and shut the door."

Rae closed the door as quietly as she could and fumbled in the dark for the seat belt.

"You are so paranoid," Iggy said, shaking her head. When she turned the key, the car engine made a horrible groaning sound like it really wanted to start but couldn't quite get there. It felt exactly like a scene from a horror movie where the next victim is trying to get away from the bad guy and jumps into some random car, only to discover that the engine is dead.

"What's going on?" Rae asked, panic rising in her throat. She didn't want to find out what would happen if someone heard them.

"Don't freak out, okay?" Iggy said. "It does this sometimes. The starter is going out." She turned the key again and the Town & Country roared to life like an old, toothless lion. "Yes!" Iggy cheered, shifting the car into first gear.

Just as Rae started to release the tension in her neck, the station wagon lunged forward and stalled out.

"Oh my god!" Rae yelled. "What's happening?"

"Be quiet! You are so totally dramatic."

"I thought you knew how to drive."

"I do, but jeez!"

Rae glanced over at the group around the bonfire and saw someone break away from the fire and move toward them in the dark.

"Hurry!" she screamed. "Someone is coming!"

"Shut up and let me concentrate!" Iggy yelled. She alternated her foot between the gas pedal and brake as the station wagon lurched forward in a series of violent jerks. As Rae prepared to open the car door and jump out for her own safety, they reached the end of the driveway and the station wagon peeled out onto the dirt road, spraying dirt and pebbles in a cloud behind them. If someone was chasing them, at least it was raining rocks on their head.

"Oh my god!" Rae screamed, clenching the seat with both hands.

"Did you really see someone coming for us?"

"I swear I did!"

"Sorry, suckers!" Iggy screamed, throwing her head back and laughing like a maniac. She drove with one hand on the wheel and the other fumbling in her messenger bag. "Here," she said, handing Rae a ziplock bag filled with loose cassette tapes. "Pick one."

Rae turned on the interior light, but it was impossible to read the name on the cassette with the station wagon swerving across the dirt road.

"I feel like I'm navigating the Millennium Falcon through an asteroid field!" Iggy shrieked.

"Then slow down!" Rae shouted. She kept reminding herself that Iggy had survived her childhood, so chances were that she would too.

"Play some music," Iggy demanded.

Rae blindly grabbed one of the cassettes and jammed it into the dashboard cassette player. The player sucked the cassette tape into its mechanical innards, making a whirring sound that reminded Rae of the silver itinerary case. She patted the belt around her waist to make sure it was still there as the interior of the car exploded with a bouncing bass line and the raspy voice of a tough, sexy-sounding woman.

"The Pretenders!" Iggy shouted. "Did you know Chrissie Hynde used to be in a band with the lead singer of Devo?"

As the station wagon careened down the road on four balding tires, Iggy cranked up the volume on the car stereo as loud as it would go. It was obvious she didn't really know how to drive, but she didn't seem too worried about it. She pulled a cigarette out of her jacket pocket and struck a wooden match across the dashboard while struggling to keep her eyes on the road. She was laughing, talking, singing, and smoking, all while attempting to steer the two-ton hunk of rusty metal as it shuddered and bounced across the transverse ripples in the surface of the dirt road. Rae's teeth vibrated in her head as Iggy rolled down the window to release a plume of noxious smoke. She felt like she was riding on a wave of barely contained chaos at its highest point, about to fall headfirst into who-knew-what.

"C'mon, Rae, sing with me!" Iggy shouted, oblivious to the danger all around her.

Tick tick tick tick.

When they reached the highway, Rae closed her eyes to shut out the rushing white lines and kept them closed until the car slowed and turned onto another bumpy dirt road that twisted and turned downward, black canyon walls looming on both sides of them. Rae felt the dark, mysterious presence of the rocky cliffs more than she could see them, and she had to fight off the sensation that she was sinking into a pit of doom. The river was right below them—she could hear and smell it—and the narrow dirt road had no guardrail or anything to prevent them from hurling straight into the water if Iggy were to lose control of the car or jerk the steering wheel the wrong way.

As Iggy sang along with her music, Rae tried to focus on the blast of fresh, cool air streaming through the open window, breathing in through her nose and out through her mouth on the count of five, over and over again, until they reached the party spot.

The first sign they had arrived was the group of cars parked on the side of the road by the Taos Junction Bridge, which spanned across the river right at the spot where the Rio Grande met the Rio Pueblo de Taos. A battered Ford truck parked at the base of the bridge had left its headlights on and directed toward the steel truss bridge, so Rae could see a group of kids sitting on the bridge, swinging their legs back and forth above the river.

As Iggy searched the narrow embankment on the side of the canyon road for a space big enough to park the green monster, Rae spotted people swimming in the lazy part of the water, near the riverbank. She knew from her earth science class that the Rio Grande was fed by snow melting off the Colorado Rockies, so the water had to be super cold, even in June.

A flash of movement drew her eyes back up to the bridge, where a boy in a red T-shirt and cutoff jeans was hurtling from the bridge and into the river below.

"Oh my god!" she screamed. "Is he insane?"

"He's fine," Iggy replied flatly. She tapped the gas pedal gently, trying to inch the car forward without ramming it into the powder-blue Buick Skylark parked on the side of the road in front of them. But without enough fuel pressure, the station wagon stalled, leaving its big, rusty rear projecting several inches onto the dark, winding road.

"That'll work," she said, satisfied.

"Are you serious? Someone is going to hit you."

"Listen," Iggy said, turning off the car and stuffing the keys in the front pocket of her Levi's. "I like you a lot, I really do. You're cool. But you're so uptight about everything! I can't handle being constantly monitored by you."

Rae let that comment sink in for a moment, biting the inside of her cheek to stop herself from laughing in Iggy's face. How many times had Rae complained to her mom of the exact same thing? She was the one who was constantly monitoring *her*, telling her to put on a jacket or sit while she ate or put down her phone and go to sleep. It sure would feel good to tell her what a horrible nag she was going to be when she grew up.

"You're right," she said instead. "I'm sorry."

"Okay. Jeez! Now let's go down and find some brewskis. That'll relax you."

"Can you drive when you're drinking? It seems hard enough now when you're sober."

She knew she sounded like a nag, but she didn't want to hang out with Iggy if she was going to get wasted again, especially without Rhody here to keep an eye on her.

Iggy jumped out of the car and slammed the door, disappearing down a sloping path to the riverbank.

"Wait!" Rae called after her. "I'll stop, I promise! I'll relax!"

Leaving her backpack in the car, she scurried to catch up with Iggy, but it was dark and she kept tripping on the bunches of weeds and river grass choking the narrow path. At last she reached the surprisingly wide, sandy beach at the bottom, where a bunch of people were hanging out. Some sat in a circle passing a joint, some were dancing to the music playing on someone's car stereo, and some huddled by the riverbank, watching those brave enough to jump off the bridge.

A group of girls sitting around a campfire toasting marshmallows looked up at Rae and smiled. She smiled back and almost tripped on the couple she had seen in line for the bathroom at the last party. Here they were again, lying on a blanket in the sand, making out shamelessly. The boy was actually lying on top of the girl, grinding his pelvis into hers.

"Is that all you guys do? Make out?" Iggy asked at her side. She had found her way to the ice-filled cooler sitting on the couple's blanket and was casually helping herself to their beer.

They stopped kissing and looked up at her. The boy held out his hand for a sliding handshake fist bump and the girl laughed.

Now that she could see their faces, Rae realized it was the same guy from the party, but he was with a totally different girl. This one had long hair in a bunch of tiny braids.

"Are we cool?" Iggy asked, gesturing with her chin to the two cans of Budweiser she held with one hand, dripping water in the sand.

"Go for it," the boy said before sticking his tongue back into his new girlfriend.

Rae thought Iggy might offer her a beer, but she popped one of them open and stashed the other in her messenger bag before walking away in the direction of the riverbank without even turning around to see if Rae was coming.

Not only was she reckless and annoying and volatile but she was also rude, no cap.

The kissing couple was so involved in their makeout sesh, they didn't seem to notice or care that Rae was standing alone by their blanket like some kind of freak. She had to start socializing before people started to think she was sus, but the idea of walking up to a bunch of strangers made her stomach twist up in knots.

Pulling her hood over her head, she took a couple of deep breaths and headed toward a group of people who had broken off from the main group and were dancing around a big boom box on the ground, away from the river. Why not? Dancing had been fun the last time she was here, and that way, she wouldn't feel pressured to talk to a bunch of people she didn't know.

She approached the dance circle casually, like she was interested but not creepily so. The group consisted of four girls and two guys, all of them seriously feeling the music, dancing next to each other but somehow alone. Their eyes were closed as they shook, shimmied, and stomped in the sand.

As she tried to decide the least awkward way to join, one of the girls reached out and snatched her by the elbow, pulling her into the circle. Barefoot with wet, stringy hair and half-open eyes and wearing only a green T-shirt that went to her knees, the girl laced her thin fingers into Rae's as she shook her shoulders and hips in time with the music. Rae stood motionless in front of her, startled.

"C'mon," the girl said. "Get down with me!"

The song they were listening to ended, and everyone in the circle whooped and hollered as the next one began.

"This is our song!" The girl laughed, scrunching her face into an impassioned grimace as she dropped Rae's hands and spun like a ballerina.

Everyone in the circle knew the song by heart and they all sang along. Their voices grew louder as they dragged out the last syllable, building in intensity until their collective voices came crashing down for the chorus.

The song was a bop. Rae recognized the lead singer's voice as the dude from Talking Heads, and she laughed out loud when she realized they were listening to a song about the river while actually *at the river*. She stopped resisting the music and let the rhythm flow through her, guiding the movement of her feet, legs, hips, shoulders, arms, and head until she no longer wondered if she looked ridiculous or corny or if she was doing it right.

Everyone in the circle cheered when she started dancing, and a boy wearing a red bandanna passed her a tiny, hand-rolled joint as if to signify her inclusion in the group.

Before she even considered what she was doing, Rae took the joint, put it up to her lips, and inhaled. The smoke burned her throat, but she was determined not to look like a total amateur in front of these people, so she sucked it way down into her lungs and held it there for at least ten seconds before exhaling. She inhaled one more time before passing the joint to the girl in the green T-shirt, fascinated by the way her hand looked as it crossed the space between them.

She stopped dancing and waved her hands back and forth in front of her face. It was like they were emitting their own light, leaving neon streaks of purple in the night sky, like slow-motion, black-light sparklers.

She was about to sit in the dirt and figure out what was going on with her hands, but some British dude in an echo chamber yelled right into her ear. The man kept yell-talking and someone started playing a saxophone, and then one of the most infectious grooves Rae had ever heard ripped through the canyon. Everyone around her roared at the sky and started swinging their elbows and kicking their feet behind them with an intense, chaotic energy that radiated in perceptible waves.

"Madness!" someone yelled.

Rae wanted nothing more than to be a part of that dance. They were all using the same moves they had used when they were slam dancing at Scum House, and she did her best to mimic them, concentrating on the way the music felt inside her. Pretty soon she was moving her body in a way that felt exactly right—kicking with one leg while swinging the opposite arm and pushing back on the other. With her eyes closed, she merged with the music and lost herself in the beat, forgetting for a moment where and who she was.

And then the music stopped.

She opened her eyes and gasped when she saw the canyon, its massive sides quivering like featureless monoliths beneath the curtain of night. Her senses were mobbed by a million pinpricks of ultraviolet light piercing the indigo canopy, by the smell of sweat and mud and fire that filled her nostrils, by the sound of the drums, bass, and saxophone vibrating on her eardrums.

"Who are we listening to?" she asked the girl in the T-shirt, panting to catch her breath. Her voice sounded strange and faraway, and she wasn't sure if she had asked the question or if she had only thought it while someone else had actually asked it. Her mouth was so dry, her lips kept sticking together.

"It's a mixtape," the girl yelled as the next song started. "I made it for my ex-boyfriend!"

"I'm so thirsty!" Rae yelled in reply. The girl laughed.

Someone passed a can of beer her way, and Rae grabbed it and poured the prickly, cold liquid down her throat. It tasted bitter and wonderful. She rolled the wet can across her forehead and rocked her hips in time with the slower song.

Someone jabbed her in the side and she turned around very, very slowly, wondering if everyone else could see that she was moving in slow motion—if they could see that she was standing outside of herself, looking in.

"Hey." It was Rhody. He had transformed back into the guy she had met on her first trip, wearing thick, smudged eyeliner and a long silver chain with dangling dog tags, his mohawk meticulously molded into long, black spears.

Without thinking, she reached out and touched one of the silver spikes on the shoulder of his black leather jacket. She pulled back when he flinched.

He wasn't exactly dressed in river attire, and while standing next to everyone else grooving in their T-shirts and bare feet, he stood out in a way that made Rae want to cry. His leather armor made him seem more vulnerable, not less, and she pulled his reluctant body against hers, hugging him tight.

"You're here," she said after he pulled away from her. Did she sound as faraway to Rhody as she did to herself?

"You guys didn't call me." He was hunched over and frowning with his hands in his pockets.

All of a sudden, Rae felt scared. She stepped back a few feet from the circle.

"I'm sorry, we . . . uh . . . we . . . uh . . ." The truth was, she hadn't thought of Rhody once since they'd parted ways at the high school. "Actually, we were never around a phone."

"There are pay phones everywhere," he replied.

She didn't know how to respond. It hadn't been her decision whether to call him. She didn't even know him. He was Iggy's friend.

"Iggy's down by the river," she suggested.

"Oh, I know. I can hear her laughing. She's already drunk."

Rae realized it was true. The entire time she'd been dancing, she'd been partially aware of the sound of Iggy laughing in the distance.

The whites of Rhody's eyes glowed as he stared at her.

"Are you okay?" Rae asked. "Did something happen?"

He shook his head and kicked the ground with his boot.

"My family's a fucking mess," he said, and his voice trembled like he was about to cry.

They stood together motionless while the dance continued around them, the unhappy center of a turbulent storm. Rae lifted her hand and rested it on his arm, overwhelmed with a feeling of hopelessness. She didn't know what to say. Her family was also a fucking mess.

"You know," he said, his face brightening, "I never drink at parties because I always take care of Iggy and make sure she gets home okay. But who takes care of me?"

They both knew what the answer was, but he wasn't going to be satisfied until she said it out loud.

"No one?" she said weakly.

"That's right," he said. "No one. So guess what, people? I'm going to get wrecked tonight."

Rae handed him her almost full beer and backed away as he chugged it. His energy was so intense, she had to get away for a minute. She had to find something to drink that wasn't beer.

He finished the beer and threw the can on the ground, staring at her with hungry, pleading eyes that sent a chill up her spine as she walked away.

The campfire had become crowded with kids passing cigarettes, joints, and bottles of booze back and forth as their voices grew louder and louder in an effort to be heard. No one paid attention to her as she located the cooler Iggy had pilfered earlier. She searched through the melting ice for a single bottle of water floating among the cans of Budweiser and Miller Lite. No such luck. People didn't drink enough water back in the eighties—or eat enough food, for that matter. She would have been dangerously close to zero health if not for the water and protein bars she had brought along with her.

Rae was going to lose her mind if she didn't get a drink of water, so she followed the sound of Iggy's annoying laughter down to the edge of the river, where a group of drunk people was hanging out and celebrating every time someone walked up to the bridge and jumped off, landing with a splash in the dark, glassy water beside them.

There she was, sitting on a smooth, black rock halfway in the water, her pants rolled up above her ankles. She clenched a can of beer between her knees and shared a cigarette with two girls wading in the river beside her, cheering and clapping like she was at a rock concert every time someone hit the water.

"Hey, Iggy," Rae shouted from the riverbank, so unbelievably thirsty she didn't even care when everyone turned around to stare at her. "I need something out of my backpack!"

Iggy's foot slipped on the wet rock when she turned toward Rae's voice, and she fell forward into the water with almost no resistance. Rae ran to the edge of the river as Iggy's friends grabbed her by her arms and pulled her out of the water, laughing the whole time.

"Are you okay?" Rae shouted.

Iggy stood in the water with her arms hanging down at her sides, staring in a daze. Her clothes were totally soaked and her hair was dripping wet. She was looking in Rae's direction, but she didn't seem to see her.

"She's drunk," one of the girls yelled to Rae.

"Can you look in her front pockets and see if you can find her car keys?" Rae asked.

The girl nodded and reached for Iggy, but Iggy snarled and pushed her away with both hands.

"Hey!" the girl shrieked, nearly falling into the river herself.

"Fuck off!" Iggy screamed at her.

Oh no. Why was she such an asshole when she got drunk? And why did she drink so much if this is what it did to her? She had been laughing all night, but it didn't look like she was actually having much fun.

Rae backed away from the scene as stealthily as possible and found herself on a footpath that ran along the riverbank. As she walked along the edge of the water, she heard voices and music coming from further down the path, on the other side of a patch of tall brush and river grass. There was a whole other section of the party over there! Maybe they had something nonalcoholic to drink.

She pushed through the brush and almost collided with an enormous rock half submerged in the river. It was basalt, the same kind of rock Iggy had been sitting on, a volcanic rock formed millions of years ago when blistering-hot magma had flowed out of the earth and cooled on its surface. This particular rock was taller than her and as wide as an SUV, with hard curves that glittered black in the moonlight and reminded her of sockets and pelvic bones, as if some huge monster had curled up and died here a hundred thousand years ago.

Rae stepped up to the rock and put her arms around it. She rubbed her cheek on the rock, which was damp and cool. She loved this rock. She needed to climb this rock.

There were holes on the surface of the rock, deep pits left behind when the gasses in the magma dissolved as the lava hardened. Rae located the vesicles in the dark and used them as fingerholds and toeholds to help her climb up the side. Once on top of the beautiful, giant throne of a rock, she sat cross-legged, in awe of her spectacular view of the purple-black canyon walls and the sprawling, starlit sky. The rushing babble of the river muffled the conversation and music flowing from the cars and people, people who seemed faraway and insignificant now compared to this fucking rock.

She took a deep breath and inhaled the odor of wet earth and river grass growing in shallow pools alongside the moving water. She could even smell the moss growing on the rocks beneath the waterline. It was like she had supersensory powers or something, like a wild animal or an alien visiting from another planet.

She felt 100 percent alive—and invisible, too, but in a good way. None of the kids passing through on the path from one side of the party to the other had noticed her sitting up there.

She could see them, though. And beyond that, she could see the little campfire and the people spread on blankets around it and the dance circle too. Rae put her hands in her pockets and watched the dancers for a while, looking for Rhody. But the circle twisted and writhed in the darkness like one big beast, and she couldn't make out any of the individual forms.

Something yellow flickered in her peripheral vision, drawing her attention to the deck of the bridge, where a girl wearing a yellow tank top stood perched on the guardrail, trying to get up the nerve to jump. Sensing her hesitation, the cheering section on the ground began to whistle and shout. "Jump! Jump! Jump!" they yelled over and over again.

The girl's face was illuminated by the headlights below, and it was obvious she was terrified. She leaned above the water, holding on to the diagonal support beam behind her with both hands. All she had to do was let go and gravity would do the rest.

When it became obvious that the girl was too scared to let go, the people watching on the ground stopped cheering and drifted back to their conversations, their beer, their makeout sessions, and their moonlight walks. As the last spectator turned away, the girl finally let go of her tight grip on the steel beam and dropped into the water below.

Rae stood to peer into the murky river and sighed in relief when the girl's head emerged from the water. She slowly dog-paddled toward the riverbank.

"She made it," said someone on the ground below Rae. She looked down and recognized the black ponytail and baby-blue T-shirt visible in the moonlight. It was Simon.

"She's really brave," Rae said, suddenly nervous.

"Do you want some company?" he asked.

Rae's thoughts flew to Iggy. *Hands off*, her note had warned.

"Sure," she replied.

Simon scurried up the side of the rock like a lizard and was suddenly there, standing right next to her. Rae's heart raced as they sat together on the flat surface of the rock, trying not to bump their elbows and knees.

"Have you ever done that?" Rae asked, pointing at the bridge.

"Oh yeah, a million times." He removed the can of beer sticking out from the chest pocket of the flannel shirt he wore over his T-shirt and popped the tab. Foam poured over the top and dripped down his hands as he handed the can to her. She took a long drink and handed it back to him, watching as he guzzled the rest and crushed the can into a disc with his bare hands.

"I thought you were going to go straight edge," she said.

He gave her a funny look before he must have remembered their conversation at Scum House.

"Not today." He shrugged. "Even though my grandma says it's disrespectful to bring alcohol to the river. It angers the river spirits." He put the aluminum disc in his flannel pocket and pulled another beer from the front pocket of his jeans.

"What is it with you eighties people and your bottomless pockets?" Rae laughed.

Simon gave her another funny look but didn't say anything. Oh my god, how stupid could she be?

They sat in a silence that was awkward at first but started to feel better as Rae let herself relax into her surroundings like another part of the landscape. The stars, the river, the rattlesnakes slithering in the sagebrush, the rocks strewn across the canyon floor like the bones of a giant god—everything was so vast and so alive. She was hyperaware of everything around her, including Simon.

"Human beings think they're so much better than everything out here," Simon said, as if he knew what she was thinking about.

"What do you mean?" she asked.

"As if building cities and sending rockets to the moon make us more important than the trout and bears and coyotes, you know what I mean? And what are we doing anyway? Just killing each other and polluting the earth and starting wars.

In the end, we eat and shit and try to get by like every other living thing. I mean, what do we do that's so special?"

"Well, what about your music?" she suggested. "Isn't that special?" The idea that human life had no meaning or significance beyond birth and death terrified her.

Simon crushed the second beer can. "You don't get it," he said, shaking his head. "All there is out here is music."

As she listened to the river burbling against the rocks and riverbank on its long journey to the Gulf of Mexico, Rae realized it was true. Even the moon in front of them, hanging nearly full and shining bright through a thin veil of wispy clouds, throbbed in the sky with a kind of music she could feel inside of her.

Time stood still as they stared at the moon together.

"Niteel Náádlee," Simon whispered. "Almost full moon. First Woman made the moon out of quartz and fastened it to the sky with lightning. But when Wind Boy tried to help push the moon across the sky, he only confused Moon Bearer, and now the moon makes strange paths." He gave a self-conscious smile and shook his head. "When I look at the moon, I feel small."

"When I look at the moon," Rae said, "I think about how there's nothing between me and it but pure space." She stretched out her arm and fingers toward the glowing, mottled orb. "Like, if my arm was long enough, I could reach out and touch it."

He turned his face to look at her and their eyes locked. Rae's hands were sweating. She knew that he was going to try to kiss her—and she was going to let him.

But as his soft lips brushed against hers, a familiar laugh pierced the night sky.

She sat up fast and saw Iggy coming toward them in the dark, propped up by the two girls from the river as all three made their way down the narrow path, elbows interlocked. She was barefoot and her jeans were still wet. She kept tripping and bursting into laughter, amused by her own inability to walk upright.

As she watched Iggy make her way down the path, the skin on the back of Rae's neck crawled with memories of her drunk mother. She used to lie in bed and listen to her mom when she came home drunk from work, laughing, always laughing, stumbling and bumping into walls on her way down the hallway to her bedroom, where she would pass out facedown on a pillow. Or, even worse, when she staggered to the bathroom, where she would collapse in a messy heap in front of the toilet and puke for hours. Then the crying would begin.

"Uh-oh," Simon said, elbowing her side as if there was any way she could have missed Iggy hobbling and hiccuping down the moonlit path.

"Shhh!" she whispered, nudging him away from her.

Praying that Iggy was too drunk to look up and see them together, cloaked in the shadow of their near kiss, Rae sat absolutely still. When she could hold her breath not one second longer, Rhody came plowing through the brush from the opposite direction, running right into Iggy and her friends.

Drunk or not, Iggy recognized him instantly. He towered over everyone else, and he was the only one in leather.

"Rhody!" she gushed, lifting her drunk Frankenstein arms for a hug. "You came!"

Rae winced as Rhody ducked under Iggy's outstretched arms and marched down the pathway.

"What the FUCK!" Iggy shouted violently after him. The girls at her side backed away from her slowly.

Rhody ignored her.

"RHODY!" she shouted again, so loud Rae could hear her vocal chords frying.

"FUCK OFF!" Rhody yelled from somewhere in the distance.

Iggy stumbled backward and rubbed her ears in disbelief. The shock of it must have sobered her up, though, because she charged after him down the path.

"Oh shit," Rae said. Was she going to physically attack him?

Simon must have thought so, because he jumped off the rock and then turned to help Rae down. He grabbed her hand and together they ran after Iggy.

They were right behind her when she caught up to Rhody and shoved him from behind with all her strength. He fell forward on his hands and knees with a loud grunt, right in front of everyone standing by the trailhead, their conversation on pause as they watched this fresh drama unfold.

Rae waited for everyone to pull out their phones and start recording before she remembered she was in 1984.

Rhody stood and thrust his arms out to stop Iggy from getting any closer to him. She kept coming toward him anyway with a weird smile on her face.

"Get away from me!" he yelled hysterically. "You're not my fucking friend!" His voice was thick and loud, and he, too, was slurring.

Rae's stomach cramped up immediately. One angry drunk was bad enough, but two angry drunks were a natural disaster.

"Stop it!" she yelled at them.

Iggy spun around. Her face twisted into an ugly sneer when she saw Simon and Rae standing there together. Rae dropped his hand, but it was too late.

"Why are you holding hands?" Iggy demanded.

The gathering crowd gasped and snickered at the unexpected plot twist, and everyone turned in unison to see Rae's reaction. Thank god they couldn't see her blushing in the moonlight.

Simon took a step forward. "Listen, we just want you guys to stop fighting."

Iggy must have momentarily forgotten what was going on with Rhody. When she turned to find him, he wasn't there anymore.

"Where did he go?" she asked.

Rae made out the silhouette of his mohawk moving toward the bridge. "There." She pointed.

Iggy glanced at Rhody and back at Rae. She looked defeated now, more sad than angry. Sensing the drama was winding down, the group of onlookers broke apart and meandered back to whatever it was they were doing before.

"I thought you were my friend," Iggy whispered, her fists balled at her side.

"I *am* your friend," Rae replied, stepping closer. "Nothing is going on, I swear."

"Wait, wait," Simon interrupted, shaking his head and walking up to Iggy. "What do you care if something is going on? You and I aren't a thing. We only kissed once, like, forever ago."

Iggy bit her lip and looked down at her feet. "It was four months ago," she whispered. "On my birthday."

What the . . . ? They had kissed? On Iggy's sixteenth birthday? And here Rae was, thinking whatever relationship they'd had was all in Iggy's head. Simon had acted like he barely knew who Iggy was, and Rae had never actually seen them talk to each other at all. Was it all a con? Was he just another fuckboy? Had he been playing Rae from the moment they met?

And to think a part of her had been secretly flattered when he asked her to come on tour with his band after only just meeting her. She was an idiot—and a horrible friend.

She could feel him watching her now, trying to gauge her reaction to Iggy's cringey reveal. Looking anywhere but his eyes, she noticed Rhody had walked to the middle of the bridge and was now standing there alone, staring down into the dark water like he was actually considering jumping, drunk as he was and wearing that heavy leather jacket. Her heart immediately started racing.

"Hey, Rhody!" she yelled, cupping her hands around her mouth and screaming as loud as she could. Iggy and Simon turned to look up at the bridge, along with everyone else.

Rhody glanced over at them before hooking his long fingers onto one of the diagonal steel beams, inching his way from the deck of the bridge toward the top chord like a skinny, black cat.

"What is he doing?" Iggy asked.

No one answered. They just stood there and watched.

When Rhody finally reached the top horizontal beam, he pulled himself up with his shoulders and arms and slowly stretched to his full height, wobbling back and forth with outstretched arms as he attempted to keep his balance. There was nothing for him to hold on to up there.

"Rhody, get down from there!" Iggy screamed. "You're scaring me!" Her voice cracked with emotion.

One of their friends—Juniper, maybe—put his hand on Iggy's shoulder.

"He'll be okay," he said. "I've jumped from the top beam before. The river is high right now, so he probably won't even hit bottom. He'll have to swim until he reaches the riverbank further downstream." He pointed to a spot in the distance. "Should we head over there?"

Iggy didn't answer. She stood there, whimpering.

"Calm down!" Rae heard herself say. "You're not helping anyone."

"B-b-but he can't swim!"

Juniper's eyes got big. "Oh shit," he said.

All of a sudden, Simon ran toward the bridge. "I'll get him!" he yelled.

Rae felt bad for scolding Iggy and she grabbed her hand while they watched Simon climb to the deck of the bridge and scale the same diagonal beam to the top. Iggy shifted her weight from one foot to the other anxiously.

When he realized Simon was coming toward him, Rhody raised his arms over his head and started hopping on the narrow beam.

"Look at me! Look at me! Look at me!" he giggled.

Rae held her breath. If he fell now, he would probably smack his head on one of the steel beams as he dropped to the water below.

Iggy screamed in her ear, "Stop it, Rhody! Please stop!"

Simon paused where he was on the diagonal beam, just a few feet from the top, and held his hand out like a crossing guard. "Please don't do that," he said. "You're scaring me."

Rhody ignored him as he hopped back and forth on the beam, his face crumpling into tears.

Simon was pulling himself to the top beam when the truck headlights that had been shining on the bridge all night suddenly turned off. Everything was thrust into darkness.

"Hey!" Iggy yelled at the owner of the truck. "Turn the lights back on!"

"My battery died!" a male voice called back, frantic. "Someone else turn theirs on!"

The silence of the somber crowd was broken as everyone started looking for their keys at the same time. Juniper started running down the riverbank and a group of people ran after him. Everyone was mobilizing—everyone but Rae and Iggy.

They were both frozen on the trail, unable to tear their eyes away from the bridge. Rae gripped Iggy's hand tighter and strained her eyes, trying to find the two moving shapes on the bridge. She thought she saw Simon pull himself up on the top beam. She thought she saw him reach out to Rhody.

"Give me your hand," she heard him say.

"Get the fuck away from me!" Rhody yelled. "Get away!"

"Jesus Christ!" Simon yelled. "Give me your hand!"

Multiple cars started their engines at the same time and the bridge was suddenly flooded in headlights beaming from three different directions. Everyone realized at the same time that Simon was standing alone on top of the bridge, staring into the water with a strange expression on his face.

Everyone gasped.

Rae's eyes dropped to the river as Rhody's head bobbed out of the water and quickly sank back under again. Before she consciously decided what she was going to do, she dropped Iggy's hand and ran to the riverbank. She unlaced her shoes and kicked them off, unzipped her hoodie, pulled off her socks and Iggy's stupid black beret, and threw everything on the ground. As she ran into the weeds at the edge of the water, she felt the soft, slimy mud squish between her toes before she dove headfirst into the glassy, black river.

The whole time, it was like she was watching someone else do these things.

The shock of cold water put her right back into her own body. The river current was much faster than she'd anticipated, and she was already yards away from the campground when her head emerged. Paddling her arms and kicking her legs to stay afloat, she spun around and around in the dark water, looking for

Rhody. At last, she spotted him by the hardware on his wet leather jacket as it glittered in the moonlight a few yards ahead of her.

She took a deep breath and lowered her face into the water, using her arms to propel her as she kicked from the hips in her best front crawl. Glancing up intermittently to keep her eyes on Rhody, she watched him get knocked back and forth between rocks in the growing rapids, his black hair plastered across his face and his dark eyes gaping in the moonlight.

She took another deep breath and dragged her arms as fast as she could through the water, willing herself to close the gap between them as she watched his head go under one more time. Her heart sang when she realized the extra effort was paying off and she would be within arm's length of him in one or two more strokes.

As she reached out to grab the back of Rhody's jacket, pain shot down the base of her skull and she slammed into a large, flat rock that seemed to emerge out of nowhere in the middle of the river, right in front of her.

She crashed into the rock with her chest first and the impact nearly knocked the air out of her. It was all she could do to grab onto the rock and breathe, and it took her a second to realize she was pinned there by the pressure of the water as it flowed around the rock and back onto itself. The whirlpool it created wanted to take her down with it, forcing her to switch her mental focus from saving Rhody to saving herself.

She tightened her grip on the black rock and struggled to keep her head above the water that rushed around her face. But her nose kept sinking beneath the waterline and she was swallowing large quantities of the nasty stuff, probably teeming with E. coli from cows and dogs and maybe some people too. If she didn't die right here and now, she was going to have a bad case of diarrhea later.

Right when she was sure she was about to pass out from lack of oxygen, someone grabbed her belt from behind and yanked her out of the whirlpool, shoving her forcefully into the flow of water on the other side of the rock. As her arms and legs twisted like a rubber doll's in the turbid water, this same person hooked their arm underneath her armpit and across her chest. Kicking his legs furiously in a lifesaving backstroke, he began to tow her to the riverbank.

"Relax," he yelled in her ear.

She let her body go limp and allowed herself to be hauled to shore. As soon as her feet touched the rocks and weeds in the shallows, she balanced herself on her trembling legs, pushed the hair out of her face, and saw that it was Simon walking beside her, one arm around her shoulders as he guided her up the riverbank.

Once on shore, she fell on her hands and knees and coughed up water until she could breathe normally again. She turned over and collapsed on the ground and let the tears stream down her face.

"Get up!" Simon said, grabbing her by both arms and pulling. She lay there like dead weight until he dropped her arms. "There's no time for this!" he pleaded. "We have to find Rhody."

But she knew.

He had already seemed nearly dead as he'd spun in the river, his eyes staring out, unblinking like a ghost. She had thought that if she could get ahold of him and somehow pull him to shore, she could try to administer CPR and mouth-to-mouth resuscitation, and he might be okay. But not now. They would never catch up to him in time. His head had kept dipping under the water. Unless the current dragged him to the side of the river and he got stuck in a bunch of river grass, his lifeless body would keep moving with the current all the way to the Gulf of Mexico.

"Please," Simon begged her.

She opened her eyes and looked up at him. There were a million stars twinkling in the sky around his head and he, too, was crying.

Never in her life had she felt so tired and defeated. Every muscle in her body quivered and ached. All she wanted to do was lie in the dirt and not think. But he wasn't ready to accept what had happened yet. She held out her hand to his.

"You saved my life," she said.

He didn't respond to her, just turned toward the canyon road.

They walked in silence along the winding dirt road as they scanned the riverbank for movement, but they were both barefoot and visibility was not good.

Rhody had looked so miserable at the dance circle, and she had been so desperate to get away from him. It was obvious he'd wanted to talk about something. Maybe she could have helped him. She could still see the hurt in his eyes as she backed away from him.

The memory made her sick to her stomach, and she bent over and puked up what remained of the protein bar in a sagebrush on the side of the road.

"This is taking too long," Simon said when she finished puking. "We have to get search and rescue down here. Did you guys drive?"

She nodded.

"Let's go back, then."

As they walked back toward the bridge, she knew, with complete certainty, that Rhody would never be found alive. For the first time in her life, she finally understood why her mother was so broken.

CHAPTER EIGHTEEN

Everyone was gone by the time they got back to the campsite—everyone but Iggy. Her big, ugly car was the only one left on the side of the road, and even though she didn't answer when Rae called her name, she found her right where she had left her at the edge of the river, curled up in the mud like a baby otter.

Rae collapsed next to her in a heap while Simon searched for his shoes. The moon was high in the sky now. She lay there, watching the rise and fall of Iggy's chest as she listened to the soft hooting of an owl in a nearby tree. She heard other sounds, too, the rustling of leaves and mysterious living things creeping along the riverbank. Her normal self would have been terrified, sitting outside in the dark in the middle of nowhere. She would have imagined hungry bears and ferocious mountain lions crouching in the dark, waiting for the right moment to pounce on her and Iggy and tear them limb from limb.

Instead, she felt weirdly calm and resigned to whatever might happen now. Let the wild things come and devour her. The worst had already happened.

She dozed off for a second and dreamed she was camping in a big blue tent with her mom and dad. In the dream, she was so small, she had to grab a fistful of her dad's pant leg to pull herself up from the ground.

Suddenly, Simon broke into her dream, standing above her. Cold droplets of water fell from his hair onto her face.

"Where is everyone?" he asked Iggy.

"They went to get help," she answered, her voice muffled from having her face pressed into a damp patch of river grass.

"We should go too," he said. He had taken off his clothes and was wringing water out of his wet jeans with both hands.

"No," Iggy said. "I won't leave. I'll wait for him here."

"Iggy," he said, crouching beside her and putting his hand on her shoulder. "If Rhody can't swim, chances are—"

"Shut up!" she yelled, sitting up. Her face was caked with smeared eyeliner and mud. "I'm staying here."

Simon shook his head and sighed.

"Why didn't you jump in after him?" she demanded.

He stood up and took two startled steps backward. "I . . . I was afraid of the river," he confessed, looking down at his bare feet.

"But you had no problem jumping in after *her*," Iggy sneered, gesturing at Rae.

Simon turned and walked toward the car.

"Justin said you pushed him off the bridge!" Iggy screamed after him.

Shocked, Rae grabbed Iggy's arm. "Why would you even say that?"

"Because it's true. I heard Justin say it. Simon climbed up to the bridge and the lights went out and the next thing we knew, Rhody was in the water."

Simon turned and walked back to them. Rae thought he might yell at Iggy and tell her how crazy she was, but he just sat across from them cross-legged and rested his hands on his bare knees. He was holding his pants and shirt and was naked except for his boxers.

Even in the moonlight, Rae could see that his nipples were hard from swimming in the cold water.

"I didn't push him in the river," he said. "I was trying to help him."

"Then did he jump on purpose?" Iggy asked. Tears were streaming down her face again, leaving fresh tracks in the mud.

"The lights went out right before he went in the water," Rae reminded her. "Nobody knows what happened."

"It's my fault," Iggy cried, burying her face in her hands. "He's been acting so weird, and I blew him off tonight. I should have tried harder to figure out what his deal was. I shouldn't have been so mean to him. How can I live with myself if we don't find him?"

She was crying uncontrollably, her face covered with snot and tears. Rae took both of her hands in hers and held them.

Simon slumped over and hung his head. The wet strands of his long hair gleamed in the moonlight.

"I have to get out of here," he said.

"Shouldn't we wait for the cops?" Rae asked.

"No, I mean, out of *here*. Out of Taos. I'm eighteen. They could send me to prison."

"But you didn't do anything!" Rae exclaimed.

"It doesn't matter. I'm a Native. They'll lock me up."

"That will never happen," Rae replied. "We were all here. We all witnessed the same thing."

"Don't be too sure about that. You said yourself that the lights went out right before he went in. Justin is going to say that I pushed him and Rhody's parents will want to believe him. They're rich white people—they'll make sure I go to jail. And I have a record."

"Like, a criminal record?" Rae asked. "What did you do?"

"It doesn't matter," he said, standing and brushing the dirt from his backside. "Can you give me a ride home?" he asked Iggy.

"I want to go with you," Iggy said, standing quickly. "I can't stay here now."

"No, no! This is crazy," Rae insisted. "You guys aren't thinking straight."

They ignored her and stared at each other, wild-eyed, brains spinning out with possibilities.

"You can come if you want," Simon said finally. "I don't care."

"Wait!" Rae yelled, panicked. "If you run away without clearing your name first, everyone will assume you *did* push him! You'll never be able to come back."

He shrugged.

"What about your music, though? How can you play in a band if you're a fugitive?"

"Nobody knows me in California. I'll change my name. I'll become someone else."

It occurred to Rae that it actually *would* be possible to become someone else in 1984. Simon and Iggy didn't have to worry about cell phones with built-in GPS or closed-circuit cameras on every corner, tracking their every move. They didn't have to worry about social media accounts cataloging and quantifying their every meal, every outfit, every change of mood.

"I'll help you," Iggy begged him. "I'll help you find gigs and I'll . . . I'll cook for you."

He didn't respond to her, just pulled on his damp jeans and T-shirt and started walking to the car. Rae wondered what had happened to his flannel shirt.

Animated by her new plan, Iggy gathered her bag, shoes, and hat from the riverbank and followed Simon to the car.

Rae sat there, listening to the river in a daze.

"Hey, come on!" Simon yelled at her. Iggy was standing at his side by the car.

Weird how together they seemed now.

"Let's book!" he yelled again, growing impatient.

She stood and found her shoes, socks, and hoodie where she had stripped them off and dove in the river to rescue Rhody. She shook the dirt out of her hoodie and dumped the sand out of her shoes before putting them back on, then looked around at everything one more time.

Empty beer cans, cigarette butts, and bits of trash littered the riverbank. Sandals, towels, and blankets were strewn everywhere. Justin had left behind his cooler. A bottle of tequila lay half buried in the dirt, and a few remaining embers glowed in the fire pit. Her big rock was a shadow in the distance. When she squinted, she saw the outline of where she and Simon had sat together, glowing violet.

She looked at the bridge last.

She, Iggy, and Simon would drive away in a few minutes. The trash would be removed by the end of the day. Someone would eventually find Rhody's body washed up on the riverbank or marooned on a rock and they would call his parents, who would take him to a funeral home, where his body would be prepared for burial. And the bridge would be here the whole time, an inanimate witness to every setting sun and rising moon.

Ignoring the calls of Iggy and Simon, she stood under the bridge with her eyes closed until she was sure she had memorized every detail of the ancient canyon and the steel beams and the way the moon reflected off the changing river.

She had to remember this. She had to remember what it looked like the night the whole world changed.

It wasn't until she'd crawled into the green monster and laid in the back seat that she felt the itinerary case digging into her stomach and realized she had jumped into the water with the belt on. Beads of panicky sweat immediately sprang up on her forehead as she pulled up her damp shirt and checked the LED display.

It was black and dead, no longer counting down the time. Black and dead like her heart.

There was nothing she could do now but see where the road took her. She was too tired to worry.

Iggy sat in the front seat while Simon drove. He was a much better driver than Iggy, and Rae was almost asleep when Iggy put a tape into the cassette player and fast-forwarded to a hyper song with a techno beat that didn't fit the mood at all. But Iggy turned up the volume and whimpered when the guy started singing. The lyrics barely penetrated Rae's consciousness. Just a faraway man asking *How do I feel?* over and over again.

She dreamed she was a baby again, buckled into a car seat in the back of her parents' car while her mom and dad sat in silence in the front seat. Her hands were crammed into thick mittens and she couldn't uncurl her fingers. She strained against the restrictive pressure of the seat belt across her chest before giving up with a sniffle. The car was silent except for the sound of the wind howling outside her window. Why weren't they talking? Where were they going?

She woke up with an intense feeling of dread and sat up abruptly. The thin, grey light of dawn was creeping over everything. Simon had parked the car outside of Scum House and she was back in her teenage body again, with a pounding headache and a dry mouth. The world she'd inhabited as a baby lingered for a minute like a thin membrane stretched over this one before it dissolved completely into whatever part of the brain memories of dreams existed.

"We're here," Simon said, his voice flat and emotionless. He slammed the car door and went inside the house.

Iggy sat up in the front seat and rubbed her eyes as if she, too, had been dreaming. She must have remembered what was real because a painful moan escaped her throat as soon as she opened her eyes and saw Rae watching her.

Rae got out of the car, opened the passenger side door for her, and held her hand as they followed Simon inside.

Scum House had been gross when she'd been here a few weeks ago, but now it looked like the "before" picture on an advertisement for a crime scene cleanup company. An industrial-sized trash bag leaking cigarette butts and empty booze bottles sat in the middle of the living room floor with a swarm of fat flies buzzing above it. There were people passed out everywhere, a tangled mass of pale arms, spiked hair, stained jeans, and boots lying motionless on top of cigarette-scarred couch cushions spread across the sticky floor if they were lucky, or on a bed of crushed beer cans and wet trash if they were not. No one moved when they entered the house, and Rae wondered how they could sleep so soundly with no covers and all the overhead lights on. The scary punk rockers looked so vulnerable right now.

Simon stepped over the bodies on his way to the kitchen, accidentally kicking one of them in the head. A black-haired girl groaned out loud and turned over, but she didn't wake up.

Rae heard him open the fridge and pop open a can of beer before disappearing down the hallway.

She and Iggy leaned on one of the walls in the living room while they waited, not making conversation. It wasn't awkward. They were too tired and too fucked up to talk. There was nothing to say.

Iggy slid down the wall slowly and curled up in a ball next to one of the anonymous, sprawled bodies before resting her head on a crusty corner of cushion. She started snoring almost immediately.

Rae tiptoed around the house and tried to distract herself from thoughts of Rhody and whether she was stuck in 1984 forever by surveying the punk-rock posters and flyers taped up all over the dirty walls.

One poster that particularly disturbed her was for the band Dead Kennedys. It showed the head of a man with barbed wire wrapped around his mouth, floating above a bunch of dead, emaciated bodies. The man's head was an illustration, but the dead bodies looked like an actual photograph. *Officer Smiley says welcome to 1984*, the poster read. Rae shuddered.

Another huge poster in the hallway had a big black cross with the red, universal no sign slashing through it. None of the posters or flyers were aesthetically pleasing. None of them made her feel good. They were all ugly with disturbing imagery: skulls and skeletons, bloody knives and zombie nuns, crying children, guns, upside-down crosses. The band names were creepy, too—Meat Puppets, the Cramps, Black Flag, Suicidal Tendencies, Bad Brains, Social Distortion, Millions of Dead Cops.

She understood the message against conformity, but why all the death imagery?

Rae wandered into the filthy kitchen and noticed a Liquid Squid flyer stuck to the refrigerator door with a toilet-shaped magnet from a local plumber. The flyer had their logo—a line drawing of a squid being blended alive—and a big black-and-white photograph of a shirtless Simon screaming into a microphone, his long hair captured mid-flip with droplets of sweat frozen in a crazy halo around his angry, howling face. The photo perfectly captured the part of Simon's personality that slammed doors and threw banana peels on the ground and kicked his friends in the head and didn't even seem to care that Rhody was dead, other than how it affected him. The same Simon who was in his room right now, drinking beer for breakfast.

The beer-for-breakfast Simon seemed like a totally different person than the Simon she had sat next to on the rock, the Simon who'd offered to share his banana with her and smelled like cedar and talked about his grandma and the moon and made her wonder what it would feel like to be a member of the Navajo Nation.

She had to admit she had a really big crush on the second Simon, and she felt shitty about that. But if Iggy was in love with the rude, angry Simon, was it really that much of a betrayal?

She took the flyer off the fridge, folded it into quarters, and put it in her back pocket as Simon passed the kitchen on his way back to the living room, wearing a fresh T-shirt and a red JanSport backpack slung over his left shoulder.

Rae walked back into the living room and stood facing him, arms crossed, staring him down, waiting for him to show some sign in his eyes or body language that he remembered how close they had been to one another last night, before everything went to hell. But he wouldn't look at her.

"Let's motor," he said.

Iggy sat up as if she had an antenna jammed in her brain that was tuned to him and him alone.

"I need to get some things from my house," she said.

Simon nodded.

It was impossible for Rae to accept that she had reached the canon event in her mother's life—the crucial decision to run away from home was being made right in front of her, and there was nothing she could do to stop it.

"Do you really want to leave Taos?" she asked, trying to sound calm and persuasive and in no way reveal the panic and desperation she felt inside. "Don't you at least want to finish high school? And what about your sister and brother? Won't they miss you?"

"They won't even notice I'm gone." Iggy sniffed.

"That's *so* not true! I saw the way they look at you. And your mom needs you too. I know you have issues with her, but—"

Before she could finish her thought, Simon walked out of the house and let the screen door slam behind him. Iggy followed behind him like a puppy.

One of the girls on the floor opened her eyes and stared up at Rae.

"Hey, man, you got a cigarette?" she asked.

Rae shook her head and walked outside to the station wagon, where they were waiting for her. What else could she do? Curl up with the crew at Scum House?

Simon had parked right beside the old school bus, and as she opened the car door to get back inside the green monster, she stopped and really looked at the bus for the first time.

Damn, was it ugly. The original yellow had been painted over with a coat of dull gray that may have looked okay at one point but was now peeling off in strips. The tires were all either bald or flat, and some of the windows were cracked or missing altogether. Mice and spiders and who-knew-what-else were probably living inside. This piece of crap didn't stand a chance of making it out of the driveway, much less all the way to California.

All Simon's talk of touring with his band had been a bunch of phony bullshit. Was this why he had agreed to let Iggy tag along with him? Was he going to let her throw away her whole life away just so he could catch a ride to California?

Rae crawled into the station wagon and stared at the back of Iggy's head.

"So you're going to steal your mom's car?" she asked.

Iggy didn't even turn around to look at her.

Simon turned the key in the ignition, which coughed and banged before it eventually started. He put his right arm behind Iggy's seat as he turned to look at Rae with those infinity pools of liquid wood, eyes that had once peered right into her soul and now seemed snuffed out and cold.

"Where are we taking you?" he asked.

Chapter Nineteen

Rae had secretly thought she was going to end up going to California with Iggy and Simon until he turned and asked her where she wanted to be dropped off. As miserable and dysfunctional as their road trip was bound to become, it had to be better than staying here, stuck in Taos in 1984. The only other option would be to find her great-grandpa and ask for his help getting home. But how, without Iggy's help?

"Hey, didn't you say your grandpa might have some medicinal herbs for my grandma?" she asked the back of Iggy's head.

Iggy found her eyes in the rearview mirror and gave her a look like she was completely clueless, like they were living in two separate realities. In Iggy's reality, medicinal herbs and stomach problems and grandmas and grandpas meant next to nothing.

She distracted herself from the panic spider hatching eggs in her stomach by counting the little hairs on the back of Iggy's neck. She was slouched over in the front seat like she was trying to be smaller than she really was, all folded in on herself. She kept glancing up at Simon like she was looking for a reaction or trying to figure out what he was thinking, smiling nervously to herself.

Rae had to do something. She had to reach over and shake Iggy's shoulders or scream at the top of her lungs or maybe even insist that she was going with them to California.

Before she could decide on any of these things, the pain in her stomach became almost unbearable, and she hid her face in her hands so they wouldn't see what she was feeling. The further south they drove, the more excruciating the pain became until she was biting on the palm of her hand to keep from groaning out loud.

Simon slowed the car and pulled over at one of the last gas stations on the way out of Taos, a beat-down Allsup's with four ancient-looking gas pumps and a handwritten sign on the glass door that read *no shoes, no shirt, no service.*

Rae's stomach pain immediately vanished.

Simon got out of the car and pulled coins and crumpled-up bills out of his jean pockets, silently counting the money while Iggy and Rae looked on.

"Twenty-five dollars and eighty-five cents," he announced. "This will get us breakfast, a road map, and a tank of gas. After that . . . I don't know."

Rae was shocked. Did he really think they were going to make it all the way to California with twenty-five bucks? Where would they stay? What would they do if they ran out of gas? How would they eat? Was he planning on robbing gas stations or something?

"I have money," Rae said, surprising herself.

Simon and Iggy watched as Rae opened the small pocket of her backpack and reluctantly pulled out her emergency stash.

"This is a hundred dollars," she said, handing the roll of cash to Iggy, whose mouth dropped open.

"Why are you helping me?" Iggy asked. "I didn't think you approved."

"I don't. Actually, I think it's the worst idea I've ever heard. But if I can't stop you, I don't want you to starve to death."

"Thank you," Iggy said, tearing up.

"Then let's gas up and blow this popsicle stand!" Simon sprinted inside.

Iggy and Rae stared at each other. Dried mud and tear tracks covered Iggy's face, which was plump the way a child's face was plump, flush with the collagen and elastin she was always lamenting nowadays. Rae could see how young she was, and how naïve and ignorant she was to the life that lay ahead of her. Iggy didn't have a laptop or a cell phone or even a TV. Rae wondered how much she knew about boys and sex and the world. She wanted to give her some advice that would make her life easier, but the truth was that she didn't know a damn thing either.

"You don't understand why I'm leaving," Iggy said.

"Not really."

"You were right when you said Rhody was my only friend. How can I stay here after what happened? I should have taken better care of him. It's my fault he's gone."

"It isn't your fault. You didn't push him off the bridge."

Iggy buried her face in her hands. "It's not just Rhody. I hate who I am here. I don't like who people think I am. Every day, I'm acting out a part in a play that someone else wrote for me. Maybe out there"—she pointed to the open road—"I can be someone else. Someone better."

"But you're only sixteen," Rae protested. "You can make positive changes right now." She held up her hand and ticked off the essential building blocks of a healthy lifestyle. "Mind your micros and macros, get eight hours of sleep every night, exercise regularly, and drink more water. Stop partying all the time and do your homework. Make a plan for what you want your life to be like in five years, and then figure out what steps will get you there—"

"*Drink more water*? Jesus Christ, you're such a guidance counselor." Iggy shook her head and turned away in disgust.

Simon opened the car door and tossed a brown paper bag and a folded road map onto Iggy's lap.

"Burritos," he said, then turned to pump the gas.

The nauseating smell of mystery meat filled the car. Iggy took two greasy burritos wrapped in white paper out of the bag and offered one to Rae.

"No thanks. I'm a vegetarian."

"Yeah, me too," Iggy said, taking a bite.

Simon got back in the car and ate his burrito with one hand while unfolding the enormous road map with the other.

"It looks like we'll be passing right through Albuquerque. Are you catching a ride with us?" He turned and stared through Rae, unblinking.

"No," Rae replied. "I guess I'll get out here." She opened the car door.

Simon nodded and started the engine. Iggy got out of the car to hug her.

"It's so weird," she said. "I just met you, but I feel like I've known you forever. And I have this really strong feeling that I'll see you again."

Rae laughed and cried into her shoulder, hugging her as tight as she could. She smelled like the river.

"Maybe you can come visit us in California after we get it all figured out."

"Yeah, sure."

"Okay, well, bye." Iggy walked backward to the car, grinning at her.

Rae hooked her backpack over her shoulder as she watched them drive away, Iggy leaning back over the front seat to wave at her and Simon staring straight ahead. She watched them until the station wagon became a dot on the horizon and then disappeared.

Which way should she go now? Her stomach had stopped hurting as soon as Simon pulled the car over because something wanted her to get out. Something didn't want her to leave Taos like this, in a busted-up Town & Country.

Apparently, her stomach was a kind of compass that could direct her which way to go if she listened to it.

Facing south, her stomach felt calm and settled. She turned around one hundred and eighty degrees until she was facing the magical mountain and the beautiful town of Taos smeared across the horizon, and it suddenly felt like there were a bunch of trolls inside her stomach, punching to get out. She turned around again and started walking along the same highway that had swallowed up Iggy and Simon.

South it was.

Chapter Twenty

Northern New Mexico in the morning was almost beautiful enough to make Rae forget about her problems. The air was ripe with the smells of nature, and the slate-blue mountain ranges on all sides of her were like bowling-lane bumpers preventing her from flying off into pure, clean, infinite space. The clouds drifting above were so perfectly puffy and stereotypically cloudlike, she felt like she was walking through a *Looney Tunes* cartoon, complete with happy birds singing to each other from tree to tree.

Still, she couldn't stop thinking about Rhody as she walked alone on the shoulder of the highway. Was she the last person he'd talked to before he jumped or fell or whatever it was? She thought of what her grandma had said about changing the past. It was not possible. Nothing she could have said or done would have prevented him from dying the way he did.

She kept telling herself this, but she didn't really believe it.

And then there was death itself. It didn't make any sense when you really thought about it. How could someone be alive one minute and dead the next? How could life stop like that? Where had he gone?

The sound of gravel crunching beneath slow-moving tires pulled her out of her thoughts, and she turned to see a light blue Toyota truck inching along the shoulder of the road a few yards behind her. Using her hand to shield her eyes from the sun, she tried to get a better look at the old man driving.

He stopped the truck next to her and rolled down his car window. "Do you want a ride, Andrea?"

"How do you know my name?" she asked, approaching the truck slowly. It was broad daylight and there were people and cars everywhere, so he probably wasn't going to jump out and kidnap her. Just in case, she kept more than an arm's length away from the truck as she studied his face.

"Don't you recognize me?" he asked. He wore his salt-and-pepper hair in a long braid underneath his yellow trucker cap, and he had weathered skin with lots of wrinkles around his warm, brown eyes.

"No," she replied. He did seem kind of familiar, though, in the way a movie you forgot you'd already watched was familiar the second time around.

"I'm your great-grandpa Ignacio. People call me Nacho."

Staring straight into the eyes she now recognized from her grandma's old photographs, she accepted her great-grandpa's calloused hand when he stuck it out of his car window and shook it enthusiastically. He looked as native to his surroundings as a piñon tree. He wore a chambray shirt, a turquoise ring on his finger, and a sterling-silver, cuff-style watchband. His words had a slightly accented, musical quality to them.

"I'm Rae," she said.

"We've met before," he said. "But that's in your future, so you might not remember."

"How could I remember something that happens in the future?" She laughed.

He grinned and leaned over to open the passenger door. "Hop in," he said.

She moved around the front of the truck and climbed in beside him. The seats and cab of the truck were worn-down but tidy. A small dream catcher woven with beads and owl feathers hung from the rearview mirror, and a paper bag of groceries leaned on the seat between them. Rae peeked inside and her mouth watered when she saw apples, dried figs, and barbeque-flavored potato chips, along with a quart of orange juice in a glass bottle.

"Are you hungry?" Nacho asked, pulling back onto the highway.

"My body is literally feeding on itself."

"Please eat, mija! It's all for you."

Rae put the paper sack in her lap and opened the bottle of cold orange juice, guzzling half its contents before she opened the bag of chips. They were delicious, especially when she alternated mouthfuls with the sweet, sticky figs.

Feeling much better after her snack, she turned her attention to what was happening outside her window.

Nacho had turned off the highway onto a narrower paved road and, from there, onto a bumpy dirt road that branched off on both sides to multiple dirt driveways, which led to adobe homes of various sizes squatting on large plots of raw, unmanicured land. In front of these houses, Rae saw old cars on cinder blocks, broken bicycles, wild sunflowers, and clotheslines hung with bedsheets billowing in the breeze. She also saw potted flowers, skinny dogs running free without collars, vegetable gardens, and gnarled apricot trees. Behind the houses, miles of cactus and sagebrush stretched across the rolling terrain all the way to the foothills.

Her great-grandpa veered down one of the longest driveways, slowing as they approached a tiny house in the middle of a big patch of dirt next to a rickety shed made out of plywood and chicken wire. As they neared, Rae realized the structure was, in fact, a chicken coop, though most of its inhabitants were huddled around the front porch of the small house, clucking and pecking anxiously for something to eat among the dirt and debris.

Nacho stopped the truck and ran out to shoo the chickens back into their coop, and Rae jumped out, too, to help him round up the angry birds, who ran in circles, flapping their wings and squawking in protest before they gave up and scurried back into their dusty pen. A big, grumpy-looking rooster waited for them, strutting back and forth across his little yard.

"I don't know how these gallinas keep getting out," Nacho said, latching the coop door. "They must be flying out over the fence." He scratched his head and wiped the sweat off his brow, then opened the door to his house, which wasn't even locked.

They stepped into a tiny kitchen with a small table and two chairs next to a potbelly stove that had a metal teapot resting on top.

Rae placed her bag of food on the table and walked over to the wooden shelves that lined one wall of the kitchen, which held a vast collection of mismatched glass-and-metal storage containers from the ground all the way up to the mud ceiling. The containers were filled with nuts, seeds, dried herbs, and spices that made all other collections of foodstuff Rae had ever seen in her life seem miniscule in comparison. The jars must have contained nearly every herb, root, and spice that had ever grown on planet Earth, each one labeled in cursive with black marker on strips of masking tape with names she recognized—echinacea, yerba mate, comfrey, calendula, mistletoe, goldenseal—as well as hundreds of other names that weren't familiar to her. Names like feverfew, mugwort, monkshood, even a root called false unicorn, and some with Spanish names like *sangregado* and *curcuma*. Plus, there were dozens of varieties of dried mushrooms and gnarled roots and rhizomes; as well as oils and nut butters and herbal teas; a slew of tins and pots and jars filled with prepared potions, powders, and pastes; and creams, ointments; and tinctures. The kitchen smelled like the herb store in Albuquerque her grandma would visit whenever she came down with a cold or an ache or when she needed to replenish her incense stash. Rae closed her eyes and inhaled the clean, comforting aroma.

"Wow," she said. "You really are a curandero."

"Sí, a yerbero. Among other things." He gave her a sly smile and opened the stove door with a metal poker, then added a piece of wood from a willow basket on the floor. "Cup of tea?" he asked, moving the teapot from the back of the stove to the middle.

"Yes, please."

Nacho rubbed his chin and studied her for a minute before selecting several jars from the sprawling wall of remedies. "Black maca root, ginseng, and rosemary," he said, naming each herb as he pulled it off the shelf. "You need stamina."

While her great-grandpa spooned the powders and leaves into a tea ball, Rae looked around his tiny home. It was made from adobe like a lot of New Mexican homes were, but the adobe bricks in his house looked like what they were—bricks of sun-dried earth, straw, and water. Adobe was one of the earliest building materials humans had developed, probably after studying the nests potter wasps make out of regurgitated soil and water. Rae knew adobe bricks were supposed to keep homes warm in the winter and cool in the summer. Considering Nacho had a fire going in June, it wasn't too bad in here.

The entire house consisted of the tiny kitchen and a small bedroom separated by a red curtain tied open with a piece of leather, so Rae could see right into her grandpa's private space. His bedroom was dominated by an old roll-up writing desk that reminded her of her grandma's writing desk, cluttered with papers and pens and art supplies. Besides a ladder-back chair, the only other piece of furniture in the room was a single mattress right on the floor, covered with a thin, yellow blanket and a small, stained pillow. A pair of shearling-lined slippers sat at the foot of the bed.

Just the two rooms, that was it. She wondered where the bathroom was.

"I use an outhouse," Nacho said as if he could read her mind. He handed her a ceramic mug. "Sit and drink this. But first, give me your belt."

Rae unbuckled the travel belt and passed it to Nacho, who crossed to his desk and sat down. As she watched him take apart the silver itinerary case with a screwdriver, she sipped fragrant tea from a speckled, blue mug with a chip in the rim that rubbed against her bottom lip. As her belly grew warm, she was flooded with the now-familiar sensation of being in two places at the same time.

She was still standing in Nacho's house, but she was somehow also in her grandma's kitchen back home. The silhouette of her grandma standing in front of her sink doing dishes, sunlight pouring through the gauzy, yellow curtains, was superimposed on the shape of Nacho as he worked on the belt. The image of her grandma wavered and radiated like a mirage, and as Rae reached out to touch her, her grandma turned to look at her. For a second, Rae was sure she was back in Albuquerque. But when she looked down at the mug in her hands, her grandma disappeared and she was back in the adobe kitchen again, and her grandpa was staring at her.

"What happened?" he asked.

As the warmth of the mug penetrated her fingers, she realized that this was the same blue mug she used to drink tea from when she was a little girl visiting her grandma. It had the same tiny chip on the rim and the same fine cracks in the glaze as the one she had dropped on the floor and smashed into a dozen pieces when she was just four years old. She could still remember how the hot tea had burned her when it splashed off the floor, and how her grandma had held her legs under cold running water and told her everything would be okay. Rae couldn't understand why her grandma had cried, then, while she mopped up the tea and swept up the broken shards of pottery.

"Do you know that mug?" her grandpa asked.

She nodded her head and stared at him, her heart pounding.

"Don't be scared," he said. "You're just time tripping."

"Time tripping?"

"Moving through time out of order. Certain sounds or objects can trigger it. Didn't your grandma warn you?"

Rae shook her head. "She told me about the belt and the cards, and the life paths and how they work and stuff, but not about time tripping."

"Always in a hurry." Her grandpa frowned. He put the case down for a moment and pulled something from the old Irish oats can on his desk. "She wants this," he said, handing her a shiny travel card with her grandma's face on it.

Rae hadn't even given him the letter yet! How had he known?

Her grandma's face was painted on the card in a swirl of green and yellow, surrounded by a border of ostrich feathers. She looked younger in the portrait than the grandma Rae was familiar with, but older than the 1984 version. Her gray-streaked hair was pulled back in one thick braid, and though her expression was serious, Rae recognized the hint of a mischievous smile hiding in her curled lip.

While she studied the card, her grandpa rummaged inside one of his desk drawers. When he found what he was looking for, he used long tweezers to replace something inside the silver itinerary case before screwing the cover back in place. The LED numbers on the display case flashed three times and immediately resumed their countdown.

Eighteen minutes left in 1984. Rae breathed a sigh of relief as she secured the belt around her waist.

"Did she tell you the case and travel cards are meant for beginners?" Nacho sighed. "We make them for young people like you who are just figuring out how to skim time. Eventually, you'll learn to travel to other dimensions without having to take this with you." He reached over and grabbed her shoulder, digging his thumb and forefinger into her flesh.

"B-but then why does Grandma need another travel card?"

"She uses those cards as a crutch. She's like a kid who learned to ride a bike with training wheels and is afraid to take them off." He shook his head. "She isn't a very serious person."

"That's not true!" Rae protested. "She gave me lots of warnings about time travel."

"Your abuela uses time travel as an escape from her everyday life. She might as well be on a cruise ship to the Bahamas for all it's worth! Since her very first trip, she's only been in it for her own pleasure." He paused and bit his lower lip, and his whole face grew sad. "It's my fault, really. She was my first child, and I waited for years to share our ancestry with her. I grew impatient. I thought, What harm could it do to teach her a little early? She was such a clever girl. So when she was twelve years old, I took her on her first trip. I let her choose a destination card all by herself, and the two of us went together. Her mom—your great-grandma Conchita—was furious when she found out! And she was right to be so angry with me. I should have waited until Lydia was of age or at least taken her someplace educational, a place where she would see how people lived and suffered in other parts of the continuum. Instead, do you know where we went? Hersheypark, Pennsylvania, in 1923. An amusement park! All she wanted to do was lollygag in the penny arcade and ride the new roller coaster over and over again. And eat chocolate, of course." Nacho rubbed his temples with both hands. "She's such a hedonista. What a waste."

"But that sounds fun!" Rae exclaimed. "What's wrong with having fun?"

"This pilgrimage we're on is not about having fun!" He pounded the table with his fists. "Nightclubs, beaches, amusement parks! These are not the places for our people."

"Where, then?" Rae asked.

"Wherever it is that you will learn what you need to learn," he replied. "Which is usually your own boring life, wherever that may be. Not some beach in Hawaii."

Rae considered this. "There's nothing to learn in Hawaii?" she asked.

His face flushed red. "Not with your head in the sand on the beach in Waikiki, there isn't!"

Rae immediately regretted teasing him. He was her grandpa, after all, and she wanted him to be proud of her. But it pissed her off to hear him talking about her grandma as if something was wrong with her. Rae's grandma was a queen! She was one of the wisest and most interesting people she had ever met. It seemed like Nacho didn't even know his own daughter.

The awkward silence made her want to squirm. She avoided eye contact with Nacho and took sip after sip of her tea until there was nothing left but leaves at the bottom of the cup.

"More tea?" he asked.

"No, thank you. I feel better."

"I'm sorry I lost my temper," he said.

"I'm sorry I was rude."

They smiled at each other.

"How much time do you have left?"

She consulted the itinerary case. "Less than five minutes."

"Are you ready to go home?"

"I . . . guess."

Her trip hadn't accomplished anything. Her mom was still a depressed alcoholic who numbed herself by watching TV all day instead of getting drunk, and her dad was still emotionally and physically absent from her life. Her best friend was still a horrible person who had stolen her crush and turned the whole school against her. That was the life she had to go back to.

"Did you have a good trip?"

"No, actually. It was awful. My mom's best friend jumped off a bridge and drowned."

The image of Rhody's pale face floating in the dark, swirling river would be stuck in her head forever.

Nacho frowned and rubbed his chin. "Did you learn anything from his death?"

Had she learned anything? What difference did it make? Rhody was still dead, whether she had learned anything or not.

"Doesn't it matter to you that people die?" she asked.

"Of course it matters," he said. "I miss my wife. But death is not the end."

"What do you mean?"

"Time," he said, tapping his head, "Time only exists inside of us. In truth, there is no beginning and no end. Imagine the time before you were born. Were you dead then?"

"Of course not. I wasn't born yet."

"Well, it's the same when we die."

Rae shook her head. "I don't understand."

"There is no time you don't inhabit. The more you travel, the more you'll understand."

"I don't think I want to travel anymore," she said.

"Oh, you will."

The air trembled and whined. Her grandpa's voice faded until she couldn't understand what he was saying anymore.

It was time to go home. Just when the conversation had been getting interesting.

She put the mug on the table and stood. Nacho crossed the room and put his hands on her shoulders.

Rae opened her mouth, but no words came out. She hadn't asked him anything about his own life. Where had he been born? Where did he go on his first trip? What was his favorite place to visit?

But there was no stopping the portal. Her peripheral vision disappeared, and the air in her lungs grew heavy and hot. She put her hands on top of her great-grandpa's hands and closed her eyes. Every particle of her flesh screamed in horror as it was converted into an energy pattern.

And then there was nothing.

Chapter Twenty-One

Rae woke up in her grandma's guest bedroom in a bed as familiar to her as her own, buried deep inside her favorite white comforter. She was still wearing her Big E's and her lucky hoodie, but her shoes were off and so was the travel belt. Her head and back hurt as if she had been asleep for a long time. She wiggled her toes to make sure they were working. Kazak opened his green eyes and meowed before falling asleep again in a ball at her feet.

She sat up and reached for a glass of water on the nightstand, noticing for the first time that it was sitting on a cardboard coaster from the Moana Surfrider Hotel in Waikiki.

Her grandma opened the bedroom door and stuck her head in.

"Back among the living?"

"How did I get here?" Rae asked, finishing the water and setting the glass back on the coaster. "Was I asleep for a long time?"

"Don't you remember landing? You were groggy, so I helped you right into bed. You slept all evening and right through the night. It's 9:30 in the morning now."

"My head is killing me," Rae said, rubbing her eyes.

"That's a side effect of time travel. I bet you didn't drink enough water when you were there, did you? Time travel tends to disrupt normal routines."

Rae nodded. "I pretty much gave up on food and water. Also sleeping, brushing my teeth, changing my clothes . . . I feel absolutely disgusting."

"You poor thing! Do you want to eat first or shower? Or would you rather I take you home? Your mom called earlier, asking when you'd be returning."

Rae was surprised her grandma would even suggest taking her home before she heard all the details of her trip to 1984. Plus, it would be pretty much impossible to see her mom and pretend like everything was normal right now. She needed some time to process.

"I don't even know what day it is," she said.

"It's Sunday, hon."

Ugh. Back to school tomorrow? The thought of it made her want to throw up. Maybe it would have been better never to have gone to 1984 at all. Except . . .

She sat up straight and clutched the comforter in her lap. "Grandma, guess what? You're going to be so happy!"

"What, dear?"

"I have your new card! I found your dad—well, he found me, really, and he already had your card ready for me, like he knew I was coming—"

"Oh, hon, I know. You already gave me the card."

"I did?"

"Yes, last night, right after you got here."

"Oh."

"It sounds like you had a great trip."

The only good thing about the trip had been meeting her great-grandpa and getting her grandma's card, and it was disappointing to be robbed of the experience of sharing it all with her grandma. She couldn't remember telling her anything about the trip, a trip she recalled now with nothing but sadness. She could still see Iggy leaning back over the front seat of the station wagon and waving like a little girl on her way to California with a guy she barely knew, a guy who didn't even seem to like her very much. Rae couldn't imagine what had happened next.

"Grandma, did you know my mom's best friend died at a party when they were sixteen? That's why she left Taos. It was awful. I saw the whole thing."

"That's terrible," her grandma said, rubbing dust from the corners of the rosewood dresser with the sleeve of her pajama top.

"His name was Rhody. You must remember him, right? They did everything together."

"That was a long time ago, Rae. I don't remember all of your mom's friends. I'm sorry." She picked up a framed picture of Rae and put it down in a different spot, then opened and closed a small velvet jewelry case.

"What did you do when you realized she stole the car?" Rae asked. "Were you there when she went to pack her stuff? Did you see Simon? Did she tell you she was running away? What did you do? What did you say?"

Her grandma spun around suddenly, her face angry and red. "I told you, that was a long time ago! Why are you giving me the third degree?"

Rae was so surprised by her grandma's response and so emotionally exhausted from her trip, she burst into tears. "I'm sorry, Grandma," she cried, wiping away her tears with hands she saw now were still creased with dirt from the river. "I just wanted to know what happened to my mom is all."

Exhaling deeply, her grandma sat on the edge of the bed and stroked her head. "Don't cry, Rae. I'm sorry too. I don't like talking about the past as much as some people do. Maybe . . . maybe you can ask your mom these questions."

"But how will I explain what I know unless I tell her about time travel?"

"Well, maybe you need to figure out a way to get her to open up."

"Yeah, right," Rae scoffed.

Her grandma stood again. "Now, what would you like for breakfast? We've got to get you home."

"French toast, I guess."

"Coming up," she said and left the bedroom.

Rae sat there, recovering from her hurt feelings. Her grandma had never talked to her that way before, and now it felt like she was trying to get rid of her.

Remembering the expression Rhody had made when she was trying to get away from him, she put her head under the covers and cried and cried and cried, expecting her grandma to come back into the room at any moment and demand to know what was wrong. But she never did, and so Rae cried until she had no more tears left.

Her grandma yelled down the hallway when breakfast was ready. Rae pulled her sore body out of the cozy bed and shuffled into the kitchen.

The little yellow table only had one place setting. Her grandma was at the sink, washing dishes.

"Aren't you going to eat?"

"I already had breakfast. I've been up for hours."

Normally, her grandma would have waited for her to wake up so they could have breakfast together. Something was definitely off. But Rae was starving, and more questions would only delay breakfast even further.

Her grandma had made her favorite. She doused her plate with maple syrup from the old-fashioned dispenser before picking up her fork and attacking the steaming plate of buttery French toast.

"Where will you go now that you have your card back?" she asked between bites.

"I don't have anything planned," her grandma said, her back still turned.

"You were so desperate to get it back, I thought you must have somewhere specific in mind."

"No, nowhere special." It seemed like she was taking an extra-long time washing each dish.

"Maybe we could go somewhere together," Rae suggested. "Maybe we could go to Hersheypark."

Her grandma whirled around, splashing suds and warm water everywhere. "Hersheypark? What do you know about Hersheypark?"

"N-nothing, grandma. Grandpa Nacho was telling me about your first trip."

"And I'm sure he was full of criticism, wasn't he? That man is impossible to please."

Rae thought hard about how to respond. She didn't want to lie to her grandma, but she didn't want to tell her the truth and hurt her feelings either. She had only met him once, but she sensed that Nacho might not have been the most affectionate father in the world.

"Yeah, I thought so," her grandma spat, storming out of the kitchen.

Rae put her fork down. She wasn't hungry anymore. Everything she'd thought she'd known about her family—everything that had survived her parents' divorce—had been shattered by her experiences in 1984. She had always assumed that her grandma had a basic, boring childhood like everyone else her age. It was hard to look at the portrait of her parents she had hanging in her foyer, two average old people stuck in a black-and-white photograph, and imagine anything else. Back then, there was no technology, no Internet, no social media or online shopping. What did people do all day, read books and till the soil? So Rae had thought—until her time in 1984 made her realize that those black-and-white people had lived full-color lives packed with as much drama, pleasure, tragedy, and despair as anyone alive today.

When she added the mind-bending complexity of being raised in a time-traveling family, her grandma was a more fascinating person than Rae could have ever imagined. She wished her grandma would put on a pot of tea and pull up a chair next to her at the table so they could talk about her experiences growing up. Rae had so many questions she wanted to ask her. What had it been like, being a kid who could time travel? Had she had any friends who were time travelers? Had she ever been found out?

But her grandma, the person who was always trying to get Rae to open up about her feelings, wasn't talking. In fact, she was acting like she was mad at her, even though Rae had gone all the way to 1984 to get her a new travel card and had probably been scarred for life in the process. It didn't make any sense.

They rode all the way to her house in complete silence, but when her grandma pulled the car up to the curb in front, she leaned over for a kiss like always.

Rae kissed her soft, wrinkled cheek. "Do you want to come in?" she asked. It was almost noon on a Sunday, the perfect time for a family visit. She couldn't remember the last time they had all hung out.

"Maybe next time," her grandma said. "I have to drop by the nursery to get some mulch for my rosebushes."

As Rae got out of the car and shut the door, she noticed the outline of her grandma's travel card in the front breast pocket of her denim shirt. She locked eyes with her grandma through the closed car window and opened her mouth to ask why she hadn't put the card back in the toolbox, where it would be safe until she needed it. But before she could even form the question, her grandma peeled away from the curb and sped down the street.

Chapter Twenty-Two

The clear morning had turned into a cloudy, gray afternoon with a cool breeze that kicked up dust and debris all around Rae. As she made her way up the sidewalk to their apartment building, she kicked aside the long, curly seedpods that had fallen from the honey locust trees in the front courtyard. She felt like she was seeing the place they lived for the first time.

The front entrance to their apartment hadn't been swept for weeks and paint was peeling off the doorframe. One of their metal address numbers was partially unscrewed and barely hanging onto the front of the door. Advertising flyers and bills were falling out of the mailbox and onto the walkway. It looked like sad people lived here.

The impression of neglect grew worse when she opened the front door and practically stepped on a pile of her mom's discarded shoes and sweaters. Except for the sounds and lights coming from the television in her mom's room, the apartment was gloomy and quiet.

Rae followed the voices of the competitors on what could only be *The Great British Baking Show* down the hallway to her mother's room, with a growing sense that she was about to discover something horrible. She held her breath and paused in the doorway, gathering all her courage before she forced herself to walk into the room with her eyes open.

The room was lit by the familiar, eerie flicker of the TV. Rae took in the mess.

The room smelled like onions. Dirty plates, paper towels, unopened mail, and more clothes were scattered across the bedroom floor. A bottle of prescription pills sat next to a glass of water and a stack of dirty dishes on her mom's nightstand.

Rae heard herself whimper as she recognized the shape of her mom under the covers.

The shape of Iggy. Iggy, who had lost her best friend when she was just sixteen years old in a terrible accident she blamed herself for. Iggy, who had run away from home with a boy she'd barely known and eventually married Rae's dad and started a family and opened her own restaurant and, somewhere along the way, become a full-blown alcoholic and lost everything all over again.

Everything except for Rae.

It was too late to ask questions. She should have realized that her mom had her own reasons for being such a fuckup. Rae had never really tried to get her to open up about her past. If she had known how much her mom had been through, she would have been a better daughter. She wouldn't have been so cold and judgmental. She wouldn't have made fun of the way she dressed or how she used proper punctuation when she texted or the way she complained about how much everything cost. And she would have told her every single day how much she loved her.

"Oh hi, honey," her mom said, poking her head out from under the covers. "I didn't hear you come home." Her hair was sticking up in messy tufts. She sounded embarrassed to be found in bed so late in the morning.

Rae jumped on top of her and burst into tears for the second time today. "I thought you were dead!" she screamed. "I thought you'd killed yourself!"

"Oh my god, Rae, are you serious? I would never do that to you."

"The bottle of prescription pills, though?" Rae reached over and grabbed the half-empty bottle of pink-and-black capsules.

"You mean the Prevacid for my ulcers? Jesus, Rae, you are so dramatic."

Her mom found the remote control in her tangle of bedsheets and peered over the top of Rae's head as she searched for another cooking show on TV. Rae closed her eyes and let the sounds of her channel surfing—a cascade of blips, beeps, partial sentences, and fragments of song—wash over her while she closed her eyes and inhaled the wonderful smell of her mother.

She was home again. Everything was okay.

"Can we make popcorn?" she asked, rolling off her mom and sitting up on the bed. "And maybe watch an old movie?"

Her mom stared at her. "What's up with you? Don't you have homework? Or some social media maintenance you need to attend to?"

"I just want to hang out with you."

Her mom sat up straight. "What's going on here, Rae? What do you need?"

"Nothing, I swear! I want to be cozy with you. I'll get in my jammies and we can have a lazy Sunday together like we used to."

"Did your grandma put you up to this?"

"Mom, I'm getting offended."

"You really want to hang out?"

Rae sighed and flopped down on the bed.

"Okay, okay!" Her mom laughed. "I'll make popcorn. Are we doing butter?"

"Extra butter, please!" Rae yelled, standing up and jumping up and down on the bed like a little kid.

Her mom got up to make popcorn and Rae looked for something good to watch on TV. AMC was about to show the movie *Poltergeist,* which, according to Wikipedia, was an eighties horror movie about a family whose five-year-old daughter was abducted by the ghosts who lived in her perfect, haunted, suburban home.

Her mom returned with a breakfast tray holding a big bowl of popcorn and two cans of sparkling water.

"On your phone, huh? Surprise, surprise."

"Chill, will you? I'm actually researching the movie *Poltergeist*. Have you seen it?"

"Oh my god, have I *seen* it? That movie is permanently embedded in my psyche. Are we going to watch it?"

"I mean, Rotten Tomatoes says it's a modern horror classic . . . "

"I swear, watching eighties movies with you is like a dream come true. Who are you and what have you done with my daughter?" Her mom got back into bed and put the tray down between them.

Rae nestled deep in the covers and wiggled her toes, too comfortable to change into jammies. She was asleep before the opening credits had finished playing and woke up in time to see a dad roll an old TV out of a Holiday Inn room and slam the door shut as the end credits started to roll. She had missed the whole movie.

From the sound of the snoring beside her, her mom had missed it too. There was popcorn all over the quilt.

Rae's phone said it was 2:10 p.m., which meant she could take a shower and still have plenty of time to work on the first draft of the research paper that was due tomorrow. It was hard to believe that she would have to return to school tomorrow—that she would have to face Cosima and Andy and try to get back into a normal routine. Her own life seemed phony now. It was 1984 that felt real.

She crept out of her mom's bed and down the hallway to the bathroom, where she stripped out of the clothes she had been wearing for more than twenty-four hours straight and stepped under a spray of water set as hot as she could stand it, amazed by how wonderful it felt on her tired body. As she lathered her hair and scalp with the same honeysuckle-scented shampoo she used every morning, she was delighted by the mounds of luxurious suds it made on her head and enraptured by its heavenly aroma. When she got out of the shower and rubbed herself dry with an oversized bath towel, she felt every nub of the terry cloth on her skin.

Putting the question of her enhanced senses aside for the time being, Rae stepped into a clean pair of pajama pants and an old T-shirt and decided to empty her backpack and get it ready for school before starting on her homework. From now on, she was going to be much more aware of her actions. She wasn't going to save things for the last minute or leave things on the floor *ever*, and she was going to be super organized with her homework and her meal prep too. Just the thought of decluttering and organizing her closet and eating a bunch of healthy food made her feel warm and secure.

As she unzipped her backpack and shook out the contents, a plain, white envelope fell to the floor. It took her a second to remember what it was—the letter her grandma had written for her dad, explaining that she had sent Rae to Taos, 1984, so that Nacho could make her a new personal travel card. Rae had forgotten about it, since Nacho already had the card waiting for her.

She tore the envelope open and read the letter inside.

Dear Dad,

I know you don't agree with my choices, but I hope that you can at least respect me enough to let me live my life my own way. I'm begging you to return my travel card. It belongs to me, and I have the right to use it the way I see fit. My memory is getting worse every day. Before long, I won't remember who I am and I'll be forced to live out the remainder of my life being spoon-fed by people I won't even recognize anymore. Please don't force this indignity upon me or them.

Your only daughter,

Lydia

Rae stood in the middle of the room, reading the letter over and over again as her heart raced.

The letter could only mean one thing, but her mind refused to believe it.

Her grandma had tricked her. She hadn't lost her card—and she didn't want it back so she could take a leisurely trip to Hawaii whenever the mood struck either.

Her mom had been right all along. Her grandma *was* having problems with her memory. Maybe she even had Alzheimer's. And she was planning on going back to a time when she was younger, just the way she had described to Rae when they were eating breakfast at the Frontier, to transfer her consciousness into a younger version of herself! Her dad must have found out and stolen her card to prevent her from going through with it.

Rae was stunned. It wasn't right. It was the same as suicide. The old grandma she loved so much would be gone forever, and Rae really needed her. She and her mom *both* really needed her. Who cared if she was losing her memory and misplacing stuff? Did that make it okay to abandon them?

She had to stop her grandma before it was too late.

She pulled her black hoodie back out of the hamper and jammed her feet into a pair of flip-flops. She had to hurry. Her grandma had the card in her front pocket. It might already be too late.

She took her phone off the charger and opened the Uber app.

A driver could be at her house in as soon as five minutes, but when she hit the button to schedule the ride, a notification bubble popped up to inform her that her method of payment was no longer valid.

She stuffed her palm in her mouth and stifled a frustrated scream. Her mom must have canceled the credit card after Rae had used the app to get to school. Damn it. Now what?

She ran down the hallway to her mother's room. Her grandma wouldn't approve at all, and even Rae wondered if she was doing the right thing, but they had left her no choice. She was going to have to get her mom involved.

"Mom!" she yelled, standing over the bed and shaking her shoulders. "Wake up!"

Her mom sat up in a panic. "What? What's going on?"

"You have to get out of bed, Mom. Grandma's in trouble. She's about to do something really stupid and we have to stop her."

"I don't understand. What do you mean, she's in trouble?"

"I can't explain right now. We don't have time. Will you please just trust me and take me to Grandma's?"

Her mom rubbed her eyes and got out of bed in a daze, reaching for a pair of jeans crumpled in the corner.

"C'mon, Mom! We seriously have to go!"

Her mom looked down at her baggy sweats and faded T-shirt and then back at Rae, who normally wouldn't be caught dead in public with her mom dressed like that. "Are you sure?"

Rae realized the face on her mom's threadbare T-shirt belonged to none other than Siouxsie Sioux.

"Positive."

On their way to her grandma's house, Rae shook her head and refused to answer any of her mom's questions, just begged her to drive faster.

If her grandma was home, she wouldn't tell her mom anything about time travel, since she would probably think she was on drugs. Instead, she would make up a story about how her grandma had sent her a scary text, one that made Rae believe she had fallen in her bathroom or something like that. Her grandma would go along with it, of course, and then Rae would have to figure out a way to talk to her in private about her plan to switch bodies.

But if her grandma were gone, she would have no choice but to tell her mom the truth about time travel and her grandma's plot to escape her dementia. Maybe together they could figure out how to stop her.

Her grandma's Honda was parked in the driveway like it always was, and the spare key was hidden in its usual spot in the fake rock by her mailbox. But as soon as she unlocked the front door and entered the dark house, Rae could feel that her grandma wasn't home.

With her mom trailing behind her, she walked through the front room to the kitchen, knowing what she would find.

The toolbox was open on the kitchen table, with a mess of cards spread everywhere.

"She's gone," Rae said, hanging her head.

Her mom picked up one of the cards from the table, with an ethereal painting of Sleeping Beauty's Castle at Disneyland. The people frozen in front of the castle were dressed in clothes from a different era.

"What's all this?" she asked. "Some game you guys play?"

"Sit, Mom. We need to talk."

Her mom sat at the kitchen table, looking like she wanted to crawl back into bed.

"Okay." She sighed. "Lay it on me."

And so Rae told her everything.

Iggy's Mixtape for Rae

"The Kick Inside of Me" by Simple Minds

"Jam on It" by Newcleus

"Double Dutch Bus" by Frankie Smith

"The Magnificent Seven" by The Clash

"Slippery People" by Talking Heads

"Spellbound" by Siouxsie and the Banshees

"My City Was Gone" by The Pretenders

"Add It Up" by the Violent Femmes

"Temptation" by New Order"

"Drowning Man" by U2

"Pale Shelter" by Tears for Fears

"Jumping Someone Else's Train" by the Cure

"Antmusic" by Adam and the Ants

"Blank Expression" by The Specials

"Too Nice to Talk To" by the English Beat

"The Passenger" by Iggy Pop

"China Girl" by David Bowie

"Lies" by Thompson Twins

"I Wanna Be Sedated" by Ramones

"This Charming Man" by the Smiths

"World Up My Ass" by Circle Jerks

"Burning Down the House" by Talking Heads

"God Save the Queen" by The Sex Pistols

"American Waste" by Black Flag

"Straight to Hell" by The Clash

"The Killing Moon" by Echo and the Bunnymen

"Time the Avenger" by The Pretenders

"Take Me to the River" by Talking Heads

"One Step Beyond" by Madness

"Blue Monday" by New Order

Listen on Spotify

About the Author

Angela was raised in beautiful Taos, New Mexico, and spent her childhood reading, daydreaming, and listening to new wave music. She currently lives with her three marvelous dogs in Albuquerque, New Mexico, where she is working on the second book in a multigenerational trilogy. Angela's writing is inspired by her fascination with human behavior, her love of philosophy, and her lifelong interest in time travel.